THE
ISLAND
WILL
SINK

BRIOHNY DOYLE

THE ISLAND WILL SINK

—THE LIFTED—
BROW

First published in Australia in 2016
by TLB Society Inc, trading as The Lifted Brow
www.theliftedbrow.com

National Library of Australia
Cataloguing-in-Publication data:

Doyle, Briohny, author
The Island Will Sink / Briohny Doyle
ISBN: 9780994606808 (paperback)
Speculative fiction
A823.4

Cover design and layout by Rosetta Lake Mills
Typeset in GT Walsheim and GT Sectra, by Grilli Type,
an independent foundry

Printed and bound in Australia by Griffin Press, an accredited ISO
AS/NZS 14001:2004 Environmental Management Systems printer

This book is printed on paper certified against the Forest
Stewardship Council® Standards. Griffin Press holds
FSC chain-of-custody certification SGS-COC-005088.
FSC promotes environmentally responsible, socially beneficial
and economically viable management of the world's forests.

This project has been assisted by the Australian
Government through the Australia Council,
its arts funding and advisory body.

ESTABLISHING
SHOT

At dawn on Thursday the 17th of February Pitcairn Island drops 0.000785 mm below its last registered sea level. An EcoEvent 24-hour live feed covers the bedroom wall. It's the first thing I see when I wake up, groggy, high above the central district. I blink and bring a detailed record of my unconscious hours into my peripheral vision. On it, cartoon lightning bolts storyboard a fitful, anxious sleep. For several minutes I lie still—clammy despite the climate control—watching a chopper circle that island like a bird of prey. Tiny children speckle the cliffs in antish processions, antennae waving at the clouds, giving the viewer the disorienting feeling of guilty, godlike voyeurism.

In the kitchen the 7am vitamin supplements assemble. The smell of coffee drifts into the room, and an ambient soundtrack featuring rare and extinct birdsong increases its volume to a bratty, insistent chirping. The apartment is programmed with my best interests. It is synchronised with the archive – a comprehensive recording of my every feeling, thought, desire and movement. The apartment thrums with pre-emptive algorithms. It communicates: wake up, it's time.

I drag myself out of bed and shower in the filtered water of yesterday's ablutions. Immediately three green ticks and the plump, animated face of Pow-Pow the Power Saving Panda appears in the steam. Pow-Pow is the latest and most pervasive in a long series of corporate motivational mascots. He is easily provoked into anger or tears, and I read somewhere that it's even possible to kill him with neglect. I'm relieved to please him this early.

'I must remember to tell Lilly,' I say out loud, and a note is recorded and logged in the archive.

I sigh at the mirror.

'Ambiguous longing 7:12am,' notes the archive, cross-referencing this feeling against all the others and their various time-coded contexts.

The apartment responds with machine-made coffee, brewed exactly so.

The corporate apartment provides unmitigated, personalised comfort. It's luxurious in comparison to my family home in Bay Heights, which responds to more than one body, and where I often find myself thrown out of sync, mismanaged, in default settings. At home I float around family life like a goldfish around a porcelain castle. And yet I'm consistently homesick on well-managed mornings in apartments like this. The archive has noted this trend, and produced a detailed report.

I wrap myself in a towel, log in to Bay Heights and watch my children scurry through the house, collecting various objects and stuffing them into bags. Lilly and Jonas look as though they are preparing for a long walk to a distant land. Their backpacks are ergonomic, with easy-to-access pouches for storing emergency items – bottles of filtered water, styluses, compasses, various measuring devices, nanocoms, smartmaps, and brightly glowing notepads bristle from the edges of their spines. The two of them whir spiky with prostheses. I watch them for a while before they notice. As they flit past the various lenses in the house they wave up at me and chirp, 'Hi, Dad,' in shrill, occupied voices.

'I got three ticks this morning, Lilly,' I say as my small daughter attends to the final fastening of her survival pack.

She smiles patiently. She has small, white, bureaucratic teeth.

'Great!' she says, unfurling a spreadsheet from her watch. 'That brings your average up, but you still need to drop six per cent. Maybe just take the stairs instead of the elevator today, or go without your 11am coffee.'

Lilly is Pow-Pow mad. She's programmed her bedroom décor with posters of his various slogans. At night, Pandas scream her to sleep from every wall in the room: 'Even solar energy is energy, so remember to Pow-Pow-power down!' and 'Take the train and hide your tracks!' and 'Keeping pets isn't cute – sponsor an endangered animal today!'

She has a Pow-Pow solar night-light, and a Pow-Pow ThermaFreeze cooling box for her MicroDynamic school lunches. Lilly diligently reminds us to surrender all out-of-date appliances by the annual amnesty date and to install tanks and distilleries. She follows us around with the EcoCouncil cooking-oil recycling tubes, though we rarely cook. She hangs about the garden with lists of five star-rated species that might help rebuild the biosphere. Pow-Pow is her closest companion. He whispers in her ear: 'Be a Deputy Panda and make sure people at school and at home are doing the right thing.'

Lilly regularly reminds us that only by obeying all of Pow-Pow's directives can we accrue the Panda Points she needs in order to progress through the hierarchy of environmental activism. Panda Points are also awarded for reporting EcoLaw violations, and Lilly polices her family officiously.

'I am giving a speech for corporate history today,' she says, regarding me dubiously. 'It's on Fleet Methane. Do you want to hear it? Mum says I should share more with you. I told her you wouldn't be interested and that really, we are both busy people.'

'Of course I'm interested.'

She gives me a withering look.

'Fleet Methane make most personal and corporate-use vehicles,' she recites. 'The company began as the only methane-fuel taxi service. In one of the first policies under EcoLaw, Fleet Methane was contracted to produce all the government cars. This deal forced other carmakers to shift to renewable energy to avoid going bankrupt. Before this, cars ran on liquid fuels such as petroleum, which were bad for the air and smelled bad too. Also everyone used to own a car for no reason and Fleet Methane made it so people didn't have to own cars and spend all their money on new tyres. When you are in a Fleet Methane car it's important you wear a seatbelt or you might accidentally die.'

Lilly beams up from her report, empowered by the force of her nascent logic.

'It's a really good speech, Lilly.'

'Thanks. I wrote it by myself.'

She refastens her pack, blows me a brisk kiss and marches off.

The archive, alert to my nostalgia, offers me a range of clips of the car amnesty. I choose a video in which families trudge home down the highway while vast machinery strips vehicles into recyclable chunks. The soundtrack is an exhausting squeal of tearing metal. It's good footage: terrifying in its own way and possibly useful as part of a larger immersive film. Mentally, I compose a rough immersion voiceover: *You leave your van on the highway and take off through the field with only a bottle of water and the shirt on your back.*

The archive can record these thoughts, file them in an optimistically named 'ideas' folder. Later, I can pull them for possible use in one of my films.

'What are you staring at, Dad?' a small voice interrupts.

'Jonas. Nice to see you.'

'You too, Dad.'

My son Jonas is a serious boy with dark eyes. He's tall for twelve. Even in the frame you can see he's beginning to display the adolescent male tendency to hunch, as though if he made himself small enough he could disappear into the background, or back into the short pants of childhood.

'What will you learn in school today?' I ask.

'It's hard to say,' he says wisely. 'I'm working pretty hard on my Timeline of Misconception at the moment.'

'What's that?'

'It's an Evolution of Knowledge assignment. We had to draw a timeline of the history of the world and mark in the things that people once believed were true but that we now know aren't. I've started it with Adam and Eve and now I'm up to fossil fuels and grey goo. It's supposed to give us an idea of how at any time what we think we know could be totally wrong.'

'Sounds grim.'

'It's okay.' My son shrugs, well versed in uncertainty.

Ellie comes out from the kitchen and Jonas turns obediently.

On the hygienic bench, beside the fractaLight fruit bowl, his school notes scroll like ominous threats: 'Corporate History', 'Evolution of Knowledge', 'Pre-emptive Mathematics', 'Ecological Economics'. 'Timeline of Misconception'.

'Have a good day, Jonas,' I tell him.

'Good is pretty subjective,' he says.

Jonas and Lilly have never lived anywhere but Bay Heights. They are safe there, but prepared for calamity nevertheless. The house undergoes three-year upgrades, adhering to eco-architectural standards. It is flood-proof. Fire-proof. Rape and pillage–proof. The SereniTech homes of Bay Heights are optimised to withstand any one of over five thousand disagreeable scenarios, from the mundane to the catastrophic.

It's a pretty house. Ellie chose and personalised it from a range of architecturally designed options. With finishing touches by renowned artists, it's a vital, intelligent dwelling for the affluent and aware. Bay Heights will not go the way of the once-promising Envirotowers development, now a shameful ghetto bordering the quiet airport.

I watch Jonas shuffle through various rooms. He lives a luxuriously unintentional life in such an intentional space. The house tracks his movements, registers his pulse and temperature. My son's entire life has been recorded: from an optimistic decision, to embryonic temperatures, to foetal handover and every stage of his corporeal development. Unlike me, Jonas will never wonder what it was like to be a child. He will never be uncertain of what his life has been. It will all be there, every minute, ready for playback in times of existential crisis. The archive will reassure him: yes, Jonas Galleon, you were here.

I narrow my eyes to slits and peer into a future where my son follows in my footsteps towards the technologically enhanced paralysis of self-analysis.

'Guilt, 7:30am,' notes the archive.

'Shhhhh,' I chide. 'Search keywords: airport, children, car.'

Algorithms eliminate possibilities, quick as snuffing candles. The room brightens, my vision filling with the still image of a plane. Today, this impossible steel phoenix is extinct, its body melted down, seats torn out and recycled to become something new, just like the smiling seven-year-old who stands in the foreground of the image; a sweet boy since transformed into my brooding twelve year old son.

I have this moment only because the archive has it. If something is not in the archive it probably never happened. All my memories are movies, reruns in third person.

'Play,' I command.

EXT. WIDE SHOT. LIFE AS IT WAS

MAX, JONAS, and LILLY sit in a refitted classic convertible by the fence of an airport. Max points at an aeroplane taking off.

MAX

Look! Maybe Mummy will see you and wave!

Jonas is looking away from the plane, captivated by looming towers at the perimeter of the airport.

JONAS

What's that?

MAX

That's a big house where lots of people live.

JONAS

Why?

I can see now how I struggled with this question, unable to answer or even change the subject. Should I have elaborated on the tower's ecoconstruction, the hope we all felt? Should I have delved into the archive, shown Jonas the headlines proclaiming a New Jerusalem? Or would it have been prudent to try to explain corruption, opportunism and finally poverty to my young son, lest he find out somewhere else?

In any case, I did none of this. After a painful pause I talked about the fireworks and singing that went on when the construction of the towers was finished. I described the tower's aviaries, and the rainforest reserves where beautiful, brightly-coloured butterflies lived and landed on children's shoulders. Then I glibly explained that sometimes when we build things we need to have a practice go. So that when we try again we get it right.

EXT. WIDE SHOT. CONT'D

JONAS

So, if the towers are bad now, who lives there?

MAX

Oh, just some people who haven't made their minds up about where else they want to live. And some people who used to live in the central district when there were still schools and shops there. You know the central district?

Where Daddy goes to work sometimes. Where the Ecodome is. Remember where you got to ride the real pony?

Jonas stares down the buckled road that leads to the decaying towers.

JONAS
Where are all the butterflies now?'

FADE

I scroll through the metadata for this recorded memory. Someone has accessed it recently and messed around with the code. They've left a sketch for an action sequence over-lay; an alternative narrative composed of stock footage and fragments from some of my other favourite memories. In this remix, the departing plane falls from the sky mid-ascent, hurtling towards the ground with a deafening scream. The children grip their ears, mouths gaping, tears streaming down their faces. Unafraid, I throw my body like a blanket across them at the moment of impact. A ball of fire bil-lows across the runway. Flame obscures the image. If this were a haptic immersion, the heat would be real enough to torrefy the skin without burning. The sound of exploding windows would drown out the cries of the children. "Ellie staggers from the wreckage, sobered and grateful for her family as the smoke clears," insist the stage directions.

I don't remember making this overlay, but I can't deny it's in my style.

In the corporate apartment I perform a series of exercises that build core strength. I do this hanging from a purpose built steel bar. My heart rate blinks opposite me – red, flashy and reassuring. Beyond the window, the Ecodome is a green jelly-mould sprinkled with people doing similar morning routines. We all build strength, break down fat cells, increase nerve sensitivity and cardiovascular health. We prolong our lives in tribute to the unexpected.

I revise my production notes from yesterday while simultaneously drinking coffee and moving through a tai-chi series promoting peace and acceptance. I know how to clear and fill my mind simultaneously.

A glance at my itinerary reveals the immediate future. I will spend 1.5 hours thinking. I'm free to imagine the outlines of buildings obscured by flames blossoming from ruptured gas lines. To consider airports melting, glass turning to flowing lava under the inconceivable heat of a second sun formed from the noxious emissions of centuries of industry. Or whole suburbs swept under a mega-tsunami, which emerges inevitably from its vast blue curtain to carry us all away. Then I will meet Jean, my business partner, to discuss the same topics we always cover: weather, women, and the cinematic merits of various disaster scenarios.

Shifting weight from right to left foot and pushing my arms outward from the centre-chest, I practise repulsing-the-monkey. I don't know when I learned this sequence or why, but I repeat it diligently every day. I draw my hands towards my heart chakra and pound it twice, bringing awareness to the pulse of my centre-being.

'Access significant moments,' I tell the archive. 'Scroll from yesterday.'

A selection of important scenes pops up in my peripheral vision. I blink to select a wide shot of me, dressed in a suit ordered from an expensive catalogue and tailored using a digitally synthesised body model. In the image, I am one day younger, seemingly staring the viewer down.

Without breaking eye contact with myself, I collapse to one knee and raise my arms, affecting a taut pose-of-the-archer. I take aim at the image. Yesterday may as well be the Renaissance, or the primordial goo. The only thing clear to me now is that this man from yesterday knows more than I do.

I pull my bowstring tight and release it in the slow motion sequence of archer-hunts-his-prey. The imaginary arrow flies through the apartment's designer air. With three quick tilts of my chin I animate the arrow, adding a convincing fire effect so that it blazes up the past.

Ellie often tells me I have too much time. She leaves helpful suggestions in my itinerary. There's a good chance I learned this yogic sequence from a book she recommended. Nevertheless, having time is a crucial part of my process.

I collect my robe from the heated hutch and sit down at the small desk. I write a word in a square of glowing light: tsunami. It translates automatically into numerous languages, accruing a context folder stuffed with centuries of news-bites and poetry. Tsunami: this is the first word of my new film. It grips the screen like smouldering debris on a damp rock. The shape of this word has wiped out countless villages, flattened eras of architecture. It is inspiring and terrible.

'We open with a montage sequence,' I say out loud, so a note is recorded. 'External. City Street. Day. Point of view: drowning man. Broken bodies plummet below vast blueness. Above the surface, an armoured jeep tumbles through the sky, its chassis split in two like a freshly shucked oyster. Dissolve. Magma bubbles pierced by shattered rock. Significant debris spiralling in waves. Big time effects reel. Stock footage. Animation. Camera bobs up above the water for a second and then: crash! A tsunami surges up.'

'Heart rate increasing, 8:40am,' notes the archive.

A glass of amino water appears beside me.

'Cut to External. Beach. Day. Wide shot. A bright and beautiful afternoon on a vacation island long ago. Families toss brightly striped beach balls across cheerful yellow sand. *You are a holidaying mother who turns to her child and warns him with friendly authority, "Never turn your back on the ocean." A wave replaces the sky, folding across the horizon and curling over your head to block out the sun. You run towards it, towards the child, but all you see is a fierce grey wall of water.* Cut to external wide shot. City riverbank. Dusk. *Now you are an old man who threads his fishing rod through a hole in a wire fence. You turn towards a far-off noise. You look up in time to see a tickertape parade of cars and people sprinkle off the edge of a disintegrating bridge and disappear into the sea. The wave tears the gigantic steel pylons out from beneath the bridge; they shatter like glass upon impact.'*

I sip my amino water. The montage seems familiar.

'Anxiety, 8:43am,' notes the archive.

Tsunamis are caused by rising sea temperatures, or sinking islands, or underwater volcanoes. Magma chambers at the base of dormant mountains fill with water. Schools of fish scatter as the sea rumbles. Explosions produce waves within waves in a continuous eruption. Deluged cities turn to wet ash in boiling water.

Deep sea fires fascinate me. They are a motif in my work.

I make cinema because I need to see these things happen. I yearn to see waves surge up against crumbling escarpment. The roots of trees etching deep crevices into the soil as they are torn from the earth. Only catastrophe can spare us from the horror of continuous history. On-screen, our last moments are a tribute to small human beauties – the softness of a kiss, the gentleness of the refrain. Immersive films like mine help us see that the things we have not done are no longer important. It's over. There's no remorse. All we know is that we have lived.

'External. Desolate claypan. Time indeterminate. A tragic throng of extras kneel to worship the very sun that draws them towards entropy.' The archive produces a quick visual mock-up while I check a Pitcairn Island datafeed.

In a simulated, retro-styled newsroom, a pretty blonde anchorwoman is propped up like a princess. Her eyes flicker subtly as she reads. I jot down her name on the tablet – a smoother, rounder combination of letters sitting next to the Japanese war cry of 'tsunami'. She is perfect. She has careful syntax, high cheekbones, a thoughtful, sculpted brow. She remains strong and lovely in the name of information. She narrates projections, complex fractals, the satellite images of demise.

'High and low pressure systems to the south. Sudden temperature fluctuations. Freezing air. Boiling sea,' she says.

'Sexual arousal, 8:55am,' notes the archive.

I could make her a star. In my film she will be the centre of the world when the weather is the only topic left, when time is stopped by the banal demon of meteorology. In the final moments of her last broadcast she will calmly abandon the script. Staring straight into the camera, her blue eyes twin moons, she will send a message of love to each one of us.

'Help each other into the brace position,' she will say, a beautiful, loving mother to the figurative children of a future order.

We are all children, nose to ankles, bracing.

'Tsunami,' I say out loud, and a note is recorded.

Suddenly, with no memory of how I got there, I'm standing in front of the bathroom mirror, brushing my teeth methodically. I can name each tooth in the maxillary and mandibular set. I can recite the parts of the teeth: enamel, dentine, pulp, root, gum. But I can't remember the final conversation I had with my brother, or my mother's maiden name.

My grim face in the mirror dissolves into a clip for a pop hit. Women in skimpy chainmail hold machetes and pirouette around a dying fawn.

I pull on a pair of circulation-support chinos, fasten my

belt around my hips. The buckle is depth-sensitive. It measures my body fat percentage. My clothes disapprove of my body and offer prudent recommendations.

'Perhaps a jog?' my pants whisper, amicably.

'Not now,' I tell them. 'Office. Real time.'

The pop dancers are replaced with a visual feed from my office. It's quiet. The room resonates with the same dull corporate hum as this apartment.

Stephanie, my personal assistant, smooths her pale hair around her face. 'Hi, Max. Will you be coming into the office today?'

'I don't know – is it in my itinerary?'

'No. But you have a distribution pitch session coming up. Approve it when you get the chance. Also, can you do a live interview link for *Entertainment News Tonight*?'

'Tonight?'

'Tomorrow.' Stephanie smiles broadly.

'I'm meeting with Jean later,' I tell her.

Her reply is another identical smile. She is one in an endless rotation of secretaries and PAs that sit in various offices in their recycled fibre pantyhose. She is educated, diligent and efficient. They all are. They are all the same gender and age, the same height. They all have the same glassy hair, the same button nose, the same open and pleasant face. I like a vintage look at the office. It's a predilection that makes my wife scoff but I've come to rely on this continuity in my employees. I need to see familiar faces, even if I'm never sure who exactly they belong to. If Stephanie has told me details of her personal life at some point in our acquaintance, I don't remember. She is a memory machine. Less like a person than a pretty, young interface that updates, but does not change significantly.

I minimise all the images and collapse them into a flat pool that flickers quietly in the corner of the room. The walls are brilliant with their default settings – several Dutch masterpieces, a Vermeer and someone else whose name I can't recall. When I leave, the apartment will commence its waterless cleaning cycle. My clothes and other items will be logged under my resident code and stored. They can be transferred to any other apartment when I'm back. Each room that I inhabit is identical, personalised by my user preferences.

The Vermeer cracks open. Its yolk is an elevator. My perspective pans slightly, the Ecodome now to my left. Each angle is a perfect tilt of the previous. In the elevator, a gentle orchestra plays an in-between symphony to cushion the abyss between inside and outside and ready the ear for the imbalanced semitones of life. The elevator is a rehearsal of a perfect birth: swift, soft and eventless, opening out to an expectant exterior.

'I love the elevator,' I say out loud, and a note is recorded.

By the time I get to the ground, my morning is already forgotten, vanished into the bare lobby of my future.

Behind me doors whir and click.

'Goodbye, Max Galleon,' farewells the elevator. 'Always remember, sustainability is key. You are a man who can make a difference.'

I leave no footprints as I step out into the world.

• •

Jean is already waiting for me when I descend into the sub-terranean bar across town.

'The Bunker Bar,' he declares as I pull back the steel stool opposite him. 'A good place to hatch conspiracies, no?'

'Quite.'

The walls of the subterranean bar are decorated with front pages from old newspapers: headlines about Vietnam, the Gulf War, the second Saudi Strike, the Water War. There are garishly framed full-colour photographs of ancient political leaders. Young women in scanty military-style outfits dart among booths made of old tanks and stools arranged in the style of an officer's mess.

Jean smiles, savouring my discomfort. He likes to drag me out to places like this. I can't access his life remotely or log in and monitor his day-to-day. Jean is secretive, with a streak of the Luddite about him when it suits. Instead of using pre-emptive programs, he manages his time senti-mentally. He writes appointments and plans on real paper, in a leather-bound notebook. In conversation, he alludes to being taken by moods, but there are no records of which moods take him where, no strategy for how to work most efficiently once he arrives.

'Look at this,' he says, smirking, keying something into the touch panel on the table between us.

Instantly, a waitress in flatteringly modified twenti-eth-century army fatigues marches towards us balancing two small tin cups and a half-bottle of aged whiskey on a tray. She lets the tray slide from her grasp and onto the table, then clicks her heels together, snapping her body into rigid, sexy attention. With a bright wink aimed more at Jean than me, and a flash of her perfectly white, perfectly sharp teeth, she brings two fingers to her forehead in salute.

'Anything else, sirs?'

An intriguing utility belt is strapped to her right thigh.

'That will be all, soldier,' Jean says lasciviously. He sings as she marches off: 'Some Yankee soldiers crossed the line, to kiss the women and drink the wine, inky pinky parlez-vous.'

'Been here long, Jean?'

'Long enough to have decided that her name is Margot and that she keeps a pet canary,' he says, gesturing to the waitress. 'Long enough to watch you battle through the throng.'

'As expected.'

'When I first stumbled on this place, I thought immediately of you.'

Jean plants words like 'stumbled' into his sentences, to evoke images of a singularly whimsical life. A meandering, artistic journey, along the cobblestones and between the cracks.

Around us, people with well-designed hair hold various beverages in tin cups, making anachronistic chatter with wartime zeal.

'Well?' says Jean, looking around.

Above the bar: an illuminated world map with stylised monsters lurking at continental borders.

'It's awful. Supremely offensive.'

'Yes! And what else?'

'A great example of the sad reduction of history to novelty.'

'Yes, yes, but more than that.'

'Uncomfortable chairs?'

Jean dismisses my glib observation with a theatrical clank of his tin cup onto the table.

'It's completely feminised. Look around you – the décor is strictly post-Disney cutesy-pie. Look at Adolf! A sweet little mousie. What commands in this place? Tits and arse. The girls are efficient little combat machines. WMDs. But, importantly, they are still waitresses. They have a discipline.'

'Protect and serve?'

'Exactly! War is always theatre: pointless but fun, with lots of funny outfits,' he giggles, wet mouth twitching and pleased. 'I would've liked to have been a soldier.'

'You still can. We can sign you up right now.' I blink rapidly, calling forth an enlistment agent, crew-cut, serious and responsible.

Jean waves him away.

'You're a cruel cynic to say that. For whom would I be a soldier now? For what? To be someone's entertainment? To be a traffic warden in a country that no longer has any streets, or even a name? No, I would've liked to have been a soldier when it was an honourable choice.'

'Nothing is what it used to be. Least of all nostalgia.'

'Who said that?'

'Me. Just then.'

'Bullshit,' he says, but Jean makes a policy of not searching networks in public. 'It's my curse that in my own time I would rather drink in this bar than fight for my country.

I mean, where am I now?'

'In a bar.'

'Who knows where? Can we call this place a country? Could we be patriots? What are politics for now? Borders shift endlessly. Territories are captured and recaptured. And what do we feel?'

'Nothing new.'

Around me, blondes in dog tags to and fro.

'East, west, blah, blah. Here is neither here nor there. War is no longer an event – now it's just endless. And if there's no real war, there can be no true territory. That's obvious. War today only signifies the endless trafficking of shanty-towns across metaphoric borders. Battle lines are drawn over what are basically cemeteries, and still there are more and more babies over there. It's become impossible to know what to call half the countries in the Middle East. Forget Africa. These are all not even countries, just anchor points. The real territories, they have names like Fleet Methane, NanoTech, Dermaplex, whatever...'

'You are an awful person.'

'You should know,' he says.

'Why?'

Jean narrows his eyes. He thinks I have become conventional and complacent while he has maintained his claim to internationalism, long after the word was drained of meaning. Jean likes to tell stories of cities visited, stakeholders met, wheels turning in exotic locales. Decisions that necessitate people facing each other across tables, holding real glasses, whispering in excited tones. Animated faces lit by the flickering embers of real fires. But these stories are polite fictions born of frustrated creativity, vignettes sketched when he should be penning screen narratives of spectacular explosion and collapse. No doubt Jean's opinion of me, filtered through the years since we were at film school, is of a man shrinking into midlife: increasingly introspective, absorbed in obsessions, hypercritical, pessimistic to the point of jubilant abandon. Balding. I can't argue.

'If you are honest with yourself you would see there is no real alternative to my viewpoint,' Jean says.

'If I'm to believe Ellie, the choice is charity.'

'If you believe that is what Ellie really thinks then you don't know your own wife.'

'Always a possibility.'

Jean snorts. 'A probability. Her charity is a strategy, not a worldview. Ellie's a crafty woman,' he says. 'She leads you, you know. Max Galleon has never walked a trail without the guidance of Ms Eloise Smyth.'

He is taunting me. He claims that Ellie introduced us. She may well have, I don't remember. I do know that, at one point or another, Ellie and Jean were intimately acquainted. It wasn't until years into my marriage that I became privy to this information. I'm still ignorant as to how they knew each other and for how long. Needless to say, Jean's insights into her character can never be completely dismissed. He is there with her, somewhere, in the half-made beds of old diary entries and love letters, in the dimly lit rooms that make the most familiar people strange.

'Jealousy, 12:02pm,' notes the archive.

As though the archive's observation was projected into the silent space between us, Jean shifts his focus from my wife to the waitress.

'Her name is Margot. She keeps a canary, a gift from a foreign friend. She whistles to it as she enters her apartment, which is small and bright, filled with vintage stereo equipment. She's a dancer. In her spare time she works on the distillation of movements, the meaning of which is entirely instinctual for her. She never reads. She never wishes she were anywhere else. She works long hours in this bar but she never needs to drink.'

I key commands into the console and 'Margot' arrives at our table with a fresh tray. She repeats her salutation ritual perfectly.

'Are you working at the moment, Jean?' I ask.

'Always.'

I respond with a presumptuous pause. I assume that, other than the work he does with me, Jean no longer writes. He alludes to his outside interests and deals. He refers to projects begun and discarded, but no evidence of them ever surfaces. Instead, he applies decades of literary theory onto his day-to-day: his walk, his mannerisms, his emotional and imaginative life where he paces through bright studios with impossibly high ceilings, painting masterpieces entitled *Nude with Yellow Canary #37*.

Conversation with Jean demands submission to the uneasy feeling of not only speaking theoretically, but becoming living theory. It's a process alternately ponderous and seductive.

'We shouldn't forget the dues that we in the cinema owe to the military,' he says. 'Every piece of technology we have is the product of war. Especially our immersive cinema! The result of a diligent quest for a total vision of war. Visibility has long been weaponised. In one sense, by writing for immersive cinema, I'm as tied to militarism as to any tradition of letters.'

'Well, that's that ambition taken care of then.'

'Yes! I should get a pension and one of those hilltop cabins for traumatised men. I could learn to hunt.'

'There's nothing to hunt up there. Not anymore.'

'Then I will simply write about the wild animals for our films – it's the same thing, more or less.' Jean takes a measured sip at his cup, looking both surprised and offended to find it empty.

'Nothing but hot air, Jean?'

He scowls and refills. His eyebrows knit a troubled wince. Somewhere far away, covert wolves howl on bald hilltops, safe, for now, from his lethal descriptions.

'Well, then, how's the war going? Are we winning?'

'It goes on,' he grimaces, making a spiralling gesture in the foetid bar air. 'There are no winners, only words.'

'Would you consider declaring war on an insurgent as formidable as, I don't know, a tsunami?'

I take a sip mid-sentence so that the word 'tsunami' gurgles behind my teeth.

Jean's eyes flash.

During the long silence Margot replaces our bottle, a woman in a red dress shrieks at a woman in blue slacks then gets up bitterly, leaving the table, and I try to imagine what is going through Jean's mind.

The tsunami has rendered him mute. Flickers of excitement play across his face but he is clearly in no rush to reply.

The woman in the red dress returns to the seat opposite her friend. They talk quietly, both of them sobbing. The woman in the blue pants extends a hand across the table and for a moment the tenderness totally disarms me.

'Longing, 12:17pm,' notes the archive.

The corners of Jean's wet lips twitch into rapid, excited smiles. His eyes are closed.

When I look back over at the women they are speaking quietly, gripping fingers. At a gaming machine set in a replica of the *Enola Gay*, a young man has fallen into a deep sleep. His friends slap him on the shoulder, shake his flaccid frame. Someone drops a soluble pill into a tin cup and puts it to his lips, but he doesn't move.

Jean speaks:

'When I was a child, around eight or nine years old, my parents and I spent almost a month living in a small town somewhere on the east coast of Australia. I remember it vividly. Until then I had lived in Paris, and had only visited the Riviera and Ajaccio in southern Corsica. These were sleepy seaside villages with bright blue water, and yellow and white stone arcades that line the esplanades. These were beaches where lovers take sunset walks with ice-cream. Everything was picture-postcard. The water in Corsica was designed to match the cobblestones. The fishermen were all perfectly placed by Spanish masters.

'In Australia, the beaches are cruel and wild and long. They snake around rugged coastline, hitting the headland and beginning again on the other side of a fierce, rocky shelf. My parents had rented a house by a beach where one morning I explored the rock pools and came back crying and swollen. My feet were raw and bleeding and my legs were webbed with a purple rash. There were cliffs that loomed directly over the swell. You could walk to the edge of one of these and get the feeling of walking across water. The only houses were built on a thin strip of land running between the rough coastline and the escarpment, which seemed to me like endless wilderness, filled with the caves and hideouts of outlaw fiends and savages. Mist hung ominously over its peak. Trees grew from its rocky face at odd angles, like barbs.

'One afternoon a storm hit. Wind whipped the branches off eucalypts, a black cloud blocked out the sun. Along the residential strip, housewives desperately boxed vicious linen into submission. Underwear, beach balls and deckchairs flew off down the road. The sky cracked open and for an hour hail the size of golf balls bombed our roof. Then the rain came thick, fast and hard so you had to yell to be heard above it, and if you got caught out in it for a second you were drenched and freezing.'

'*On the Beach* was set in Australia,' I chime in, eager to have some frame of reference, some way to contribute. 'The first psychological disaster film.'

Jean ignores me, lost in the sharpened peaks of his imagery.

'We watched a man running up the street, his suit so wet you could see his feeble body and his waggling little prick. The lightning over the escarpment lit green-black crags of split rock. The storm stirred passion in my parents and they had a terrible fight.' He breaks off for effect. His stubborn refusal to outsource the work of memory makes his own unverified past vivid and enthralling.

I close my eyes to lose the world around me. I want to slip into Jean's memory.

'My mother put me in the car and we skidded down to the beach. The windscreen wipers bent under the barrage of water. We sat in the car while my mother sobbed and heaved. The storm subsided and we watched the waves. I had never seen anything so violent. The ocean was charcoal and frenzied, the waves jagged peaks. They reminded me of a painting of Neptune that had made an impression on me. The brute god had a plump, milky white girl tucked under his huge arm. He was stirring up the sea with lightning from his trident, parting its frothy surface like bedclothes, ready to submerge with his plunder and rape her in some murky cave. Sitting there beside my mother, it seemed that only a god could move something as powerful as this ocean. We got out of the car and stood transfixed and dripping at the edge of a cliff. I stared, shivering and excited, while my mother wept and stamped her feet and yelled things that were swallowed by the storm. And then, just as suddenly as it had rolled in, the storm was gone, leaving a still winter twilight in its wake. The tide seeped like an oil spill over the damaged dunes, the house lights flickered like flash fires around the escarpment, and the hot breath from our mouths puffed white smoke into the frozen night. The world had rehearsed its ending before our eyes and it was beautiful.'

Jean's voice trails away everywhere but in the archive, where it becomes mine, to do with what I want. I'm at home now, though I have no memory of leaving the bar, nor of walking home through lamp-lit streets. I'm sitting in my haptic chair, sandwiched between two images, two lives. On one side of my body, the archive shows a real-time recording like a mirror, exposing me in wretched full-colour. On the other, I compose and recast. I steal people's memories and inhabit them as my own. I am the camera and the subject. This is total visibility. Total war.

INT. OFFICE. NIGHT

Max is vacant, strapped into a black haptic chair. There is a sick fog in his eyes. A wire extends from his wrist as though his circulatory system is creeping out of his skin, making a desperate attempt at wrapping around some greater structure. Max watches a flickering image, as big as the wall, as big as vision. He whimpers like a child as he replays.

PAN TO:

INT. APARTMENT. POV MAX

The projection depicts a handsome grey-eyed man reciting a monologue in a dimly lit room.

JEAN
...puffed white smoke into the frozen night...

In a close-up of JEAN'S eyes, waves of pixels froth on a treacherous shore. The flickering image changes, becoming the story of the monologue, though now it's MAX'S MOTHER crying and pounding on the steering wheel while old boots, bicycle parts and other secret objects from childhoods-gone fly past. The items bounce across the windscreen, threatening to crack the thick glass. Max is suddenly standing with his mother at the edge of the cliff as the rain shoots through them, giving them energy. A voiceover plays for immersion.

VOICEOVER
This is what you remember: You are alive and violent as paintings of gods. Your skin is luminous and piqued by lightning. You peer over the black rock face and squint to see death, lashed with white foam. Houses like fires. Your mother touches your cold skin and together you laugh electric, forever and without loss. You are caught in the eye

of a timeless storm. Allow the storm to spill from
your eyes. Live, for a small moment, in the ecstasy
of real memory.

FADE

• •

These days, to drive one's self is decadence. In many ways, the self-driving car is the seminal technological development of our times. Human scepticism, the main obstacle to its widespread adoption, was easily dealt with, as usual. Still, what kind of mass psychological metamorphosis was necessary for a mother to finally feel at ease putting her children into a self-driving vehicle and waving as it pulls away from the kerb? What kind of process did we as a species go through to finally accept that in the case of an accident an algorithm is more equipped to take evasive action than we are? Do we even remember the change? I don't, of course. But somehow, I do remember how to drive.

I climb into the empty car and the cabin adjusts in response to the unique pressure of my butt on the driver's seat. It's incredible, and it makes me proud, to have maintained the archaic skill of driving. The windscreen tint lightens almost imperceptibly. Schwerbut, my favourite Viennese dub collective, is already playing.

I mode the car into total manual operation. If I have an accident today, driving along the highway to see my brother Tom, there's an 89.9 per cent chance it will be entirely my fault. I'm never more in control than when I'm driving and subsequently, I am never more precarious.

Lilly has done her due diligence – I have heard the lectures. That automatic vehicles don't crash. That by refusing to relinquish the driver's seat, I am putting lives in danger. That if I want to know about my inefficient acceleration, just ask Pow-Pow, and he will compile a report.

'I love to drive,' I say aloud, so a note is recorded.

The Ecodome becomes a shimmering green blob in the rear view. At the invisible gate indicating the border of the central district, radar registers my identity and intention, and I pass through noticed and approved.

Some time in the past decade, a once-sprawling and dangerous suburban wasteland was flattened into a quaint pastoral. Beyond the central district, wind farms glitter the clear-felled land. Regeneration zones are demarcated with fluorescent borders. Tiny native saplings bend on their skinny trunks – easy prey for rogue gusts and small twisters.

The plan of the region resembles a fractal daisy. From directly above, the central district is a pollinated centre. From an angle, it is a connecting petal in a blossom of other zones—residential, corporate and natural—none more central than any other. The silver train lines and the almost transparent solarbitumen road connect each blossom into a trellis and, in the space between (what designers refuse to think of as 'negative space' anymore) there is the outline of a tiny bud. Every development needs to leave space for the future, a more essential, more intelligent, bristling green world. But each new growth raises the question: are we too late?

Some old quotation emerges from the fog of my psyche.

'By its fullness, the future is propaganda,' I say out loud, and a note is recorded.

The archive crosschecks it against the network. Several Joseph Brodsky books are placed in my reading queue. Have I read him? The question floats up into my periphery feed; I wave it away dismissively. A series of other suggestions are made, all classics from the Classicbooks Antediluvian Ideologies Collection. I make a show of looking like I've read them, though I know the archive doesn't judge.

I'm twenty minutes' drive from the central district when the first trailer pack rises up. From a distance it looks like the scattered bricks of a recent ruin, but as the sedan speeds along the road it grows into formation: hundreds of caravans and tiny houses on flatbeds, all jigsawed together. Tents are strung up in neat lines. Children jump across guy ropes. The largest buses have ComDishes strapped to their roofs.

On the bed of a truck sits a huge government-issue water tank. A screen curved around it shows Pow-Pow, wagging his fluffy finger at the playing children. Vandals have damaged pixels in a pattern that cuts through the image like a trail of articulate ants. POO POO, reads the graffiti. Further afield, rows of self-composting toilets have a familiar logo stamped on their doors, along with the corporate motto 'Waste Not Want.'

Nomadic communities remind us all that we are in the initial phases of a new kind of social structure. Moved on from place to place to ensure a sustainable strain on the land, here are the people for whom a stake in the new interurban lifestyle is not an option.

These scenes have become part of the national character: we of the sprawling wind farms and trailer lots. They are as iconic as Hong Kong's fierce towers, towers with rooftops so mirrored with water tanks and solar panels that daytime plane passengers used to have to close their cabin windows when flying over the city due to the risk of blindness.

The pack stretches for over a kilometre. As one group of trailers fade, another grows in the rear-view, chasing after me like a forgotten child, running to keep up, waving desperately.

I'm not stopping.

Tom's care facility is located in an area dominated by retirement villages: clusters of condominiums, their faux–Native American designs marking the proximity to my destination.

Instead of the glistening ultra-modern aesthetic of the central district, the elements of technology-assisted life-style in this place are candy-coated, like children's medicine. Old men and women ride through the wide streets in obscenely technicoloured electric buggies and four-wheeled motorcycles. Native shrubs and grasslands are manicured around teepee-shaped 'Harmonic Convergence Huts'.

In mud-brick workshops, ancient hands build pots on the wheel, play ukuleles, weave baskets, or perfect the seductive Cambodian finger dance. In a candlelit theatre a long-retired actor reads Huxley to an attentive audience.

Finally, after all the botched apocalypses, it is the dawning of the Age of Aquarius.

I park the car at the commuter station and walk through the vehicle-free zone. There's no Pow-Pow here, but the smug air of point-scoring still lingers. I trudge down the pleasant streets, breathing in patchouli, humming along to the ambient soundtrack: some obsolete, tinny optimism.

Century-old bodies in batik running suits lounge on the grass outside the 'Centre for Human Potential,' giving the impression of students at an old-time university. The hospice is exiled to the far perimeter of the compound, its mere existence a sign of ultimate defeat. For most of us, there comes a day when there will be no more macramé, no more investment portfolios. We will not live long enough to live forever.

In the foyer of the hospice I tell the receptionist that I'm here to watch my comatose brother sleep.

She doesn't smile.

Years earlier, regeneration crews found Tom sleeping in a tent in an open field recently vacated by a trailer pack. The medical report said it was likely the residents had been harbouring Tom. When the police called me, it was probably the first time I had heard my brother's name since Jonas's birth.

I can't remember if I thought of him much during his absence, but his reappearance fuelled an obsession. I need him, I think, because in many ways my brother is a human archive containing all the missing parts of my life: the parents I do not know, the childhood I cannot recall. All the unrecorded parts of my life; hazy moments that burned up in the critical caesura between 'now' and 'then'.

A navigator directs me to an elevator via a networked micro-speaker in my ear. I've been here hundreds of times but I never remember the location of Tom's room. It would be gratuitous to remember; all these small things are taken care of.

Scanning the key at the door, a latch clicks and a friendly female voice on the speaker gives me a status report. 'Last peak activity reported over seventy-two hours ago. Patient remains stable and unconscious—'

'Mute.'

Tom's mechanical breathing is an assisted ocean, washing away. Initially doctors advised us to read to him, talk to him, tell him about our lives. They said anything could trigger a return: the more personal the better. They said the human brain is one of the world's last remaining mysteries. That its complete capacities are almost unknowable. Months passed, and now the doctors have very little to report.

Tom doesn't speak either, but that doesn't mean he has nothing to say. I stare at his face, for hours, breaking it apart into concentric circles and allowing them to bounce onto the white floor. We share genetic code. Also, childhood. And, nothing. My deepest fear is that he will not remember me when he wakes. He will walk from the hospital the same stranger who arrived. Tom's face is an ancient map to a place I have forgotten.

I sync my breathing with his. Moments slip away like breath when I'm with him. The archive notes the time, and also my increasing alertness before I do. I turn to see Ellie's face, giant, floating by the door.

'Sorry, Max.' My wife's even voice surrounds me. 'I didn't mean to disturb you.'

'You haven't. I'm fine.'

'You looked so peaceful. I don't want to interrupt.'

'That's okay, Ellie. I'm pleased to see you,' I lie, keeping my voice even.

'I watch him a lot. For you mostly, because I know you're busy, but also, it's become a habit. Watching him is...' she says, 'hypnotic.'

'Yes. It is.'

'It's not just him. It's the whole rhythm of the place. The pulse of the monitors, and that noise, the electric squeal.'

'When I first heard that I couldn't stand it.'

'Neither could I. But now I find it soothing. How funny.' Ellie stages a rapid laugh, and then says, 'Jacqueline Cochran described the first experiments with high-speed aviation like that. She said all vision is made impossible and a high-pitched squeal fills your ears. It's horrifying, apparently, to break the sound barrier.'

'I imagine it would be.'

We both watch the body on the bed, imagining a ball of Tom-ness inside it, flying through steadily-circulating fluid at supersonic speed, never reaching the surface.

'I would've left you alone,' says Ellie, 'but I'm expecting someone.'

'Here?'

'Yes.'

'Who?'

'I heard about her through an acquaintance at the

Philanthropic Union. A doctor who specialises in coma states. Apparently she has had some success.'

'Success at what?'

'Reaching.'

'Which is?' A graph in the archive contextualises my defensiveness. Ellie, of course, can access these resources at any time.

'It's a process for communicating with someone who has lost consciousness.'

'Why didn't you tell me?'

'I didn't want to cause you unnecessary stress.'

'What is this doctor doing today, exactly?'

'Just looking, I expect.'

The door clicks and a hospice nurse enters the room, eyes glued to a glowing image in her palm. 'Mr Galleon?'

'Yes.'

'I'm acting as intermediary for Dr Gabrielle Stern.'

'I'll be observing too,' says Ellie from above my head.

'That's fine,' says the nurse. 'I expect we will have contact from Dr Stern soon. Will you be present for the examination, Mr Galleon?'

I feel invaded. Usually when I visit Tom my time is empty. I just watch him until I feel like we will both shatter.

'Yes,' I tell her.

'I have contact with Dr Stern,' the nurse says and Ellie nods, hugely.

'Hi.' A new voice. 'Can you hear me okay?'

Both Ellie and the nurse exchange pleasantries with this new voice and I tune out, shut my eyes, and focus on the electric squeal.

'...this is my husband,' Ellie says, suddenly bringing me into the exchange.

The speakers pick up some atmospheric noise, a sharp ping, and the voice changes register somewhat, becoming a little softer, a little higher.

'I'm very glad to meet you, Mr Galleon,' says the voice, as though noticing me for the first time.

'Hello, Doctor,' I say.

'Call me Gabrielle,' she says. 'I'm sure that your wife has filled you in on what we are here to achieve today.'

'Briefly,' I say, sounding peevish.

'From everything she's said, I really think that this could be a mutually beneficial endeavour. But actually she told me she only met the subject once, briefly. I assume you have had more time with him.'

'Yes, I have,' I say, adding, 'though in another lifetime.'

'Do you think you might have any additional information for me, something I might not have discerned through physical and neural examination? Anything might help. Do you remember your brother ever complaining of headaches?'

'No.'

'Did he have obsessions and fixations?'

'I don't know.'

'Are you sure? Do you remember what he was most interested in as a child?'

'No.'

'Did he have any learning difficulties? Do you remember if his speech was well developed at around age eight?'

'I have absolutely no idea.'

'Okay.' The syllables of her words are careful, loaded with the weight of their letters. 'We'll start the examination then.' She sounds disappointed.

'Shame, 12:57pm,' notes the archive, registering my temperature.

The nurse plugs various monitors and electrodes into Tom and begins to list figures and names of obscure body parts.

'Six over 981.'

'And under forty?'

'I have two to eleven.'

'That's good. Thalamacortex?'

Incomprehensible data washes over me like a numbing salve. Tom's skull looks wrapped in vines. The nurse shaves a small patch of hair from behind his ear and smears a thick conductive jelly onto the bare skin. A tiny camera on a wire is inserted under his left eyelid.

'We have a movement of 0.772.'

'And with an open valve at three sixteenths?'

'The same.'

'Okay.'

The doctor deals with these numbers carefully, repeats them as though a sudden recitation would risk spilling their potency across the plastic floor. I imagine her in a lush indoor garden somewhere, emptying numbers into fertilised water, growing an organism of Tom against the soft stream.

'Five millilitres. Good glutamate levels,' says the nurse.

Ellie smiles at me generously. If she were really here,

she might squeeze my hand. We might, I suppose, take a walk in the sunshine after.

'I think there are number of ways we can perform a reaching,' says the doctor eventually. 'Mr Galleon, you're the obvious choice for a connection considering you may be the only person to have common neural patterning. But your wife told me that you hadn't spoken to the subject in several years.'

'About twelve.'

'Twelve. That decreases the likelihood of recognition.'

'Recognition of what?'

'The connection.'

'Connection to what?'

'The subject.'

I rub my temples, which throb as if it were me who had been penetrated and explored. 'I don't know what you are talking about. I have no idea what you do.'

'Max, I...' Ellie is embarrassed. She hates when I don't play along.

'That's okay, Ms Smyth,' says the doctor. 'I think we should schedule a meeting to discuss the procedure, once I've had time to format the subject's data.'

'I find expert-speak irritating,' I reply. 'I'm never sure whether anything is actually being said.'

'I'll give you a brief spiel then, in non-specialist language,' Dr Stern continues, undeterred. 'I'm here because I've had some success reaching coma patients through electronic linkage of neural pulses, exploiting principles of connectionism, and without AI modelling. What I'm concerned with primarily is the transference of brain pulse images from a conscious party to an unconscious subject. I suppose you can look at it as an electrically mediated synaptic conversation. In any case, there's evidence to suggest that reaching is more successful in cases where the conscious party has some kind of emotional connection to the unresponsive brain. The possible interactions that can come from the process are very impressive. Of course, we're dealing with cutting-edge technology. It's all very new.'

'Are you saying you'll be able to wake Tom up?'

'No. You've misunderstood me. What we're generally able to achieve is communication between the subject and another system. In this case, you. Your system. This can contribute to the likelihood of regained consciousness, but the results are varied.' The doctor coughs. 'And of course there is always an ethical consideration.'

The nurse, who has finished packing up her various instruments, exits without a word.

I look to Ellie, trying to extract some hidden knowledge from her face. She blinks, her eyelids like blinds dropping over pretty green glass.

'Ethical consideration?' I say.

'Well, there may be a considerable amount of trauma.'

'For whom?'

'I'll know more as soon as I've finished Tom's profile. Shall we say two weeks and then we'll meet again?' A pause. 'Mr Galleon, I'm looking forward to working with you. I'm very optimistic about what we can achieve here.'

I don't respond. Ellie and the doctor conclude the

meeting with politeness. The room clicks and then the doctor's voice is gone.

'Well,' says Ellie.

'Well,' I say.

'The children will be home soon.'

'Yes.'

'And you?'

'I'll stay in central.'

'Yes.'

'Ellie, why did you contact that woman?'

'I just heard about her. I'm curious.'

'Curious about what?'

'About Tom. And you. About you and Tom. And about the technology. It's good to keep abreast. Cutting edge...' she lets her sentence trail off, then her tone hardens to an accusation. 'Aren't you curious?'

'Of course. You're fully aware that all I want in life is the certainty of knowing exactly what happened to me in the past and exactly what's going to happen to me in the future.'

Ellie laughs dryly. 'What about what happened to Tom?'

'What happened to Tom has happened to me, too.'

'Such a self-centred view.'

'It's exhausting.'

'I suppose it's not so bad. All you used to want was fame and artistic freedom.'

'Those things aren't as satisfying as they sound. The only thing worth wanting is total absolution.'

'From what?'

'Responsibility.'

'Well, I hope all your dreams come true.' Ellie's eyes appear to blink back tears, or perhaps it is an emotion after-effect, keyed in to make me feel guilt.

'Guilt, 1:20pm,' notes the archive.

I want to get back in the car and drive until I hit the ocean, wherever that is.

'I'm trying to help you, Max,' Ellie says. 'You know, you used to want me to help.' She shakes her hair as though casting off a bothersome fly, then vanishes.

I sit numbly beside Tom's bed, watching a newsfeed. It takes only a minute for the residue of conflict to fade away. On average, I hold emotion for just less than fifty-two seconds. This is far lower than the global archived average. Far lower, I expect, than Ellie, though she does not log this kind of data in her archive. Not for me to access, anyway.

On the newsfeed, experts pit speculative outcomes against one another, occasionally gesturing to the monolith of Pitcairn Island projected in the background.

'There are experts for every occasion, Tom.'

My brother says nothing, but it's true. There are the big experts, for Pitcairn and every other narrowly avoided annihilation. Then there are the down-home types, for projections of stock futures and the weather, experts on what to eat and how to comb your hair, when to panic, when to sleep, when to stockpile glue and beans.

'There's even an expert on you,' I tell him.

Tom says nothing, needs nothing.

The comatose make great listeners.

• •

When you have no memory, nothing is a surprise and yet, in an even more important sense, true surprise isn't really possible. You simply move forward through time. One activity is no more relevant than any other.

It sounds calming. It's not.

I'm in the car, heading back to the central district, when Stephanie's face materialises across the sprouting landscape, a helpful dossier hanging from her clavicle like army dog tags.

'Where are you?' she asks, unnecessarily.

I look out the window at the carefully landscaped nothingness and consider a myriad of responses, ranging from the obnoxious to the trite. I compose a montage of possibilities to lend gravitas to the scene: a mountain, cleaved into a quarry by a trade road. Emaciated refugees clinging to wire fences. Tiny figures tumbling from a collapsing skyscraper. A hail of missiles speckling a perfect blue sky. And in the pasture, one thousand genetically identical sheep, heads moving in perfect unison to watch the single car pass.

'I'm on the road,' I say.

'That's not ideal.'

'No?'

'You're scheduled to be at the office. We prepared a remote rig. For you. For Cindi Mac.' She narrows her eyes with concern. 'Are you still able to do the interview? Connection is in half an hour. It's in your itinerary.'

'I don't doubt it,' I tell her with a tone meant to remind

her who's the boss. Then, ashamed, I add, 'I can stop the car if that's best.'

'It's a three-way conversation in quarter-realtime,' she says, as though this decides everything. 'You and Cindi Mac, the host, and a young filmmaker, Sullivan. You know him? He has an experiential epic to be released this summer. He's well regarded.'

A dossier springs up in my periphery. I blink it into the foreground. A young man and his accomplishments obscure my horizon, and the car knowingly switches to autopilot.

Sullivan is a bright star of the Neo–Copenhagen School. Reading about him makes me feel stiff, rusty. In his press picture he's a young man in his twenties. The image depicts him in some unfamiliar museum, standing in front of one of the first ever MiniCine Immersive Environments, a vicious halo of coloured pixels exploding around his head. I was twenty-five when MiniCine was launched for consumers.

The car pulls itself over to the side of the road, just beyond a trailer camp. Pow-Pow springs to the dash to ask me whether we can turn off the lights and if I really need to leave the microclimate on. I run my fingers through my hair and lighten my teeth with a touch. I take off my jacket, affecting a nonchalant slouch against the backrest.

Stephanie returns to the windscreen.

'I've got the producer,' she says.

'Fine.' I wriggle a little in my seat. The car feels crowded.

The producer says a few quick, gushy words to me then it's down to business. 'Where are you?' she also asks, looking dubiously at the aubergine Ecofibre interior.

'I'm on the road.' It still seems like a hopelessly out-of-date phrase.

The producer has nice blue eyes.

'Oh, cooool,' she says, suddenly far too young. 'I'll have you "relaxing on set".'

On the windscreen Cindi Mac and Sullivan bookend the road. Cindi is being tended to by a small army of stylists. Sullivan may or may not be sitting on a metal stool in an open, tastefully decorated warehouse, with artfully exposed solarbrick walls.

I pretend he is really sitting on a toilet. I imagine bowel movements, internal decay, a hideous water-born pandemic.

For a few seconds, a countdown covers their faces, dissolving at one. Music fades out and Cindi begins her introduction.

'I'm so excited about this!' she squeals. 'Today we have two generations of cinema stars joining us via remote to discuss their upcoming film projects and the future of movies as we know them. What a fantastic treat!

'I'll start off by introducing a man whose film credits include *Shock Wave 1, 2* and *3, Burn, No Future* and *Then Rest*. He was a pioneer of the new cinema, and is one of the high-est-grossing filmmakers the box office has ever seen. He joins us, relaxing on the set of his new picture. Here he is folks: Max Galleon!'

Cindy Mac beams through canned applause.

'Hi Max!' an artificial audience greets me in unison.

'Hi!' I'm far less convincing. 'Nice to see you again, Cindi.'

'And our second guest this evening is a rising star filmmaker whose new film *Teardrops* is due for a summer release – and I've got to say, Sullivan, the hype on this project is huge.'

'Thanks, Cindi, it's been a wild ride.'

'Oh, I'm sure everyone is just too excited, Sullivan. And Max, you've been just too quiet lately. What can you tell us about your new project?'

'I don't want to reveal too much, Cindi, but I will say that it's another immersive disaster film, and this one will be the biggest to date.'

'Oh, come on! You've got to tell us more than that!'

'I'll give you one clue, Cindi, just one word.' I pause, ready to break out the bonanza. 'Tsunami.'

Cindy squeals and claps her hands on her knees. 'Oh, I'm sooo excited!'

Canned applause pours all over my body.

'Excuse me, Mr Galleon,' Sullivan interrupts.

'Max.' I wink.

'Okay, Max. What do you say to people who claim that you make the same film over and over again?'

I pause, possibly for much too long, before answering. Behind the scenes Stephanie is undoubtedly having words with the blue-eyed producer.

'Sullivan, most mornings I can't even remember what day it is, let alone what happened in the last film I watched. Am I right, Cindi?'

The host bats her glittery, feathered lashes. Some electronic whooping distinguishes itself from the generally agreeable laughter. It bolsters my confidence.

'But truly,' I continue, 'life today is so uncertain. If you go see one of my films, you know what you're in for. You will have to forge an existence in a returning ice age. You are fighting for breath in that burning underwater tunnel. You are walking through the irradiated aftermath of a city. You are the survivor hurtling through space to find a new world for the human species. This is all happening to you. That's right, Cindy – to you.' For effect, I point suavely at the windscreen, fingers on both hands cocked like pistols.

I turn to look at my opponent. He's unimpressed.

'If you think all those situations are the same,' I add, coolly, 'I'd say you're unprepared for catastrophe.'

Someone in the synthetic audience tsk-tsks.

Sullivan offers his palms to the lens in a gesture of supplication. I can't tell if he's being sardonic. I glance down at my own pistol fingers, and attempt a smooth transition by running my hands awkwardly through my hair.

'Don't get me wrong,' he says, with perhaps a hint of smugness. 'I'm a fan. *Then Rest* had a profound impact on me. But I'm wondering when you will decide to turn your talents to something new?'

'The point of my films is not the content. It's the experience.'

'But even that's the same. You are an everyday nobody living a meaningless life until you encounter the horrific catastrophe which makes sense of your whole life while you surrender to the sensual pleasures of annihilation. There's no revelation. Nothing changes.'

'In an amnesiac existence, remaking the same film is a voyage of infinite discovery,' I mutter, catching myself at the end, making an effort to speak louder, to look directly at the windscreen with confidence. I switch into pitch mode. 'The narrative of the disaster film has disintegrated. Instead we try to focus on creating a properly immersive simulation. Experience beyond the limits of the basic human senses. Simultaneous multiple-perspective engagement. Light flickering at the exact pace of your panic-stricken heartbeat. Inaudible sound waves causing physical reactions akin to a trance state or drug-induced religious ecstasy. The aim is to strip back all sense of identity. For the viewer to attain a state of pure consciousness, so close to the calm euphoria felt at the onset of death, while maintaining an emotional core which then allows the subject at the end of the movie to disconnect and re-enter their lives. Complete surrender while you're watching, because it will all be over too soon.'

'But that's just it, Max,' Sullivan says, unmoved. 'It's not real. And meanwhile, real things are happening in the world that we are completely disconnected from.'

'Who is to say what is real experience, Sullivan? Living through a firestorm, or filing your emissions returns?'

Canned laughter pokes regular holes in our tense exchange. Sullivan is undeterred.

'It's about what we do with our lives. What you do, Max Galleon, you, is manipulate our ability to connect to the real disasters that are occurring every day. For many consumers of your films, events no longer seem real unless they can be distributed as an entertainment product, optimised for a fully haptic immersion.'

In the fake crowd, someone coughs and apologises. I start to reply but Sullivan stops me.

'You say your new film will give the viewer a real experience of living through a tsunami,' Sullivan says, 'but you don't actually care about what that real experience is, and has been. After the third mega-tsunami in Indonesia, Lombok was completely destroyed. Not just because of the wave. There had been three vicious floods even before the tsunamis, each ripping the islands to shreds. Each yielding more gruesome, blood-soaked images. I believe you recreated some of these in your own work, no? We couldn't get enough video from the floods. The coverage generated a lot of international aid. Good footage always does. We gave for the clean-up. We donated for the rebuild. We all did our part and after each clean-up effort new fishing boats arrived, donated by big-time corporate interests. It's charity, right? But soon, after the cameras had moved on, there were more fishing boats on that tiny island than there had been collectively in the past thirty years. A corporate trade-up scheme was inaugurated. Three fishing boats for one StellaTrawl – if people were willing to sign a contract regarding the sale of the catch, that is. The whole area was over-fished. People starved, Max, but not fast enough to wow the newsfeed. Slowly and terribly. That was the real experience of tsunami. Meanwhile, we had moved on. We couldn't care less about the experience of disaster unless it's a spectacle.'

'Oh wow! Isn't this exciting!' Cindi says but she looks stricken. This is supposed to be a bubblegum video show.

There's an option to hug her at the bottom of the screen but I'm feeling too prickly.

'I'm not sure what point you're trying to make, Sullivan. Do you want me to make a starvation film? Believe me, I've looked into it, but preliminary research says that the haptic immersion to make it work would wreak havoc on the viewer's metabolism.'

Some weirdo cheers.

'I'm just asking: at what point do filmmakers have to take responsibility for the experiences they are creating?'

'Disaster is something that we feel a primal attraction to. In uncertain times, experiencing disaster is cathartic.'

'But the viewer of your films is passive. You're a pornographer.' Sullivan makes an obscene thrusting gesture from the stool. 'That's the kind of catharsis you mean, right? At least you're honest about that.'

'I'm interested in the primal side of experience. I don't make narratives. I make films that are immersive. Of. The. Senses. If that makes me a pornographer, well...' It's my turn to affect the palms-forward gesture of false supplication. It's not unlike the repulse-the-monkey stance, I notice from pure muscle memory, breathing deeply to steady a quaking pinky. 'Well, I think Hitchcock would disagree. He talked to his friends about a time beyond production. When we could just beam the picture into the audience's skulls. That time is now. It's yesterday, even.'

'Your simulations erode our ability to connect with the world.'

'I'm working in a genre with a rich history. You want a

feel-good family drama? You make it. People can draw their own line between fantasy and reality.'

I want a drink. I want to close my eyes and sleep until the heat-death of the universe.

'Every disaster recorded over the past decade is named to tie in with an immersive cinema release,' Sullivan says. 'By coincidence, it was one decade ago when *Shockwave*, your first fully immersive disaster feature, took the third-highest box office gross ever recorded.'

'And didn't we all love that movie!' Cindi Mac interjects.

Applause spills once more.

Sullivan continues. 'My question is: what kind of experience do you think your films create? I think your films are narcissistic. Nihilistic, even.'

'Oh my gosh,' Cindi interrupts again. 'Sullivan, we are sooo sad to hear about all those fishies.' Her tone switches from sorrow to a kind of sexy scolding. 'You are so bad for saying we don't care. We sooo care!'

The canned audience echoes the catch-phrase.

'In fact,' she says, 'there's a care-code up right now that you can all use to instantly make a difference in Cindi Mac's I Sooo Care About Fishies Appeal.'

The audience applauds.

Twelve toddlers do the I Sooo Care dance in a rain of glitter. Cindi beams.

'So, Sullivan,' she changes tack. 'We really want to know all about your new film, *Teardrops*. Sounds like it might be a sad film?' she blinks.

Sullivan looks miffed.

'Not really, Cindi. With *Teardrops* I hope I have created an immersive cinema experience that allows us to once again look at our responsibility to each other, and to the world around us.'

'Wow,' says Cindi.

'I suppose, to get a bit of contrast going here, the question I want people to ask themselves is more like: what if the world isn't about to end? How can we continue to be useful in a perilous time? We all think there has to be an origin leading fatedly to an ending – but what if there doesn't?'

'Well that would be sooo much better,' says Cindi.

Sullivan isn't listening. 'We want to expose the inherent artifice in films that offer conceits like catharsis. We are committed to showing the gaps in the timeline, the glitch in the total image. Our immersions are incomplete – they leave a space for you.'

'Glitch!' Cindy says, blinking. 'That sounds totally amazing.'

She flicks her blonde bob and parrots a scripted question in a tone that almost sounds tired. 'Max, you have been described as the godfather of immersive cinema. What advice do you have to any aspiring filmmakers?'

'At some point the pioneers of any movement are replaced by younger innovators, those who grew up with the technology and are able to advance it, to push its limits or find a new way to make it work.'

'Dismissive, masking deeper hurt, 3:33pm,' notes the archive.

'I welcome the future with excitement,' I continue, 'but

one of the difficult aspects of the future is the way it erases its own past. If you want to make films, just make them. And, like Sullivan says: be real.' Before I can stop myself, I affect another pistol pointing gesture.

I feel ill.

'Awesome!' Cindi says. 'Thanks Max, thanks Sullivan. We are all looking forward to the release of...' I blink rapidly to fade her out.

A concerned query from Stephanie pops onto the screen. I turn off the interface, rest my fingers on the wheel, and feel the engine click over. A real thing. Circuits and wires. I let the car guide itself back on to the road.

A calming montage springs up in front of me: lazy Sundays, kittens with wool, a field of rye rippled by a breeze. I swipe it away. The windscreen is empty, except for an algorithm of potential routes.

There's no such place as the road. Not really. There are only arrows and numbers to put us back in our place.

I search my recent locations.

'The Bunker Bar,' I say, and a course is plotted. I sleep until the car gently wakes me, its door opening straight into the entrance of the bar.

Fortunately, Jean is right were he should be, an imposing countenance amidst the faded flags of long dead dictators. He peers across the room, pre-empting my navigations with a bemused squint.

'Max,' he calls, gesturing at the seat beside him, and at the bottle and second cup.

I say nothing, just sit, sip, let the warmth wash over me.

'Never mind,' says Jean. 'I saw the interview. It was not so terrible. He's a young man, Max. We were young once.'

'I don't remember that.'

Jean shrugs, taps on the console. 'You can't have a breakdown every time someone challenges you. It has been a long time since artistic integrity was at the forefront of your mind.'

'Was it ever?'

He sighs.

A combat cutie swishes towards the table.

'Ah! Margot!' he beams. 'Whiskey my dear, we must get drunk or we can do nothing at all.'

Jean swings his arm around Margot, sweeping her onto the stool beside him. She giggles, and I get the impression Jean has been frequenting The Bunker Bar regularly. 'Where's my kiss?' he asks.

Margot coyly plants a peck on his stubbly cheek, and in one deft move replaces the canister of Scotch and is back on her feet. I try to zone them out, but I don't have adequate strategies. To fall off the world for a moment, to really stop it penetrating, you need to take drastic measures. You need to be prepared to follow the example of someone like Tom.

'She's incredible,' says Jean. 'She's a painter. She paints weather. Rain, clouds, hail, snow. She paints on ice with water, nothing else.'

'Who?'

He shakes his head in mock despair. 'You know, you should have a hobby.'

'I do. I make immersive disaster films. When I'm not

doing that, I overfish villages, apparently.'

'Work is not a healthy hobby,' Jean snickers. 'You need a passion of innocence. A diversion. Me, I collect things. I collect late–twentieth century kitsch and celebrity culture. Fan letters, gossip magazines, that kind of thing. You know, it was an age of innocence then. Everyone was obsessed with super-people, as if they were royalty, chosen ones. If we were of age then, we would have been among this royalty. We would have been respected. You remember?'

'No.'

'Oh, come on, Max. This is the world of your childhood nightmares. How old were you when the twin towers came down?'

'I was never a child. Where is the record? Who bore witness? I have no memory, Jean.'

'There is Tom.'

'Tom's sleeping.'

'You are so stubborn.'

'I'm not stubborn. I'm afraid. Once upon a time we wanted to see humanity triumph over nature, raising the sword and fighting until the best man discovered the way. We believed there would eventually be something we could do to prevent nature winning: fly south for the winter, drill through to the Earth's core to produce an eruption to counter the blow, turn out the lights to reverse centuries of environmental devastation. We invested faith in research groups so that we might have a warning of impending doom.'

Jean nods nostalgically.

I continue. 'We used to love knowing there was an

Antarctic Temperature Research Team. It felt like someone was taking care of us. Some hero. Now we all have our eyes on Pitcairn. And all we can hope for is an easy drop from the gallows, or a safe place to wait out nature's fury. You're lucky if you can bunker down, vowing that if you make it you will be a better husband, father, worker, consumer. Salvation lies in surrender. We've tried everything else.'

'It was just one interview,' he says.

'The interview isn't the point. I've forgotten the interview. The only way I could remember it would be to watch it.'

'Sullivan's a young man. It's not the time for a young man to think the way you're thinking. What's left if a young man thinks like you? Hysteria? Bitterness? Why rise in the morning? Why eat, drink, create, fuck?'

'I was never a young man.'

'For god's sake, Max.'

We don't speak for a long while. The room buzzes. I have two more sips of whisky. Pow-Pow appears on the table between us and instructs me not to drive home.

'It's not an environmental issue,' I slur, but Pow-Pow disagrees.

A combat cutie brings coffee, but wakefulness is the last thing I want.

'I also collect old diaries. You can pick them up for a relative pittance. They are wonderfully banal. Cheaper than any other paper artefact, and totally disposable, therefore utterly collectable. They will be worth good money soon, Max; I'm not alone in this,' Jean says, but I am already drifting out of the scene.

• •

You emerge from the darkness and step out into a bright day. You don't know where you are, or who. Trailers dot the landscape and beyond, the field is filled with windmills. You take a step, and then, not knowing which direction to go in, you stop. There's a footprint in the dirt. A shape that belongs to you. Quite deep. As though you have been standing still for too long, through a rain-storm or a drift. Something worse, perhaps. Something unspeakable that you either failed to notice or can't remember.

Ants pace the perimeter of the imprint. It's a world in there; a footprint civilisation. For a while you're so intent that you fail to notice the people around. None of them looks familiar. They're staring at you like you're a movie. You swallow drily and stare back. You want to regain the power of communication without words. You want to interface. Transfer the data and shut down.

'What did you see?' someone asks.

You point. As though you might point a line across the plain, the fields, the wind farms, the overgrown scrub, the lines of text. Right back through the slit window of the barn and into a sleeping body's open mouth, then all through the nervous system and into a brain.

A certainty strikes you: this is Tom's memory. And then, just as suddenly, you can't be certain at all.

• •

It's been a long time since I understood what people actually do to make my films. At the collapsible warehouse which serves as a studio, I'm surrounded by young people saddled with utility belts. Executives gesticulate wildly into geographically vast conversations. Sitting in a chair with my name on it, I feel like a child placated just enough so that the adults can get on with their jobs.

To cement my feelings of worthlessness, I hole up in the production office and research Sullivan. The campaign for his new film, *Teardrops*, is ingenious. The best I've ever seen. Somewhere beneath his hessian outfits and throwback politics he must be hiding a team of the best association designers in the world. Every clip I watch is carefully managed, subtle, viral, and composed of what appears to be almost one hundred per cent real footage. They are embedded in video feeds, often without context. I can't say how many I'm exposed to before I realise what I'm seeing – that everything is part of a much larger campaign.

The first clip is a long, almost-still shot of the Great Wall of China. The camera draws back so slowly, so hypnotically from the deepest crack in the rockwork, to reveal the panorama. Even when I'm aware of the device being used, I'm captivated, and it's not shock or intrigue that does it. I'm familiar with the Wall as a sacred site for secular pilgrims to come and grieve: to grieve misfortune, mistake, and mistreatment. The Great Wall, guttered by tears—bodies young and old, all grimacing and gnashing and waving white silk—has long been an iconic part of global consciousness. But what makes this clip so much more remarkable than a tourism immersion is the rhythm. The slow, heaving rhythm. A gentle keening from one thousand throats fills the production office. The room becomes a pit of moan, which pulls me down into the basest experience of emotion. My tears flow, and for a moment I feel as though I am truly a part of something, some great, ancient, weeping communion.

Many seconds pass before I'm able to split my attention. I hear that the moaning is a reactive drone-note. The Great Wall, when focussed on minutely, is cocooned completely with the dancing pixels that have drawn me into trance state. Once I manage to get control of myself, I can see the immersion is almost primitive, and I wonder how I could've been so easily taken in. The technology is old, the aesthetic practically vintage.

'Almost no action within familiar image,' I say out loud, so a note is recorded. 'Image with strong emotive links. Drone sound cues and slow-cortoscopic registration of light.'

But the stillness. The understatement.

After two shots of amino water and a brisk circular breathing exercise, I shake the heavy shadow of the immersion and consult my emotional map. Predictably, the archive has recorded jealousy. But the word falls short of what I'm really experiencing – a thrilling competitive urge that makes me feel like heading out to the lot with some of the crew and kicking a ball around, something I almost certainly have never done.

'Search: Sullivan, *Teardrops*, media pages.'

There was a time when young aspirants saw the keepers of their craft as valuable teachers, heeding the words of their forebears for decades, before, inevitably, crucifying them in the town square – or in literature, which is worse but at least it's an acknowledgement. I watch the record of the Cindi Mac interview. I search every sentence Sullivan utters, seeking signs of grudging respect.

Around me, the production office is filled with various prototype headsets. Streaming lists flow down the walls – abbreviated production notes like hieroglyphics. Look at all this stuff – even if I could cultivate my Platonic ideal with Sullivan, even if I could reach this aggravating young talent, what would I teach? I'm a dictionary of abandoned vocabulary. On the other hand, my surrounds do remind me of something far more enticing to the modern artist than any hackneyed wisdom. In my endless, unethical repetition, I have made a lot of money.

'I have a notion...'

Stephanie's small face pops up instantly.

'Yes, Mr Galleon?'

'Have you seen the promo for *Teardrops*?'

'I don't think so.'

'The Great Wall thing.'

'Oh,' she says, blue eyes misting somewhat. 'Yes, I think I have.'

'I looked it up. The Great Wall clip is forty-eight in a promotional opus. No doubt we've seen others. I just can't remember them.'

She's poised for instruction, head tilted like a classic cinema starlet.

'I need you to find out who Sullivan's association and branding designers are.'

'Of course,' she says. Her irises reflect search terms and a rapid fire of imagery.

The filmed components of my movies, which are minimal, are done in the studio. There are new effects included in each picture, but otherwise Sullivan is technically right: the formula is identical. High frequency sine waves, stroboscopic light particles, sensations programmed into a haptic interface. New and stock images. Ultra-predictive associationism. The genius of the genre happens in a lab. Animators and immersers, Indian mainly, some Korean. The best in the world. At least, I thought they were.

'Ambition, 10:20am,' notes the archive.

A copy of *The Art of War* moves to the front of my reading queue. I open it and then blink my way to the crib notes. I do, in fact, want victory with no battle, to subdue my enemy without having to actually fight him.

'Can you get Sullivan to come out here?' I ask Stephanie.

'I'm on it,' she smiles broadly, patronisingly, in a way that makes her look like a completely different person. How long have we worked together? Who was my assistant before her? I put the question on a list of things to look up.

'He accepted your request immediately,' she says. 'Haven't found names for the designers yet, but I'll keep looking and let you know.'

When her face drops from view I flick through some pages of Sun Tzu. I feel accomplished. Control has been restored. I read the same few lines perhaps a dozen times and then check in to my real life battle locations. I log in to the hospice and and gaze momentarily at Tom's inert form before moving on to Bay Heights. No one is home there, and I stroll through the rooms, examining objects, listing them, locating their origins.

'I own all these things,' I say out loud, and a note is recorded.

Today Ellie has draped a gold robe over a cane chair in such a casual manner that it can only be interpreted as intentionally provocative. She's attempting to communicate something. I crosscheck the item in our personal inventory. There's no trace of it, though I have a definite sense of having seen it before. A film perhaps? It unsettles me.

A mid-morning organic fruit salad appears beside me. I pick it up and begin to eat, naming fruit methodically: pineapple, fig, cantaloupe, orange, Chinese gooseberry, and something pale green I can't quite grasp. I touch a tentative tongue against the firm, cool flesh.

'Honeydew melon, 10:45am,' notes the archive.

I let the fruit drop back into the bowl and push it aside. It's time to move swift as the Wind and be as closely formed as the Wood. I quit my view of Bay Heights, put the unfinished book in my finished pile, and march forward into the fray.

Beyond the office, the production looks like an ant colony. The whole is an astounding work of creative genius unknowable to any one of the parts. I am the best evidence of this. I am an auteur, and I have no idea what is happening. I decide to wait prudently in the chair with my name on it. Pretty soon I fall asleep.

A gentle whisper in my inner ear wakes me just in time

to see a tall figure in a loose, dark linen suit walking across the lot.

'Mr Galleon,' says Sullivan, extending a hand.

The hair on the crown of his skull is shaved into a symmetrical patch, and when he puts his hands together in a yogic salute and nods to me, I see that the shape is a bulls-eye target.

I stand up. My head meets his chest.

'Thanks for coming,' I say, shaking his hand firmly, sensors poised to register his pulse and temperature, interpretive software ready to chart his emotional state.

'I wouldn't miss it,' he says. 'I'm surprised you asked me actually. I got the feeling you didn't enjoy our time together on Cindy Mac.'

'Oh? All forgotten, I assure you.'

'Well, regardless, I'm excited to see what you're working with.'

'Of course. The technics. I'll attempt to give you the grand tour.'

I look about desperately at the maze of holograms, cameras, motion sensor units, feeling like a SynthoCritter in the hunter's quarter of the Ecodome.

Sensing danger, Stephanie appears by my side. She extends her delicate hand to Sullivan.

'I've just been watching your series on the archipelagos,' she says, beaming. 'You can count me as a real fan,'

Relief is expunged from my blocked sweat glands and soaks into the advanced fibres of my casual wear.

'This is new generation haptics,' explains Stephanie, gesturing to a shell rig where five young women, bodies lacerated by sensors, are measured for ThermoShock latex playsuits.

'Mr Galleon decided we need to get more from our sensations, so we are applying an interface to the entire body at each nerve site. There will be no more illusion transferral through the fingertips in this film. We are looking at sensitivity definition right down to the pinky toe.'

'An entire-body experience,' I add.

'So your main goal is still the sensual experience?' Sullivan asks.

'Of course,' I say.

'We are working with a higher-definition biogram here,' Stephanie continues. 'Each cell in the object is filmed and then created as its own individual model, then all patched together. The result is realer than real, with no interdependence or crumbling cells.'

'Flawlessness,' I add.

'An anathema to life,' Sullivan mutters.

'That's the point.' I try to look him straight in the eye and gauge something other than youthful arrogance and dissent. I could shake his hand once more in order to measure his vitals, to really know my enemy on the level of blood pressure and sweat viscosity, but there's no convenient excuse for contact.

We wander through the clusters of activity. Orders blast out of speaker points, lights flicker and dim and brighten again. Systems soundlessly enhance. Sullivan becomes captivated by this or that process, yet always retains his same grim grin, while Stephanie fields questions on mechanisms and purpose.

Jean, whom I had not realised was even on set, crosses the floor towards us. He is scowling.

'This is Sullivan,' I say.

'Of course,' Jean snarls.

'It's good to meet you, Mr Di Vita,' says Sullivan.

'Stephanie, will you give us a minute?' I swat my saviour away like a fly. Her face shows no sign of hurt or neglect; it is as smooth and generic as pearled silicon.

I subtly arrange my body and mind in attack stance.

Jean cocks an eyebrow.

'Sullivan,' I begin, 'I've been watching your trajectory with real interest. I want to make you a proposition.'

The eyebrow drops and Jean looks at me, horrified.

'Have you seen the promo for *Teardrops*?' I ask him.

'No, I—'

'It's the Great Wall of China thing.'

'Oh,' says Jean, slowly looking the young man over with a new, grudging respect. 'It's very good.'

'Thank you, Jean,' Sullivan says. 'That's very meaningful coming from you.'

Jean narrows his eyes. Clearly he too has trouble reading the young man.

'I want to know who your association designers are,' I break in.

'Max, with respect, everyone who is working on *Teardrops* is doing so out of love. We don't have labels like 'association designer' – it's so reductive. We're on a collective mission.'

'Alright, what do you want then?'

'You asked me here, Max. I thought you wanted to show

me how much you already have, to teach me some kind of lesson, not to pillage my slender resources.'

'Is the Alaskan-melt clip a *Teardrops* promo too?' Jean asks, still looking at Sullivan appraisingly.

'Yes.' Sullivan smiles.

Jean nods.

'Sullivan, your film is undoubtedly going to be good. But the reality is, mine will be the one that makes money,' I say. 'It may gross higher than any film I've ever made before. In the end, it's those figures that show how valuable your work is, not any critical voice declaring originality.'

'You have quite a career behind you,' Sullivan scowls.

I repulse the monkey, shift my tactics. 'You have a point. I'm not stupid. I have good reason for asking you here. I want to see more of what you could do, if, say, you had more resources. Besides, I'm looking to add something a little experimental to this next picture of mine. Some personal touch.' I cringe inwardly, deliberately angling my gaze away from Jean. 'I want you on board, Sullivan.'

'On this mega-tsunami disaster epic? I'm sorry, Max. I'm flattered, but I'm dedicated to my vision for a cinema of empathy.'

'What if I redesign the whole thing?'

'Include more explosions?'

'I'm being sincere, Sullivan. *Mega-Tsunami* doesn't go in for full immersion for another eight days. I could pause production, or even pull it for a little while. It will only feed the hype to do so. We could rearrange the items on the drawing board. Look around you. I have the means to take any direction I choose.'

Sullivan's mouth twitches.

'I've been thinking a lot about Pitcairn Island and what it represents,' I continue. 'There's this looming uncertainty right now, and I think it's a cinematic uncertainty. Seems like a shame to try to resolve it with big explosions. It gives us a chance to do something new. I've been thinking about a film the scope of which will be the whole world, not its cathartic death but rather all its adaptations and possibilities. I see what you are doing with the *Teardrops* promo. You have an innovative style. I think we can learn from each other. A mixture of your earnest homage to the history of the image and my—'

'Your money,' says Sullivan.

'—my considerable experience. My desire to reinvest in the industry, and to reinvent it.'

'Max, I want to be clear on something. I'm a committed artist.'

'We established that,' says Jean.

Sullivan continues undaunted. 'In my work, I'm committed to the uncompleted form, to the interrupted composition.'

Jean stifles a snicker.

Around us, million-dollar holographic glaciers melt, water breaking across the conductive floor. Vibrotactile tremors manipulate our skins.

'I want co-designer, co-director and co-producer credits,' says the committed artist, licking his lips.

After Sullivan leaves, Jean corners me between

fractaLight evocations of dying penguins.

'I hope you know what you're doing,' he says.

'I never do, you know that.'

'Yes, but you don't need him to show you. And you don't need empathy either. You have me. I'll tell you what you feel. I've been doing it for years.'

'We may have had our day, Jean. We need to step into the future.'

'You have no idea what you are talking about.'

'I wonder what it's like to actually be on a sinking island?'

'You tell me,' says Jean in a bored, bitter tone. 'You're the expert.'

'I plan to find out, I hope you will come with me.'

Jean snorts.

'What do you think of these penguins?' I ask him.

'I think they should explode. And I think our reaction to that should be fear, not empathy.'

••

Ellie is crouched over a hose replenishing the hydrogarden when I swing the Fleet Methane sedan up to our Bay Heights home.

'Hello, Max,' she says, unsurprised. 'What a surprise.'

Rows of cloned crocuses fan out around my wife in symmetrical patterns.

'You look so elegant today, Ellie,' I say, approaching her gently so as not to disturb any order. I have come home to have my wife hold me, and now that I'm here, it's reassuring to see that Bay Heights is an actual house, a thing of stone and wood rather than a series of domestic sets for a family sit-com.

'The camera adds ten pounds,' she says, turning and stalking in to the house.

In the kitchen she makes a show of manually logging me into the household management system. My settings kick in. A state-of-the-art Oji machine begins to drip coffee through a sheet of thermaglass into my favourite cup at a rate of forty-eight drops per minute.

'You look tired,' says Ellie.

'I am. The film is taking over.'

'Creative strain. But something else, too – you look weary in a deeper way.'

'Maybe. Perhaps disappointment. I usually love the initial period of making a movie, when I have complete control.'

'You're lonely?'

'Maybe.'

Ellie retrieves my cup, sliding it across the bench towards me. Then she opens another hutch, producing a loaf of just-baked almond bread.

'Thank you.'

Ellie smiles graciously. If she isn't pleased to see me it's impossible to tell.

'Jean tells me you two are taking a trip?'

'Oh, yes?'

'Yes, he says you are going to take the tsunami project to Pitcairn. He also told me that you have started sleeping with the enemy. I thought he was joking about an affair with your assistant or some minor TV personality, but apparently you are courting a protégé.'

'Ah, yes, the young idealist, Sullivan. Jean hates him, of course.'

'Of course.' Ellie smiles with affection that's not meant for me. 'Jean thinks your admiration for him is evidence of some kind of midlife crisis.'

'I suppose that could be true.'

'I told him it was nonsense, that you need a memory to have a midlife crisis.'

'Do you?'

'Of course. If you have no past, how can you know you have reached midlife?' She looks at me searchingly. 'You are immune.'

'To crisis? We could sell that, Ellie.'

Ellie does not reply.

'Where are the kids?' I ask.

'School wellness carnival. Remember to congratulate Lilly, she's on the gymnastics team this year. I added a copy of her routine to your itinerary.'

'Thanks.'

'Jonas didn't sign up for anything,' she says, nodding at our son's complex tangle of hapticwear, hanging on a hook in the corner of the room.

'Boys love games. It's nothing unusual,' I say.

'I know. I'm not worried. He has a lot of friends in the games. They're from all over the world. I haven't played the one he's into now, but judging from the last one they haven't changed very much since I was a kid. Of course, they are much more realistic now. But what bothers me is the stigma. I mean, when we were children, games were for – well, they weren't for socially adjusted children.'

'I'm sure that I played them.'

'I have no doubt.'

'We should take the kids out later.'

'Sure.' Ellie looks apprehensive.

'Just for a little while. We could go and sit by the bay.'

'That sounds lovely, but, you know, Jonas is quite upset with you.' She gazes off to the horizon. She's finished our current interaction and set her sights on future worlds.

'Anguish, 2:45pm,' notes the archive, but Ellie isn't paying attention.

'Why?' I ask.

'Pitcairn, of course.' She narrows her gaze as if she could catch a glimpse, just beyond the decorative rooftops, of the sinking island.

I go to our bedroom, take off my suit and change into a pair of soft Italian jeans made from recycled polymers by some ingenious textile engineer. Our original art deco dressing table sits against the wall at the foot of our bed. Its huge circular mirror has been replaced with a screen. In it, a pristine landscape glitters. It's a forest, deep and enduring. To a child of another time, it would seem magical, as though you could jump through the mirror into another world. Our children barely notice it.

'Log in.'

Pitcairn Island rises in the mirror like a ghoul in an old horror film. A graph describes a drop of 0.0014 mm, the biggest this year. I choose a commentary option. Two pre-senters, a male and a female, interviewing an expert.

'Well, I'm shocked, Mary,' says the male presenter. His expression is electroderm-steady. 'These are hard facts. It's sounds to me like there's a one hundred per cent chance that this new data may or may not signal the beginning of the end for our planet.'

'It sure sounds like that, Wayne,' says the female present-er, nodding. 'But I think we should defer to an expert, don't you?' She addresses the question to an imaginary crowd who bay and hoot like a pack of mechanical wolves.

'I'm glad to be here,' says the expert, offering no further introduction. 'What's important to know, Mary, is that we are in the presence of potentially real devastation. The plau-sibility level on this scenario outcome is through the roof. I'm not going to lie to you – that's bad.'

'How high have plausibility levels reached?' asks Wayne.

'At this point we can't confirm figures, but I can say this: we have never seen a plausibility level this high. Probability levels, yes. Plausibility? Never.'

'Can you give your expert opinion to the viewers at home?'

'Based on the new data and statistics, my expert opin-ion is that this isn't good. We are talking about at least two major factors. First is rising sea level. Our estimated yearly sea level expansion rate is higher now than it ever has been. It's exponential. The South Pacific is registering an increase in sea level at almost three times higher than it was just five years ago. That might not sound like much to many of you, but if you just think of a glass slowly filling with water at a tiny fraction of a drop per second, and then the water begins dropping at three times that rate, you'll have an idea of how much damage that can do. It's not good. It's potentially devastating.'

Wherever the expert is, it is coded night. A studio moon sheds a grave light onto his projected catastrophes.

'Now,' he continues, 'if you think about that slowly filling glass of water floating in a sink, itself almost full, you tell me what happens when the weight of that glass of water eventually causes it to drop completely into the brimming sink. Overflow. Fact.'

Mary looks shocked. A helpful rendering of a sink, splashing tides of blue-green water onto a polished kitchen floor, appears above her like a thought bubble. Pow-Pow stands opposite the sink, hands on hips, a droplet splashing from his own fathomless pupil into the spill below.

'The second factor here is volcanic activity. The island itself is volcanic. We know that. That it is dormant is meaningless. We can't be complacent. I'll tell you why: of the sixteen largest explosive eruptions during the nineteenth and twentieth centuries, twelve occurred with volcanoes which had almost no known historical activity. Fact. And they caused the deaths of one-hundred and ninety-three-thousand people. And that was at a low plausibility level. Imagine what the potential is now that we are recording plausibility levels of five or six times that amount.'

'What are the global ramifications of this?' asks Wayne, his forefinger and thumb hooked around his chiselled chin in a gesture of serious thought.

'The ramifications are conceptually unlimited, Wayne. What we have to understand is that everything is connected. This is just one link in the chain. There are credible models that suggest the rising sea levels, followed by the dramatic increase in ocean temperature, once exacerbated by the engulfment of not one but potentially three islands, could lead to the complete destruction of the already endangered icecaps. And this would just be the beginning. What am I saying here? Potentially: rogue waves, floods, earthquakes, ice storms. There is even a strong argument for this event signifying the final catastrophe.'

Mary claps her hand over her trembling lips as she has done millions of times before, catching any vocal appeal to a higher power just behind her tangerine-lacquered fingernails.

'Now, we can't say that this is what will definitely happen, but let's begin to think hypothetically and say: this will happen...' The expert's cadence leaves us with only the end of the message. 'Let's say the sinking of Pitcairn means the end of the earth. Okay. The earth is going to end. What will that look like?'

'I think we all need to put on our headsets here to get a bit of an idea of what we might be in for,' says Mary. All the fear has dropped from her voice; she now sounds excited, as if the lights are being turned down for a party game.

A headset appears beside me on the bedside table, but I wave it away. I choose to hang back in the shadows of the bedroom. I live in the flickering neon of the 1280×

multi-interface. I surf, I sample, I store, I skim, I direct, I occupy, I link, I associate, I pattern, I save, I load, I send, I generate, I log, I shuffle, I repeat, I edit, I option, I accept, I ignore, I hype, I share, I subscribe, I comment, I rate, I choose, I dwell.

I swing out over the infinity of images: a sinking island to a genetically profound dung-beetle, a sadistic game show to a ruined dustbowl town, to the fastest man on earth, to cartoon children and pandas singing 'Ring Around the Rosie', and there is the option to join them, now, before they all fall down.

• •

The clattering of bags being dropped to the floor downstairs snaps me out of trance-state. Almost three hours have passed. I switch views and watch my own children as they enter the house, continuing their shrill conversation, calling out for Ellie.

The kitchen crunches complex equations before churning out spirulina and organaproteinberry smoothies, just in time for hungry children to descend. I head down to meet them, hovering in the hallway until they sense my presence.

'Daddy!' Lilly yelps.

She beckons me into the kitchen where she and Jonas are gulping their snack. Each mouthful adds calories to their daily quota, producing complex nutritional charts in the background. Future eating plans are constantly being constructed, ensuring future Lilly and Jonas are of stable weight, nourished, satisfied, and fully able to attend to the events of their lives.

'Hello, little Lilly.'

She scampers over to me and I bend down to receive a kiss on the cheek.

'I'm on the gym team,' she says. 'We might be going to China.'

'That's exciting. At this rate you will have seen the whole world before you turn twelve.'

Lilly gives me a withering look. 'Not the whole world. That's impossible.'

Something in the near-distance bleeps and my daughter's face becomes distant.

'Sorry, Dad, I have to take this,' she says, and scurries off to her bedroom-cum-office at the back of the house.

'She's very busy,' I share with Jonas.

He shrugs, pulling on his gaming headset.

I peer in at him through the silvered lenses. My face is probably floating like a cloud in some compelling post-apocalyptic wasteland, an obstacle to completion far less significant than ammunition inventory or vitality points.

'Jonas?' I place a hand on his shoulder and he flinches.

'She's highly involved in several groups at an organisational level,' he says in an irritated monotone. 'She has a natural aptitude.'

'I can see that. How about you?'

'Not really my thing.'

'What's your thing?'

Resigned, Jonas pushes his headset back onto his crown. 'Seriously? Who knows? Besides, what my thing is today might be totally opposite tomorrow. Best not to go on record with a for-sure-thing this early.'

'What's the game?' I gesture at his skull.

'*Glacial Assault 5.*'

'Is it enthralling?'

He shrugs. 'It's not as good as *Mutiny*, but I can't play that until my friend logs on. *Glacial Assault* is a good solo game. It's simple.'

'What's *Mutiny*?' I ask, and immediately regret it as his small eyes narrow and lock on mine.

'It's the one that's set on Pitcairn. Remember?'

I stare him down.

Eventually he says, 'How's your film?'

'Good.' I ignore his accusing tone. 'You'll be pleased to know two things: tsunami...' I pause for effect. '...and Pitcairn.'

'I already knew that,' he says, furrowing his brow. 'It's dropped again, you know.'

'Yes, I saw,' I say. 'Potentially real devastation.'

'That's a stupid phrase. What does it even mean?'

'I'm not sure. I guess I haven't thought about it.'

'You should.'

'Have you?'

'Of course. I talk about this stuff all the time with my friend in Lutsk.'

'You have a friend in Lutsk?'

'Dad,' he says, impatiently. 'That's why I have to get up

early sometimes.'

'You get up early?'

'I have to. Because of the time difference between here and Lutsk.'

'You'd have thought they'd have done something about time difference by now.'

'It's an oversight.'

'How did you make a friend in Lutsk?'

'We met through online petitioning. We play *Mutiny* together. He's really into monitoring Pitcairn's drop. He has a lot of theories.'

'What does he think?'

'He's torn between the fatalist view that the submergence of the island will mark the beginning of the absolute reorganisation of the earth's climate, and the view that it won't make any difference at all, that it's just another doomsday conspiracy. Still, we won't know either way for another fifteen years or so – that's what he thinks, that's when we can get the measurements, trends, patterns, blah.'

'What do you think?'

'I think it's dumb to align yourself with any one position. The predictions are all over the place. But no matter what, either the island will sink and lead to the end of the world, or it will sink and the world will be fine. Or it won't even sink. It's dumb. As if thinking about it does anyone any good. Who cares?'

'That seems like a pretty grim perspective, Jonas.'

'All we do is place stupid bets and then invent big-story outcomes that may or may not mean anything anyway.

I mean, what about complexity?'

'Indeed.'

'And some people say that all this is just a by-product of successful evolution, and that the worst possible thing we can do is to try to slow the process, because it's inevitable.' He shakes his head like a tired old man.

'Shame, 4:50pm,' notes the archive, adding to my emotional map.

'And some people still believe in God, which is so weird,' says Jonas.

'It's important for people to have faith,' I say, parroting the prepared slogans from the *Building Tolerant Offspring* guide.

'What the hell is faith?' counters Jonas.

'Faith is how people believe in God.'

'Is that an answer?'

I hold my ground.

'My friend in Lutsk says your films are part of the problem.'

'He watches my films in Lutsk?'

'Why wouldn't he?'

'I just never thought about it.'

'Exactly. If you think about it, what's the difference between Lutsk and here? How many things do you think about that might not happen and might not even matter anyway, and meanwhile people are watching your films in Lutsk and you don't even bother considering it.'

'That's true,' I say, beginning to feel uncomfortable. 'Hey, I thought we could go down to the bay.'

'I'm not scared, you know. If it sinks, it sinks. We'll know what it means when it happens. Or we won't. Whatever.'

'Maybe you should go and have a shower.'

'Fine. Block me out. Your loss.' He turns away.

'Jonas,' I call after him. He stops but doesn't turn back. 'You can come,' I say, and it's as though I've said some words of pure magic, words that allow the bright young child to leap free from his prison of old man's fatigue and worry.

'What?' he almost shrieks.

'You can come to Pitcairn with Jean and I. You can be a consultant on the film. It has become clear to me that you have considerable expertise.'

Jonas is dumbstruck.

'Am I your hero?' I ask.

'I don't have heroes,' he says, recovering some of his grimness. 'Heroes are stupid. It's statistically improbable that you would choose the right one. And even if you did, you couldn't rely on them to be consistent.'

'Sound logic,' I say gravely, but the emphasis is lost when Jonas suddenly barrels his small body into mine, wrapping his arms around my hips in a tiny bear-cub hug. We stay there for a long while, my son dreaming of flight and adventure while I wish silently to be able to remember this: please, just this one moment, even if the rest of the archive burns.

• •

Evening is marked by an enhanced, oversaturated sunset. We choose a spot by the water that has tables and a swing set. Ellie lays out an impressive picnic spread and administers various vitamins and antihistamines to the kids. We begin eating, tentatively at first and then with gusto, as though reacquainting our bodies with the action of eating, forcing them to recall its pleasure. Initially the food circulates strategically. First nut loaf, then garden salad, then fruit. But soon the order is mixed. We reach over each other for more of one thing or another. And when we are finished the table looks like the remains of a village after a war is over, when all interest is lost.

While the kids play, Ellie and I sit on top of the table with our legs touching, like teenagers. Lilly busies herself on the shoreline, measuring salinity with her Trainee Waste Watchers kit. She taps data into a logbook. Jonas, headset on, enthralled in a game with his friend in Lutsk, darts around us.

'Reset possibility,' he says. 'Exchange salted pork store for native wife. Engage possible scenario outcome.'

A small parental view window in my periphery shows me what he sees. His arms jerk around his torso, cutting through thick scrub. His hands shield his eyes from dangling serpents and the splash of poisonous sap. He stabs a home-carved oar into choppy waters, uses a halved coconut shell to bail water from a leaking canoe. Thwarted by the fierce waves, he plunges into the swell, one thin prepubescent arm wrapped around his newly acquired wife, the other paddling furiously through the foaming brine. He is gasping. He tumbles in a wave and is dumped, left reeling under the picnic table. His eyes are covered by the headset, but the position of his jaw indicates a steadiness of concentration. Each strange tableau is a strategic move, conceived from discipline and insight. In another context he would look as though he were fitting and needed medical attention.

'New decision. Bury my wife. Paddle the strait at low tide,' he says firmly, decisively, standing like a soldier before a drill sergeant.

'It's good you're taking him,' says Ellie. 'If the island sinks he can build you a canoe.'

'Real or virtual?'

She laughs. 'Whichever is more practical.'

'You're not worried? It might be dangerous. I might not be a fit guardian.'

'Oh Max, don't say that on record. Of course you are. I think it will be a marvellous adventure. Secret men's business.' She laughs again.

'You don't think it will sink?'

'Of course it will sink. It is sinking. Just very, very slowly. We might not even notice. Besides, I don't need to worry about the end of the world. You do it for me.'

'And here's me, feeling so redundant.'

Ellie and I fall silent, content to watch blue foam lap against glass dunes. Further out, little sailboats made from light rock gently. I wrap my arms around my wife's shoulders and she gives me what seems like a genuine smile.

'This was a nice idea,' she says, and something tangible flashes between us.

'I evoke the hardy endurance of the ravaging drought,' says Jonas from under the table.

'Yes,' I say to Ellie, and then: 'I'm sorry.'

She shrugs and closes her eyes for a second, covering up some deep sea that we might have plumbed the depths of together.

'Will you stay here tonight?' she asks.

'Yes.'

I want her to ask me to stay forever. I want her to designate tasks for me, tell me how to spend my life. Great spiritual callings. Or at least masculine, husbandly things. Lawn mowing. Minor carpentry. Fucking. But all that is taken care of by expertly designed machines – combinations of metals, plastics and nanochips that know my children, my home, my wife's body, with the benefit of centuries of research and design.

'I am the sharp burn of the returning ice age,' says Jonas.

Later, at home in our bathroom, my wife and I wash up, getting ready for bed, rinsing in Panda Approved portions of water and soap.

'Do you want to have sex?' she says, just like that – as she always has, as though asking me if I like salt on my soybeans; a benign indulgence.

'Yes.'

'Okay then.'

Ellie heads into her closet and returns draped in a golden-threaded robe that looks like a chrysalis. If I bought it for her for some distant anniversary, I can't remember now.

'Suspicion, 11:10pm,' notes the archive.

We undress next to the bed, removing our clothes and placing them in a cleaning hutch by the door. Then we lie down. There's no awkwardness or embarrassment. We know each other's bodies. Only our desires are unknown. I insinuate my body into hers until we are making strange love. As though two bodies entwined were enough. I push our cheeks together, smell the age-fighting enzymes of her face, the Maxishine pigment of her hair.

'Your breath is hot,' she says, pushing me away and moving on top.

In the mirror I regard her elegant form above mine. Her buttocks are a perfect china-bowl curve, her even shoulders flow into the muscles that pull at her breasts: beautiful muscles, muscles the names of which I surely must once have known.

On top of me she conducts herself perfectly. Her timing is precise and calculated. I concentrate on locating myself within her, on merging our intentions in a mutual outcome.

Her face is blank and serene. Frightening in low wattage. There's no deep sea, no abyss of reaching hands. Nothing. We are a proxy network.

Somewhere in the future of our coupling: an anticipated disconnection.

• •

Ellie is gone from the bed when Lilly launches onto me like a demented animal.

'Morning!' she proclaims, her tone more drill sergeant than small girl. She clutches my shoulders.

'You're very affectionate this morning, Lilly.'

'It's something new I'm trying.'

'It's nice.' A bright sky shines in the art-deco mirror.

'I'm still not convinced,' she says.

'And how are you this morning?'

'A little B12-deficient, but otherwise balanced.'

We lie still after the initial burst of movement. We're a cubist rendering of family, grotesque heads sprouting from a chest.

'It's off-peak time,' says Lilly, suddenly loosening her grip and scuttling back to the floor. 'Now, Dad.'

I peer over the end of my bed at my small daughter.

'Off-peak time for what?'

'Water.'

'Oh. Okay, I'll get on it soon.'

'You have thirteen minutes. Seriously.'

She turns on her heel and heads out of the room. I shut my eyes for another few seconds. When I open them Lilly's face looms like a storm cloud in the blue sky of the mirror.

'Eight minutes,' she yells. 'No need to hurry, it's only the ecological status of our species at stake.' She looks at me like a surgeon might at a benign tumour. 'And Mum says to tell you to check your itinerary. You have an appointment.'

From bed, I look over my coming day. I have a meeting with Sullivan, and a meeting with Tom's doctor. I'd like to skip both, or at least have already attended them.

'Seven point five minutes,' yells Lilly.

I turn my attention to the tasks of the present. I certainly don't want to be held accountable for the ecological status of our species. Not before breakfast.

I walk sleepily to the shower where hot water splashes on my back, loosening tight muscles. Invigorating jazz plays and the motivational smell of coffee is puffed into the steam from vents near my feet. My shower is three-and-a-half minutes too long though, and when I arrive in the kitchen, dressed neatly and ready for a new day, Lilly is not speaking to me. She makes a lot of noise packing her bag, smashing various devices around, kicking her feet along the tiles. She leaves without saying goodbye.

'Panda Points?' Ellie enquires, sashaying into the room as I am scanning through channels of news bites and noise.

'Afraid so.'

'You know it's important to her.'

'I know.'

'She will learn to analyse your apathy soon – then we will be in real trouble.'

'I'll get more.'

'Apathy or Panda Points?'

'Whichever my family requires.'

'Thank you. Always the provider. Did you look at your itinerary?'

'I did.'

'And are you nervous?'

'About what?'

'About seeing Dr Stern again.'

'Who?'

'The doctor who is helping you and Tom to connect. Come on Max, I really want you to commit to this.'

'Yes. Sorry. But why can't you do it again?'

'It's not about me.'

'Right. So what is it about then? Is this just you trying to have me assessed, Ellie? It's not necessary, you know. I have a complete psychological profile logged for you to peruse at any time. And feel free to add to it if there's some glitch, if you think there's anything missing.'

Ellie laughs coldly. 'There's nothing missing, Max. Nothing that is not in plain sight.' Then, perhaps regretting her cruel tone, she adds, 'I just have a feeling about this.'

'Fine. Okay. And what are you doing this morning?'

'An awareness-raising lobby.'

'Raising awareness of what?'

'Not sure,' she laughs, almost nervously, as she floats out of the room.

I sip my coffee and wait. At nine I accept the connection query from Dr Stern. This time, when her disembodied voice fills the room, I feel instantly irritated. Outside the hospital, and far from Tom's placid presence, her intrusion is amplified.

'Mr Galleon, can you hear me?'

'Yes,' I grumble.

'Is Ms Smyth there too?'

'Coming,' yells Ellie from somewhere behind me.

'Great. Our next meeting should be face-to-face if we are going to get serious about the procedure.'

'My wife still thinks it's a good idea.'

'Do you?'

'I do,' yells Ellie from somewhere.

'Do you, Mr Galleon?' Dr Stern asks.

'I have no idea.'

'Well, we'll have more success if you have an open mind. Now, I'm afraid I've got a few questions to get through.'

'About Tom?'

'Not yet. For now I just want to focus on you.'

'Why?'

'Because you're the connection. We need to follow on from where we left off last time. I sent through some articles, did you...'

'Sorry, Dr Stern,' Ellie says, 'we haven't had time yet.' She saunters back into the room, wearing a dark green satin sari with a crimson sash that puts me in mind of forest fire.

'A busy morning. You know, children...' She puts her hand on my left shoulder as though we are posing for a portrait.

Undaunted by our demonstrated lack of interest and by our performed family bliss, the doctor continues. 'Read them when you get a chance. They explain the grounding theory.'

'Okay,' I say, picking at some dry skin on my hand, unwilling to take up Ellie's enthusiasm for whatever project she's embarked on.

I tune out as the two women ramble through polite dialogue. I feel like a child, dragged to the doctor, beset with an illness the symptoms of which his young mind cannot name or understand.

'...okay, Mr Galleon?'

'Call him Max,' says Ellie, snapping me back to attention.

'Okay, Max – so can you?' Dr Stern asks.

'What?' I sound defensive.

'Describe your most vivid memory.'

'Probably not a good idea.'

'Sorry?' says Dr Stern.

Ellie jabs me in the ribs.

'Memory is not my strong suit.'

'It can be any memory, anything at all.'

I pause for a moment, scathingly appraising the situation, feeling a hot flush spread over my cheeks.

'I'm not sure I even consider memory to be a credible category,' I tell her.

'It doesn't have to be credible, it just has to be yours.'

I look down at the floor, at my hands, out the window, but the doctor's attentive face is everywhere thanks to that ominous front-gaze interface setting my wife likes to activate when making a point.

'Fine,' I say, giving Ellie an 'I surrender' look, and seeing, for a second, Dr Stern's soft features blur over her sharp ones.

I half-heartedly try a deep-breathing sequence, and say, 'I'm in Tom's room. It's filled with photographs, toys – a bunch of generic childhood artefacts that could have been ours. Tom's asleep. Faceless people begin to file in, two by two. They kneel at his bed, speaking to him in desperate sounds. The room gets too full to move, but they keep coming. I'm pushed against the wall. People crawl on top of the bed. They claw at Tom's skin and hair. I try to yell but find I've forgotten how to talk. I start to panic, my mouth gaping like a fish, pushing through the people towards the bed. Then, suddenly, Tom gasps, wrenching himself up as if from underwater. Without opening his eyes, he yells, "We need the disaster! We need the final catastrophe!"'

I open my eyes and see the doctor's broad, sympathetic face.

'I'm not sure if you understood me,' she says, slowly.

'No?'

'Well, is that a memory? Did that really happen, Max?'

'Gabrielle.' I use her name pointedly, meeting her gaze and feeling oddly better. 'That's precisely my point.'

Ellie coughs. The doctor does not break eye contact.

'It's important that we have a good understanding of each other going into the process,' she says, 'because we are talking about a process, not a procedure. It's something that you are going to have to work at – almost as hard as I am, to ensure that we see results.'

I try to blink as slowly as possible to avoid both the doctor's imploring eyes and Ellie's disgruntled shadow, rigid in my periphery. A soothing cup of herbal tea appears on a coffee table between my wife and I. I'm not sure who it's intended for.

'Of course, I've gone through Tom's files,' Dr Stern presses on uncertainly. 'But before I start telling you what I think, I'd like to hear your impressions. Often there is something more in the intuition of someone who knows the subject. Mostly the information is unconscious, but it can be telling. I have some unconventional methods, Mr Galleon.'

'I really have no idea about our childhood,' I say. 'And even if I could conjure up something that you might approve as a memory, there's no way to assure its accuracy. These days I rely almost entirely on a networked memory. I monitor everything, so I always know what has happened and how I felt about it. It's a much more reliable system.'

She looks a little deflated, and changes the subject. 'There must have been a few theories batted around as to how Tom got to his current state?'

'Of course. That he was hit by a car and then dumped outside the trailer pack,' Ellie replies, eager to provide something useful. 'That someone from the pack beat him unconscious...'

'Do either of these hold true?'

'I couldn't say,' my wife admits.

'And how about you, Max – what do you think?'

'I'd say something happened to him that was singular and violent and shattering. Something completely beyond my comprehension.'

The doctor is dressed plainly. A grey skirt and a crumpled cream blouse. She's younger than I am, early forties maybe. She has almost-black hair, pinned back from her face with silver combs. It's an oddly out-of-date look, but she is pretty, I suppose, like a wilting flower.

'The fractures in his bones were already partially healed when he was found. If he had injuries from a car crash or a beating, then he sustained them at least two weeks before he was found,' I tell her, reading from a report that I have blinked into view.

'Yes, that's what we've been told,' she says, and pauses. 'Have you heard of THLE?'

'No,' I reply. The archive cross-checks the anagram against the network and pins a highlighted article to my research board: Temporal Lobe Hibernation Epilepsy.

'It occurs when the brain shuts down following a state of prolonged neural overload,' says the doctor. 'It was quite common a decade ago.'

'Do you think that's what Tom has?' asks Ellie.

'It's another theory.'

I sigh and Ellie pinches my arm hard. 'I'll leave you to finish up,' she says. 'I have an appointment.'

The doctor looks away politely as Ellie leaves. I watch my wife drift down the stairs and into the rest of the house, like she's a blazing maidenhead on a distant ship.

When she's gone, the doctor speaks again. 'Oh, Max,' the doctor says, with too much familiarity. 'Don't worry about it.'

On the screen she's unexpectedly relaxed and easy, as though we are old friends.

'Déjà vu, 9:45am,' notes the archive.

'The issue is translation,' she says. 'To fully understand the patterning of a single human brain, you need to transfer those unique patterns onto a processor. Either an artificial processor, like a computer that can decode the patterns into data, which we then have the task of decoding, or we can transfer onto a conscious biological substrate, like another human, who might be able to experience those patterns. A good comparison is the translation of language: the actual translator is as important as the text. A translator needs to have an intrinsic, contextual understanding of the subject. Do you follow me?'

I nod, and she continues. 'Outside of this model, we have no way to measure subjective experience – we can only measure its external correlates, like behaviour. But the comatose have no behaviour. Even a dilation of the pupil, an irregular breath, a cough or a sneeze, would be behaviour in this case. Tom exhibits none of this.'

'You are talking about turning me into a computer?'

'No, quite the opposite.' She smiles with disarming affection. 'Though from how you describe your reliance on external memory, I wouldn't think you'd be worried about that.'

'No?'

'I get the impression...' Gabrielle's smile wavers. She searches my face and then changes tack. 'What we are talking about is not a mechanical translation, it's a deep intimacy. Perhaps the most profound connection possible for human beings to establish.' She looks at me unblinkingly as she says this.

'Just twenty years ago we knew nothing about consciousness,' she says. 'It was barely even an experimental parameter. We didn't understand what kind of neural activity allowed categorisation to occur. We treated it as little more than a decision in an algorithm. Not long ago, leading neurologists talked about brains using computer metaphors. They didn't even have the language to begin to describe the kinds of procedures that are fairly common today. The technology I'm working with can allow you to access your brother's consciousness and experience it as your own. More importantly, it allows him to experience an external stimulus that may force into action those brain functions that his coma paralyses. If we are successful, then you close your eyes...' She blinks finally, slowly. 'You close your eyes and you become someone else.'

••

Twenty minutes after the doctor logs off I've forgotten her name. I know this because I need to check the archive and watch our encounter so that I can explain the whole thing to Jean. The obligation I feel to run things past Jean is heavily ingrained in me, no matter the pomposity or obscurity of his view.

'The idea, I think,' I tell him, 'is that I have some kind of dream conversation with Tom. He's given access to my brain and can let me know how he's feeling, what's been happening out there in the nothingness.'

'You will be tapping into his unconsciousness,' says Jean, impressed.

'But: can a person have an unconscious if they are unconscious? Isn't it all consciousness or nothing at that point?'

'There's always repression,' says Jean, and then: 'I suppose it might be interesting, professionally speaking. For us, I mean.'

'Oh yes?'

'Well, it's a pure immersion. No one is in control. It's an ultimate surrender. You don't even know what genre you will be dealing with.'

'Memoir, I hope.'

'You have such mundane dreams. I think Tom will turn out to be more interesting than you, even unconscious.'

'Thanks,' I say, but I only sulk for a moment. I can't afford to lose Jean's attention, or my own. 'I have misgivings.'

'Of course you do.' He now looks bored. 'What if Tom

can confirm nothing, can give you no more idea of yourself? Or what if he does not recognise you – how then are you to know he was even your brother in the first place and not just some elaborate hoax?'

'Exactly.'

'You will be afraid no matter what you do. You may as well do something rather than nothing. Besides, I expect this is all Ellie's doing, yes?'

'Yes.'

'Then there's no point debating it. It's already in motion and has its own design. Let's talk about our film.'

'Okay,' I say. He's right, of course. 'I've invited Jonas to accompany us to Pitcairn.'

'A child? What moves you to take a child to the end of the world?'

'It's his legacy.'

Jean looks amused.

'He feels quite strongly about it,' I say.

'I don't doubt it. Alright, I suppose we need him, in that every apocalypse story needs a child. Actually, he might be good as a body sketch for animations. Can he feign gruesome deaths?'

'He's a heavy user of haptic gaming networks.'

'Good!' says Jean. 'Have you spoken to the script supervisors?'

'I don't know.'

'Well, they've reorganised the narrative elements around the island. They've designed the algorithm to incorporate all real time data. Apparently this can continue even after the film's release.'

'So it will always be current.'

'That's the idea.'

'What happens if the island sinks?'

'Exactly! It's an exciting prospect. We might have a film on our hands that eventually incorporates an immersion of its own demise. There's no way to imagine what that looks like until it occurs – but it can't hurt the takings.'

'No, not until there are no takings left.'

Jean smiles wistfully. 'The last film,' he says.

●●

It's rare and strange to have the chance to sit beside my wife on our tasteful lounge suite. Our children are sprawled out before us as though posing for a twentieth-century domestic products advertisement. Lilly busies herself with a complex chart. Jonas is temporally jacked-in to Lutsk, having a conversation in a pidgin language I don't under-stand with a person I can't see. Beside me and yet not, Ellie keeps abreast of social engagements while simultaneously teaching herself botany.

'Do you know where your children are?' I say to her, in a mockery of delinquency prevention campaigns.

She gives me a half-laugh.

'Never,' she says. 'Thank god.'

We look at them for a while. They are totally absorbed in their elsewheres; breaking back into where we are only for the occasional grab at the snack bowl.

Pitcairn Island is spread across one whole wall of the family room.

'Funny to think it's an actual place,' says Ellie. 'Somewhere you can visit. It seems so unreal to me. Or rather, so much a part of my life here that it can't exist concretely somewhere else. Somewhere far away, I mean.'

I nod. 'My itinerary has us logged on an airtrain with a boat transfer in New Zealand,' I say.

'For anyone else, going there would make it more real.'

'What do you mean?'

'Well, most people take trips for the memories. But you're more of a colonial reconnoitrer. Once you're done with that island, it will belong to the empire. People will have total access to it because of your film. Even after it sinks.'

'Yes. If there are still people around to watch my films.'

'You can add that clause to anything. Might as well do nothing.'

'According to Jean, we've worked up an algorithm to incorporate the sinking – so I won't only be taking possession of the island, but also it's sinking.'

'Disturbing.'

'I've started to think of the film like *The Picture of Dorian Gray*; the real location must, sadly, sink. But its representation will be here forever.'

'You have it round the wrong way. In *Dorian Gray*, it's the artwork that ages. The real Dorian stays young and carefree – at least for long enough to be driven mad and to destroy himself.'

'Sounds like it needs an update for modern audiences.'

Ellie smiles oddly. 'You're the expert,' she says. Then she tempers the compliment with a reminder of my basic impotency. 'I'm feeding all your vitals through to Dr Stern right now. I've set up a few new observation parameters.'

'Like what?'

'Just more emotional stuff. No big deal. She wants to see if there's any unconscious connection, or any remembrance of yours influencing everyday behaviour.'

'She knows how to read that?'

'I suppose so.'

'I don't know how I feel about you doing that without telling me.'

'I did tell you,' she says.

I wince.

'You know,' she says, 'in some respects your two obsessions have a lot in common. '

'Which obsessions?'

'Tom, and that island. They are both impassive, and yet so much depends on them. On some decoding of them. On working out their past and future. You interact with them like you are playing one of Jonas' games, and yet they are totally uncommunicative, sinking, sullen.'

'Alone,' I add.

At this, Lilly, who I'd forgotten was even there, swings around to lay a blazing, admonishing look on her parents.

'Pitcairn isn't alone,' she scoffs. 'It's an ecosystem.'

ROMANTIC
SUBPLOT

'Why did my wife send me to you?' he asks.

'She was curious,' Dr Stern says.

'About Tom?'

'About you and Tom.'

'Which part of my brain is still in love with her?'

'There is no part. You are in love with her when you experience a particular pattern of neural fire.'

'Which part of my brain is in love with you?'

'There is no part.'

'You are the fire in my neurons.'

'Scientists hate it when you construct lame metaphors from biochemistry.'

'There's love in my cortex.'

'Stop, or I'll sedate you. You're just experiencing a chemical, electrical, and hormonal synthesis.'

'Is that why I can't remember any of this when I leave you?'

'You can't remember because you believe you are a

zombie. You don't know how you feel.'

'What does it feel like to be you?'

'Like blotting paper.'

She falls back on the paisley bedspread like a moth camouflaging. Max perches at the end of the bed, waiting for the uneasiness to rise up again. Outside, rasping voices sing folk ballads to the strum of an acoustic guitar.

'This place gives me the creeps,' says Max.

Gabrielle smiles. She's tired. Lately she feels as though she is running at half-capacity, overloaded and apt to crash.

'Doctor,' Max says. 'I need talk therapy.'

She sighs. Max's inability to recognise the needs of others, without having it logged in some database of his, constitutes a block. She troubleshoots it methodically.

'Let's just be still for a moment,' she says.

Max fidgets. He has the attention span of a toddler. In their early meetings he used any downtime to minutely review the seconds just passed. Gabrielle let it happen, partially to test him: know a person's compulsions and you know what they need. And it was convenient too, that he was occupied while she worked on other things. It seemed odd to her, though, that Max, locked in his revisions of moments past, was unconcerned with missing moments present.

He explained that the archive took care of the present. It was hard to get him to switch it off. Another troubleshoot: she cited reasons that the archive didn't belong here. That it couldn't capture complexity of the work, that it experienced technical feedback issues, and, finally, unbuttoning her blouse, she pointed out the most obvious reason not to record their appointments: Eloise Smyth.

Beside her now, post-coital Max is restless. He needs continual stimulation. She considers turning on a feed of the island, letting him slip into the hypnotic trance of watching points of points of angstroms drop portentously into the sea.

'What's the worst thing you've ever done?' he asks, seemingly eager to get back to a more gloomy normality.

'Really?'

'Yes. I'm interested.'

Gabrielle yawns.

'Fine, I'll go first,' says Max. 'I've blown up cities to make cinema.'

It's a conversation loop they've had before.

'Do you regret it?' she asks.

'I don't know. No. Nothing really exploded. Not in any real sense. But then, it feels the same, like it did happen. I guess that's the point.'

'I'm not sure that's true.'

'Your turn.'

Gabrielle sighs again. She stares out the window, watching a couple, matching prosthetic hip-joints rippling under their track pants, jog across the commons. She can see their joints connecting with the polymer under their skin.

'Four of my patients have died,' she says.

Max looks thrilled. 'Was it your fault?'

'Not entirely.'

The hip-joint couple finish a lap and come back past the window – a background loop.

'People die, Max,' she says. 'If this was twenty years ago, half the people at this facility would already have been dead. Your brother...' she starts and then stops.

In the adjacent room, Tom bleeps significantly.

'I know. Tom would be dead.'

'Yes. But he's not now. We have the resources to give him a new kind of life,' Gabrielle says.

She secretly envies Tom. A quiet life, restful and respected.

Max feels Gabrielle reach out to stroke the thin line of hair that runs from his chest to his abdomen, as though pulling a string to crumple and guide his body towards her.

'Remind me what we know,' he says, resisting.

Initially, Gabrielle was convinced his amnesia was a nervous performance. Eloise always laughed it off, unconcerned. Max obsessed on it, but didn't actually want to deal with it. Gabrielle decided it was a game. She wondered, briefly, if it was a game for the couple – Eloise setting the sexual challenges, Max obeying, but claiming amnesia after the fact. But his conversation loops are constant, and he avoids having to come to his own conclusion at all costs.

'Something is blocking Tom's thalamacortical system from functional reconnection with external stimuli. It isn't a tumour, or a lesion. Your brother is healthy. Fast activity patterns at medium voltage across the whole brain indicate a different neural activity to slow wave sleep.'

'Will he remember me?' asks Max, again.

'It's not important, Max. What's important is that he recognises you, or at least your neurological pattern. I think we're close to establishing a protocol.'

'Mmm,' he mumbles, aroused by his own anxiety. He crawls towards her. 'A protocol of sneaky liaisons in empty hospice rooms.'

Gabrielle slips out of his grasp, anxious to be back with her real patient.

'Time to say goodbye,' she says.

'I still don't see why.'

'Because if you don't remember the affair you won't feel guilt.'

'I don't feel guilt.'

'You will eventually.'

'And then?'

'And then you will look for the source of it. And you won't find me there.'

Reluctantly, Max lets his eyes drop and rise in a secret pattern that the archive recognises.

'I never met a woman so hell-bound on turning me off,' he smiles grimly. 'I really don't know why we have to do this.'

'Because I need you to. Because if you don't erase me, I can't continue with this. Professionally, it's disastrous. And then there's the rest of the fall-out. The brain is so plastic. Emotional attachment can be as simple as repetition. Did I tell you I spoke to your wife the other day?'

'Probably,' he grimaces, eyes wide for the retina scan. 'Find. Keyword Stern,' he commands.

The peripheral statistics window shows the last access date as yesterday.

'You spend too much time in review,' says Gabrielle, again.

He flushes. The past few hours, the archival record of their love affair, falls between them, an uncanny valley. Apart from this, the only other records of their time together are clinical.

He sits rigid at the end of the bed, staring down the projection as though a hard stare might imprint it on his mind's eye. In the image, Gabrielle extends a hand over the top of Tom's prostrate body. The future lovers shake hands and a cascade of information is logged along the side of the image. The angle of the camera renders the handshake surreal: faces are out of frame; shaking hands animate the body between them.

Max turns away from the picture. He looks like he is in genuine pain.

'I don't want to erase this,' he begs.

Gabrielle says nothing.

'I want to watch it one more time then. Erasing this is the same as scheduling eternal first dates.'

'Sounds fun,' she retorts.

'It sounds terrifying,' he says.

Max stares at the picture. Gabrielle, bored, tries to work out if it she looks older or younger in the picture compared to other pictures, but finds she has no frame of reference. She runs a quick speculative animation of Eloise Smyth aging, but somehow it doesn't look true.

These days you can get minute bacteria that can chew away wrinkle-causing fissures in the muscle. And people use nanocells derived from fish scales that brighten tissue from the inside. But there's still no foolproof personal technology available to tell if you are being lied to.

'I'm hardly worth looking at,' she says.

'I like to look at you. You look like a beautiful woman, one with needs.'

On the first day they met in person, Gabrielle took Max's EEG, stretching the cranial net over his head like the most attentive of hairdressers – and then, also like a hairdresser, she listened to his problems. It set a precedent.

'Tell me about your mother,' she'd asked him.

In the typically evasive manner he'd used for at least their first five meetings (three of which were single-purpose: clinical, by the book) Max replied that his mother was 'like a mother', 'like her photograph', 'caring', 'slim', 'a little worried' and, finally, 'dead'. This kind of answering didn't bode well. Later, teasingly, after their first flirtations, Gabrielle asked him to describe a situation in which he would experience love. 'I love my wife', he said. When asked about fear he said he was afraid of 'earthquake'.

'I don't think I can watch any more of this,' he says now, pausing the entry.

'It wasn't my idea, Max – you wanted to say a proper goodbye.'

'There's no point. I won't remember anyway.'

'You might. You can.'

'I won't,' he says, and then addresses the archive. 'Delete entry. Discard item keyword Stern from all files.' He blinks to moisten his irises, repeats the breathing pattern that matches the security code.

The system processes the erasure.

'I hope my next first impression is more charming,' he says.

'I've made my own assessments.'

'They'll become lore – I have nothing to refute them with.'

'And yet you have a great imagination.'

'What are you basing that on?'

'You're a filmmaker.'

'My films aren't imaginative. They're formulaic. All the same. Ask any critic.'

To prove it, he summons up a folder of reviews and hangs it above them like a string of flags.

'I'm not interested in critics. I think you're imaginative. And imagination and memory are basically the same neural process.'

'Whatever,' he says, tightening his intelligent belt across his abdomen.

'Are you okay?' Dr Stern asks, switching her tone to sound less like a psychologist and more like a concerned lover.

'No. I feel injured. Like you cut me.'

'You're being dramatic.'

'You asked.'

'Nothing has been cut. Remember, I've seen your brain.'

'That does seem like an unfair advantage.'

'Max, the kind of memory loss you believe you suffer from is incredibly rare. It's generally more of a plot device than an actual neural affliction.'

'Tell me why I can't remember, then.'

'Dramatic effect?'

Max laughs grudgingly.

'Perhaps memory would expose holes in your story,'

she says.

'There are holes in my story now. Some days there are more holes than story.'

'Max, you can remember. You just don't.'

He grimaces.

'Please don't misunderstand me,' she says. 'I'm not here to judge. I don't necessarily think not remembering is bad or wrong. One day, when everyone carries their memory peripherally, we'll all be able to edit out pain and suffering from the past. We'll replace unpleasant experiences with joyful revelations. We'll be less afraid of the consequences of our actions and the actions of people who hurt us. We'll be immune to trauma. We'll sleep like babies.'

Max focuses on threading buttons through tight holes.

She continues: 'The work I'm doing will eventually lead to the possibility of linking directly into the memory of another. We'll be able to experience things like love and empathy fully, and they'll be experiences that transcend language and even embodiment. I don't think the technology is far away, either. Twenty years perhaps. Maybe less. It'll happen in your lifetime. I see the possibilities every day.'

'You see them in me.'

'I experience them with you. You claim that I've erased myself from your memory. You believe that every time we meet is the first time.'

'Yes.'

'Well, that's liberating.'

'But you believe that I can remember.'

'But you say that you don't.'

They stare at each other, both fully dressed now, stalemating.

'My mind is prosthetic and enhanced,' Max says in a tone of which Gabrielle has grown tired.

'Yes. But in the mind, a memory is not a representation. It's not like a photograph. A memory is a reflection of the way your brain's dynamics have changed to allow the repetition of a performance, conscious or not. I believe you have real memory. You have experiences and impressions – they influence the way you are in the world. But you can't prove them, and that bugs you, so you outsource the task. It makes sense. But you still conceive and create. More than most people.'

'Does it comfort you?' he asks.

'What?'

'Your expert status,' he says, cruelly.

'Conceiving a future in which I can isolate pain and remove it like a weevil from flour – this is an enduring activity. And you are a comfort to me. I can't say anything beyond that. Now, let's go and see your brother.'

Tom's room is less claustrophobic – the monitors open it up into the wider space of data.

'I would never cast you as a doctor,' says Max, watching Gabrielle check Tom's rhythmic activity, a monotony of delta frequencies.

'No?'

'No. You would confuse the viewer. To create a good film you need clear symbols. They create boundaries.'

'What would you cast me as?'

'Mysterious girl with haunted eyes, waiting in the subway before an explosion turns everything to rubble.'

'Flattering.'

'Those caps on Tom's neck make him look like Frankenstein's monster. Like we're experimenting on him.'

'In a sense, we are.'

'You aren't supposed to say that. That's exactly why you could never play a doctor.'

'Give it up, Max. I know you're frightened.'

'But do you know how frightened? I mean, what if he wakes up and he has no memory of our childhood? It will mean we never had one.'

'All the better for you. Children are like sponges, as they say. Which means adults are just old sponges. If we're lucky, we dry out. If not, we sop and moulder.' Gabrielle sees that she is not getting the right reaction, but continues anyway. 'If he wakes up and doesn't have the answers to your questions, Max, then you can just erase him. Or you can erase him now and save yourself a lot of time and money.'

Max steps back, sending a steel trolley skittering across the polished floor. Gabrielle focuses her attention on a cranial wire so thin it's almost invisible.

'If I can just erase him,' says Max, 'how can I be sure he was ever here at all – and, for that matter, how can I be sure of you?'

'Let me concentrate,' she says, connecting the wire at the site of a fine drill-hole in Tom's temple. The hardware is satisfyingly clean and sensitive. A sharp tone indicates chip connection.

Max hangs around the edges of the procedure like a child dragged to work by their parent. Gabrielle grounds the wire in dielectric putty and adjusts the charge. An image spreads across the air.

'Come and see, Max,' she says. Her tone is patronising and bright. She registers that this is probably what she would have sometimes sounded like if she'd had time to become a mother.

The panel of thin branches spreads around them like a trellis of fine, twisting roses.

'The cerebellum is a beautiful structure,' she says.

As the signal disperses, Gabrielle isolates frequencies. She turns the volume right up. Max reaches out for her hand, wishing that he could read something from the temperature of her fingers, the rhythm of her pulse. Instead, he focuses on his own breath, then on the sounds in the room, the sounds from Gabrielle's machine that is plugged into Tom, and soon it seems to him that the room is filling with a vast tidal river. The sound is like rapids crashing across rock. A great body of water, a river that narrows and then expands again, swelling, running fast with infinite momentum. Every drop in the river has sound, contributes to the cacophony. Electric eels spark through the slimy deeps. Plankton split and multiply. Alligators feed on turtles and drinking birds and then die and decay, becoming food for the same small creatures. Schools of thousands of shimmering pink fish jump into the air, which is not air at all but more and ever more river. In some distant, primal pool, Max's chest swells. His lungs remember how to breathe water. The river is running through him, and is him, and runs through everything.

Max stands beside his brother with river coming out of his eyes, flowing down his cheeks.

'It's so beautiful,' he says.

'It's the sound of consciousness,' the doctor says. 'Of billions of neurons firing.'

• •

A room of 243 bodies. 151 male, ninety-two female. Four of these children.

1,944 litres of oxygen intake per minute, then, suddenly nothing. 243 bodies gasping. Or not. You can't remember gasps.

When forty-five peacekeeping personnel arrive, five medical officers confirm the absence of 243 heartbeats, 243 bodies not breathing. Three beds are bodiless, masks on the floor, drip chambers dangling cannulas like too-small fish. Because of the spectacle—the long hair hanging, the stillness, the smell—no one notices these three empty cots at first. Later, two experts record and report the aftermath of the event that will now be known (though mostly unknown) as the Sleepers Cult Catastrophe. The word catastrophe is used, even though these kinds of events are commonplace.

The two experts observe similarities with other such catastrophes. The IV bags containing a known, non-fatal drug combination, and the use of sine wave drone and other non-pharmacological hypnotic techniques. But they find no charismatic paraphernalia, no slogans or prayers scrawled on the stark walls of the isolated old barn. One remarks how the group resembles an audience laid out in an immersive cinema. But they are not immersed. They are dead.

You remember none of this. You only remember waking with the impulse to run, consciousness rising above you like a wave.

• •

After an hour of intimacy, Gabrielle leads Max into the therapeutics lab, where she injects a radioactively tagged isotope into a vein to produce a crude colour-coded map of his brain activity.

'It's like finger painting,' says Max.

'The associations you make depend on the operation of dentate and pyramidal cells. Here and here,' she says, indicating luminous splotches on the scan.

She gives him a copy to take home.

'My children will like it,' he says.

'Try to imagine a cube,' she tells him, injecting equal levels of the neurotransmitter glutamate into both Max and Tom's systems and setting electrodes to record directly from neural cells. 'There are three stages in a successful reaching. This is linking. You send a cube, and if he conceives the cube it signals recognition of external stimulus. He'll be unaware of where the cube is coming from, but if he's receptive it won't matter.

'The next stage is binding. In a single neural system this process occurs naturally when two functionally segregated brain areas are integrated. For us though, it's different. It's

118

a process where functionally similar brain areas from two separate neural systems are integrated.'

'How do they separate again?'

'When you're no longer connected. But Max, technically, you never completely separate. You are bound.'

'Right, okay.'

'And the third process is adaptation.'

'Who adapts to whom?'

'There is no who, it's what. There are two neural systems. You are passing information stimulus between one system and another. Adaptation signifies the brain's acceptance of the stimuli as part of its own system of impulses. As though a part of your brain is an accepted and utilised part of Tom's, and vice versa. It shouldn't affect you too much. I imagine you will have more vivid dreams, and possibly enhanced or apocryphal memory function. Maybe even some unexplained phobias.'

'Nothing out of the ordinary then.'

'It depends how much information you transfer,' she tells him. 'It is unlikely to be more than an image or two. The point is contact.'

Max feels something on his neck, a reassuring pat.

'Max, we need you.'

'Gabrielle...'

'It's strange – the computer model shows us how metaphors can become ingrained in the way we understand things. Because we once described the brain as a computer, we thought that a computer could accurately measure brain activity. But only another brain can truly measure brain activity. Only another embodied brain can form a descriptive system of what it is seeing.'

'So, a bit like love,' he says.

'Love is an equivalent metaphor.'

Max looks desolate.

'I mean,' she says, 'I don't want to replace the computer with love, because we can talk about it without resulting to poetic comparisons. It's experience, at a cellular, neuronal and chemical level. We need to be careful with metaphor. At a certain level we are the description.'

'Well, let me describe what I'd like to do to you then.'

'Why don't we have a look over your last week instead? Let's take a little stroll down memory lane.'

'Very funny,' he says, and activates playback mode, scrolling through time-codes broken down to microseconds.

'Strange,' he says, after a while.

'What?'

'Not there.'

'Misfiled?'

He shakes his head. 'Not possible.'

Gabrielle waits.

'I must have erased it,' he says finally.

'The whole week?'

'It's becoming compulsive.'

'Be careful, Max.'

'You started it.'

'It's not me heading recklessly into your memory and erasing at whim.'

'So now it's a memory?'

'I never said it wasn't. I only said you had your own as well.'

'It gives me an indefinable feeling,' he says. 'Like a high.'

'A free feeling.'

'Exactly.'

'Making tiny cuts, incisions that give the cutter a feeling of control.'

'Who is using metaphor now?'

'Perhaps it's metaphor, perhaps it's love.'

'Perhaps it is,' he says, putting a hand out to touch her.

She turns away.

'I suppose, in a way, erasing the mundane, the joyful, the well-organised and the achieved is another homage to your obsession with disaster,' she says.

Max shrugs. He looks faraway, calm.

'How is your film going?' Gabrielle changes the loop.

Max looks at her oddly, as though experiencing a lag in perception.

'The film is good, I think,' he says eventually, eyes snapping back into focus. 'Though, who knows? I vacillate.'

'Will everyone still die?'

'Of course. Except for the survivors.'

'Who are the survivors?'

'Everyone is. Every viewer. Every protagonist. On their own. That's the point. Don't you even watch movies?'

'Not the kind you make. I've had enough surviving.'

'What kind of movies do you like?'

'Documentaries.'

Max nods.

'My movies are documentaries, sort of. This next one is about a real event. It's about the sinking of Pitcairn, which is real – it just hasn't happened yet.'

'Will it sink?'

'In the movie or in real life?'

'Either.'

'In real life, as my son would say, who cares either way? Either it sinks or it doesn't.'

'And in your movie?'

'It will sink like nothing has sunk before,' he grins. 'But this will be the only real divergence. Everything needs to be something we have already seen, except the catastrophe. That's the key to achieving a high catharsis rating for an immersion,' he smiles. 'Not everyone agrees with me on that any more, though. Did I tell you I have taken on a protégé? I'm poised to break into the future.'

'A protégé for the future. Tom for the past. Now you just need someone for the present.'

'I told you, I have the archive.' Max's grin twitches. 'Or perhaps that's what you are for.'

Something flickers across her face.

'Are you alright?' he asks. 'Low blood sugar? Let me switch on and check.'

'No. I'm okay.'

'Did I upset you?'

'No.'

Max conjures a cup of water.

'Let me be the doctor,' he says.

Gabrielle surrenders, sitting down and pretending to sip

the cool water. Max is a handsome man. He looks younger than he is, bearing all the advantages of a good diet, a mon-eyed life. Tom too looks excruciatingly young, as though he shut his eyes on aging along with everything else.

Max puts on a lab coat, pretends to take Gabrielle's temperature.

'Hot as hell!' he says, enjoying himself, leaning down to listen to her heartbeat. 'Ah, yes. As I expected. It's beating for me.'

He scrolls through unrelated graphs and spreadsheets, pretending to read.

'Ms Stern,' he says, pushing safety goggles down on his nose. 'Describe your most vivid memory from childhood.'

'I had no childhood,' she says, but he doesn't get the joke.

'It's important to let go,' he teases. 'We need to build con-nections to achieve a successful reaching.'

'Okay, Dr Galleon. Well, I grew up in an extremely vi-olent period on the fringes of the old city, what we used to call the suburbs. I watched everyone on our block hand their homes over, and then mortgage their time on work-lease schemes. The transport system shut down and people could no longer afford to run their cars. We were isolated. Couldn't get money out of the bank. Couldn't get to the hospital or to school. And that was just the beginning. Our neighbours gassed themselves in their lock-up garage. We looked at the news and saw tableaux of people we knew sit-ting around card tables, holding hands, Bibles spread open on their laps, slumped heads trickling blood from the ears. My mother was a believer.'

'In what?' Max closes his eyes and rocks gently between toe and heel.

'In anything. But when the energy crisis hit, we realised it was useless. Even she did, finally. I was in city crisis housing when the lights went out. Do you remember the Covenant of Noah?' Gabrielle scans Max's face for a spark of recognition, but all she sees is the blank look of someone scrolling an in-eye network.

'You don't need to look it up, Max – I'll tell you. I'm a witness. I remember the plumes of smoke rising into the sky from towers on fire. I remember the queues of people selling their stereo equipment and TVs to second-hand dealers for pocket change.'

His irises contain a reflection, blurred and partial, of the most iconic image of the period: a woman sitting in a bloodstain outside a city hospital, stunned, cradling her stillborn baby. Gabrielle knows the image inside out. She places her palm over Max's face, allowing him to watch without any real-world interference.

'I saw it with these eyes,' she whispers, letting the light back in, steering his gaze to hers.

'I don't remember,' he says, shaking his head.

'Maybe that's why you are here.'

Gabrielle leads Max back over to the electrograph. She carefully reattaches his hood. When she is done he flicks his head around like a model in a shampoo commercial.

'I'm here for the star attention,' he says.

'Close your eyes. Try to conceive a cube,' Gabrielle instructs, pushing him down onto the gurney.

'How about a sphere? For variety?'

By way of reply she injects Max with one millilitre of Meritas, watching his eyes flicker and fade. She turns up the audio track and shifts her attention from body to data. This is a delicate procedure. To dose with both sedatives and alien stimulus without pushing the brain to the point of seizure takes practice, and a machine precision. After twenty-seven minutes she brings him to. Max gasps like a man coming up from deep water.

'Count backwards from fifty,' she instructs.

An electrolyte solution appears next to Max.

'What did you see?' Gabrielle asks, when he is finished counting.

'Nothing,' he says. 'Static. I can't remember. How many times will we do this?'

They eat a late dinner of soybeans and rissoles in one of the communal dining halls. It's the closest thing they have to a date. They don't think about the minute lenses and sensors tracking them.

A resident, a woman of at least one hundred with a shock of grey frizzed hair, wheels herself to their table

'Did you hear the music?' she says, and then continues without waiting for an answer. 'Every night they have such lovely music here. All the old songs. You know, I'm quite the rocker. It's nice to see a young couple come out here to enjoy the place. I never dreamed after all these years...'

Max shudders.

'Do you play an instrument?' the woman asks, smiling indulgently.

'A little,' says Gabrielle. 'The piano.'

The woman keeps looking at Max expectantly, as if she didn't hear Gabrielle.

'I don't play,' he says.

'Do you like rock 'n' roll?'

'Sometimes,' he says.

The woman sings a few tuneless bars before an old man waves her over and the two of them begin chatting, jerking rhythmically in their chairs.

Max watches them roll out into the night.

'Is it possible for a man like me to get old?' he asks. 'Could I be like them? Retire to some vast garden somewhere, and just prune and weed? Do the crossword puzzle? Reminisce about some good old days that never really were? It's not something I could do alone, and I can't imagine Ellie going in for it. But maybe with you?'

'You can't leave your wife for me.'

'Why not?'

'Think of me as just a good way to warm up your romantic pathways. The brain is so plastic, it needs the right kind of exercise. Then, when you leave, just forget all about it and go back to your life. It shouldn't be too hard for you.'

'Sometimes you sound like her.'

'Who?'

'Ellie.'

'I assure you I'm someone else entirely.'

The dining hall slowly empties. Residents gather for a poetry reading in the amphitheatre.

'We keep old people very busy, don't we? They're almost

as busy as my children,' says Max.

'Music, poetry – these are binding agents for the network. The trick is to create shared experience. This comes to us from Hertzberg and Krauss. My supervisor studied under Krauss,' Gabrielle says. 'This is what you are looking for in Tom, right? Shared experience.'

'It's what everyone looks for,' says Max. 'What are you looking for in Tom?'

'I'm interested in the possibilities for the reaching protocol,' Gabrielle says, too quickly.

'Reaching. It's a telling name,' he says. 'But I think you want to know something else.'

'Like what?'

'You tell me.'

'I already have,' she says, monotone.

Max grins, 'Or maybe it's not Tom you are interested in at all.'

He shuffles closer and she lets out a strange laugh, both shocked and relieved.

'You and I,' Max says, 'should probably leave poor Tom alone.'

Gabrielle doesn't reply. She tries to connect to real sensation, but instead, as always, she is hit with a barrage of random memory. Her mother in the final, gabled house. The fog in her eyes, the pattern of hemlock posies on her dress. The dark, smudgy cobra on her arm. A dream with too many symbols strung together. Herself as a teenager, running down the steps to the garden, trying not to see the chipped porch swing, the pond with two young trout, the wormwood trees, the field beyond with two goats, two calves without spots or marks, two fat swine and two young boys playing shepherd. After this, she will only see her mother in a newsfeed.

'If you won't grow old with me,' Max says, 'at least let me take you to the movies.'

Her vision returns, jarringly. She doesn't want to look at Max, or talk. She goes over to the piano and begins to play the only piece she knows, a section from the 'Blue Danube Waltz'. She plays it just as she was taught, perfect pauses between each phrase. When the movement is finished, she returns to the beginning.

Without speaking, Max leaves the table and comes to stand beside her. He places his hands on the keys and she immediately sees the practised positioning of the fingers, the high arch of the palm.

The hands remember.

He plays a complementary phrase, just as her mother once did. They continue faultlessly in duet as though they are one instrument. The piano extends from their fingers.

Max leans in to kiss Gabrielle, and, with or without players, the 'Blue Danube' continues.

• •

Remember how we used to build our houses? The wood and plaster, glass and steel? Remember flame lick, salt rot, deluge? Remember how the world around us used to yield? Turned to mush beneath the levees. Corroded in acidic air.

Split apart until shards become the arsenal of the storm. Your home, a weapon turned against you.

Weather, poisoned, comes unstuck. Adheres to nothing, spills over and tosses up all the carefully sowed flowerbeds.

Remember dust clouds?

Remember dogs?

Remember how national edicts came to be replaced by scar-words? Ravaged, scoured, burned, sodden, smashed.

Remember the slow rebuild? Is there before and after, or only now and then, and then again? Everything now is mirrored, and reinforced and strong. Capital letter everything, everything permasomething. Everything now is powder-coated and pre-emptive. The only poor materials left are skin, flesh and organ meat. Human remnants. The final permeability, the traces.

Remember _____?

Gabrielle peers out her small window into the world. The flowers have grown back. Residents frolic around the hospice grounds. They sniff up fields of colour. People aren't surprised by this bright restoration. They see the colours and forget the endless brown and grey. This is nemesis, the principal that makes human tragedy morally intelligible. Nature goes on until it goes on without us.

'Do you like my penguins?' Max asks, coming up for air from his work, casting a clip from a storyboard across the wall.

'Very real,' says Gabrielle.

'Yes. I thought so. They will explode beautifully.'

'That seems like a shame.'

'Oh yes?' he says. And then, 'The effect will be marvellous.'

Gabrielle gives him a series of identification tasks. Then behavioural tasks: the gambling task, the lying task, the coloured blocks task. But not the memory task.

Tom still does not stir: not in body, not in data.

Max multitasks, half-attending to the coloured blocks, half-monitoring a feed from Pitcairn. One of Gabrielle's feeds shows his brain is a shimmer of green and red. She is too overloaded to get him to focus. She keeps glitching out and freezing mid-process.

She turns to the island. Greenery ripples in the wind. Overhead shots make the landmass look like the splotch of a Rorschach test. A magazine-style inset report takes the viewer into the homes of Pitcairners, the lens zooming in minutely on their wooden carvings and taxidermied birds. A room crowded with hammerhead sharks, monkfish, mullet and dugongs, all carved and stuffed. A small marsupial sits patiently on a bedside table. The reporter picks up a conch with a landscape engraved on it and holds it close to the lens. Links to information on crafts of the region roll across the feed. Then the reporter is inside a small wooden church, gesturing towards a large steel bell, the original bell from HMS *Bounty*. The frame lingers on frayed prayer books, an ancient candlestick, and then a quick cut shows the church at night, lit by flickering candle-flame. A small and motley congregation line the pews. The descendants of mutineers and primitives. Funny, Gabrielle thinks, looking at the peaceful scene, how much we all know about them and how little they know about us, about what the rest of the world looks like. It's a museum, this island.

The heads of the worshippers are tilted towards the altar, singing the word. On impulse, Gabrielle accesses the sound. A hymn in exultant and discordant voices, words misshapen but still clear:

Brightly beams our Father's mercy,
From His lighthouse evermore,
But to us He gives the keeping
Of the lights along the shore.

Let the lower lights be burning!
Send a gleam across the wave!
Some poor fainting, struggling seaman
You may rescue, you may save.

Max turns to look at her, and, for a moment, he's attentive. The swarming colours of his brain slow.

'You know what, Max – I have an idea. Let's take a little trip.'

• •

He watches the flat landscape roll by, nervously. Like the windmills beyond the train, his body is in constant motion, a foot twitching rhythmically, two fingernails flicking. He sits far across from Gabrielle. Nothing touches. Not even gaze. It had been difficult to get him to leave the retirement zone. Gabrielle had used several strategies. She'd had to flirt, to cajole, and then bribe. She'd explained to him that his lack of concentration might be what is preventing connection. She showed him his brain.

'That's all noise, all compulsive stimulation.'

He'd made a dirty joke, but looked ashamed.

They disembark at the central district. Walking along the platform, the music follows them, some personal choice of Max's rolling in soft waves through the pleasant, peaceful environment of the central district Electrorail. Lights flicker on as they pass by. Max is encoded and anticipated in all his everyday spaces. They take the stairs to the street and three green ticks spring up beside them.

'I think I finally understand the challenge Tom represents for you,' Gabrielle muses.

'Oh yes?'

'Yes. He doesn't respond to you. In fact, the past as a whole doesn't respond to you.'

They reach street level and several floodlights activate, shining up through the branches of the shade trees that line the road. A car pulls in, the word 'Galleon' spreading across its windscreen in a bold serif. Max walks towards the car automatically. Relaxed electronic music seeps from its doors.

'Max!' From nowhere, a tall figure approaches.

Max weaves about on the spot for a moment, seemingly taking in his environment for the first time, now that something unanticipated has penetrated it. He looks at Gabrielle. He is panicked, rabbit-like.

'Do you know him?' Gabrielle asks.

'Max!' yells Jean again, taking long strides along the

pavement, lights dimming and flicking to a dramatic violet tone as he passes by.

'Shit,' says Max under his breath.

'You are a strange phenomenon,' Jean yells, almost panting from his walk.

'I just arrived by rail, from the retirement zone,' Max stammers. 'I've been to see Tom.'

'Yes, yes, I know. Ellie tracked you as soon as you re-entered visual mode, she let me know where you are. I hoped I'd catch you. Max Galleon, storm rider! Let's say it all out loud, eh? For the archive!' Jean tips an imaginary glass in a mock toast.

'What are you doing here?' asks Max.

'I needed to talk with a man I can slap if he offends me. And you are impossible to catch lately. All that off-lining. The invisible man. Quite unlike you.'

Max flinches.

'I had to see you,' Jean says without addressing Gabrielle. 'In the flesh.'

'Why?'

'Two reasons. First: congratulations.'

'For what?'

'For the masterful *Mega-Tsunami* pitch you presented. It's incredible. Never has a storm surge so devastated the psyche! You're a magician of destruction. Watching that pitch, it is impossible to imagine a storm ever managed to break without you to direct it! You're a conductor of experience, a charismatic! You're the perfect opposite of your true self.'

'What a compliment.'

'Are you making a joke? Stick to action sequences. I just gave you the greatest compliment. But it was well-deserved. You are an impotent man, inert, frustrated, apathetic, tired, balding. And yet—'

'Jean.'

'I'm sorry,' says Jean. 'Though I was just getting to the flattery: and yet you are completely transformed by the promise of art. Your passion is beyond your personality. It's phenomenal.'

'They liked the pitch?'

'The world likes it. This film is necessary. It has to be made before it's too late! You communicated this like no one has before. And though I know different, it really sounded like you yourself had never emphasised this before. Amazing! To pull that off! They were shaking. Too unhinged to applaud. We will storm into the next stage of production. It will be our finest immersion yet.'

It begins to rain. Jean pulls a disperser from his pocket. They stand in the dry diamond while the rain falls.

'There's another reason I needed to see you. It's a personal matter,' Jean says gravely. 'It regards love. At its most unexpected and dangerous.'

Max steps back into the rain, a soft blue dispersing light pulsing out from his shoes.

'Jean,' Max stammers. 'I hope you don't have the wrong impression. We're just...'

'Love, Max!' Jean interrupts, regarding his friend critically. 'Only the most basic and yet impossible to simulate emotion.'

'I'm not sure if Ellie—'

'Ellie!' Jean shouts again. 'Always with your suspicions. Ellie is born to be loved, and so has no understanding of its value. You, however. Well, you will know what I mean. But come, let's go somewhere we can sit down.'

'We don't have time. I mean, the doctor and I need to—'

'No time for what?' Jean protests 'For me? Rubbish. Some matters are too delicate to discuss on the street. And in the rain, no less. Better we sit down with something warming.'

He slaps Max on the back, and for a moment the disperser ray splits and some rain seeps under, refracting the blue light like tiny sapphires on the pavement.

'I'm very tired,' says Max.

'I can't begin to approach the subject out here on the dismal street.'

'Try.'

Jean narrows his eyes. He examines Max minutely, as if deciding something. After a while his mind is made up. He says, 'I am in love.'

'You?' Max's relief is palpable. 'You are in love?'

'With Margot.'

'Who's Margot?'

'Margot is not her real name. But it does not matter. I love her.'

'Where did you find her?'

'You've met her, Max. At the Bunker Bar. She's not beautiful so much as perfectly made. Everything fits together. She's exquisite in every last detail.'

'How long have you been seeing each other?' Max stammers, trying to regain himself.

Jean waves his hand in dismissal.

'Not long, not long. But I am in love! Max, is it fair that I should have to answer such questions in my state? This is jumping-from-skyscrapers love, it's fearless-grand-gestures love.'

The rain gets heavier, forms walls around them like a wedding marquee. Water drifts into the recycling slips and is tanked.

'There is more, Max. Look.' Jean unfurls a notepad, flicks through pages and pages of text, real ink running in the rain. 'If it were possible I would have filled forests of paper with my ideas. I needed surfaces. Real surfaces, something I could feel.' Jean removes his jacket. Its white lining is covered in scrawling longhand. He turns around. His shirt too, stained with cursive. 'I used Super B Beetroot Complex.' He takes off his shirt, revealing cerise ripples on his skin.

'Stop. I understand,' says Max, laughing now from relief or hysteria.

'Do you? Can a man who is transformed each time he speaks of his ideas understand what it is like to be unable to create? And then, as suddenly as you dried out, to be fertile again? She is my muse.'

'I'm very happy for you.'

'Margot!' he shouts. 'I am going to see her. You have to come. The doctor can wait. It's too late to work anyhow. I want you to see how I change when I'm with her.'

'I can't, Jean.'

'You have to.'

'No.'

Max turns and walks into the sharp, noisy rain. His jacket glows slickly, beading water and absorbing it instantly. He looks back and sees Gabrielle lingering just beyond Jean, the rain making her skin flicker.

The Fleet car pulls up slowly alongside Max. He holds the door open for Gabrielle. Once inside, they sit in silence, rain sluicing the windscreen, Jean, grey haired, grey eyed, wrapped in text, diminishing in the rear-view like the wild, highway prophets of old.

'I'm sorry about that,' says Max eventually.

The stereo plays the same music they heard in the train station.

'It's fine. It's nice to see someone from your life. Other than your wife, I mean.'

Max winces.

'It has been a long time since he's written anything other than the requisite explosions,' he says.

'He seems like a fascinating man.'

'He's a bore,' says Max. 'We all are.'

Another train rolls in and Max regards it anxiously.

'Do you think he suspects something?' he asks, then answers for himself: 'No.'

Max's hands rest inertly on the steering wheel as the car navigates itself away from the station. After a few moments he shakes his head and climbs into the back seat.

'Input the location,' he says, reclining across the seat for a nap.

'Envirotowers,' says Gabrielle.

'What?'

'Desperate times, desperate measures.'

'Why are we desperate and what are the measures?

'You'll see.'

'I hate surprises,' Max says, then after a while adds, 'Jean should know that, too. There are too many of them, and somehow, as well, nothing is that surprising anymore.'

He sighs theatrically.

'It sounds like your film will be a great success.'

'Yes. Maybe. I need to see that pitch.'

'You don't remember it at all?'

'Of course not.'

'Why don't you try? We can go through one of the breathing exercises.'

Max looks at her with real anger, but in less than a minute she sees the emotion drain from his countenance and he becomes serene.

The road winds around the silent airport, the place where Gabrielle last saw her father. He'd turned to wave, heading down an aerobridge with a suitcase in one hand and a newspaper in the other. What was the headline that day?

Ahead, the towers rise up to meet them.

'I'm frightened of this place,' says Max.

'Why?'

'Lots of reasons. It's a powerful symbol of failure.'

'Xenophobia?'

'I'm not xenophobic – I'm not frightened by the real place or the people, just the idea of the place.'

'That's definitely xenophobia. When I was a kid my mother took me to live here.'

'You lived here?' he says, shocked.

'While my mother studied to be a nun.'

'A nun?'

'A pseudo-nun.'

'Jesus.'

'That's right. It was the thing to do.'

They park at the side of the tower. Max hesitates before following Gabrielle through the courtyard, walking on hand-painted ceramic tiles, the art of long-gone children: stick-figure families, long-gone too. Chipped and purposeful rocket ships, now retired. Well-loved pets, now dead. And flowers. And dolphins. A lost world under grime.

They pass the solar gates and enter the left tower via the atrium. Inside, the building is hollow, like a pyramid. Each floor is a cell. A hive construction. This was the radical model for the first architecture to take its cue from the cellular organisation of insects. Bees: industrious, but also vibrant. Better than the drudgery of ants or the abject, hidden, over-fertile world of worms. Gabrielle counts hexagons top to bottom, left to right, to find the one she lived in, now crumpled and sagging.

'It's big,' says Max, staring up at levels and levels of balconied floors.

The tip of the pyramid splits the reflected light of the moon and sends fractal packets of it sprinkling down through the many residential floors. From there the shadow of trickling water is picked out by the light. The water tanks must be underused and overflowing.

'Pow-Pow would be unimpressed,' says Max.

'Pow-Pow's not such a big deal here.'

A rustle from behind makes Max jump. He turns in time to see a goat galumphing through the foliage.

'They must stick around because of the water,' says Gabrielle. 'And pest control,' adds Max, pointing at the side of a broken pipe embossed with the Waste Not Want logo. He leans back against a diseased palm tree to steady his nerves. 'When are you going to tell me why we're here?'

'Be quiet, okay?'

Gabrielle listens for the sound of children scurrying around the garden.

'Pieeeeeeyeeeeeee,' she calls out.

'Pieeeeyeeeeeeeeeeeeeayee,' comes the shrieked and giggled response.

'Are you serious?' says Max.

'Relax. It's a game. The kids like it.'

'Are they from the prairie?'

'In some sense.'

Gabrielle ushers Max over to an old steel elevator and they ride it to the sixth floor. Stepping out onto the balcony, they tiptoe over ladders of moonlight. Gabrielle knocks three times on one of the mirrored honeycomb cells.

'Yes?' says a voice.

'Fine weather we're having,' she replies.

The door opens and they step into the large, open room. Around them, bird cages rust and creak. Torn doors hang limp like broken promises.

'The aviary,' says Max.

'That's right.'

A group of twenty to thirty people mill, chattering in low voices. In the corner five men hold hands, staring upward, emitting a sustained, inhuman hum.

'What is this?'

'It's a cult based on the Japanese principle of *mono no aware*.'

'What?'

'It translates vaguely as "the ah-ness of things".'

'Right,' Max says, nervous, trying to activate his databank – but the Envirotower zone has long since been declared an excluded zone. All data signals are blocked in an attempt to flush out the malingerers.

'I brought you here because I thought it would help you open up. Focus your attention.'

'I see,' he says.

Gabrielle smiles. 'We need to try another approach. There's nothing to worry about. It's just a harmless party game, really. A kind of immersion, I suppose.' She signals to a woman in a long blue dress with embroidered silver webbing at the hem. 'They believe that certain objects contain knowledge. That the stuff of the world remembers, in a way that we can't.'

Interest piqued, Max looks about properly for the first time. In the centre of the room there is a large pile of old junk, circled by tea candles and guarded by another web-robed woman. In the flickering light he makes out an unstrung violin, a rocking horse, several old paperbacks, a plastic abacus. All old and faded scraps, saved from a time of large-scale production of goods. Pre-Cornacoprint. Some even pre-MNT. Has he ever seen such objects before?

'It's a genius model, and ecocorrect too. A psychoactive recycling depot,' Gabrielle explains, leaving out the more controversial aspect of the practice: that the whole thing falls apart without the drugs.

'I thought you would be interested in it professionally, in any case. There aren't many people who know about this.'

A small boy with a tray approaches, offering tea in chipped but pretty cups.

The milling people gather around the pile of junk, humming a low drone note. Max sips the sticky tea, and doesn't notice when Gabrielle deliberately spills hers onto the ground.

A woman recites a poem and then selects people to come forward and choose an object. Once close to the pile, the people look like burrowing creatures, like rodents, scratching at the edges. They cradle the objects they select. The ones that speak. A wooden carving. A locket. Ancient paperbacks. A broken chair. A football. A piece of mirror. A creature picks a torn red dress from the pile, transforms back into a man, and weeps for joy. He dances across the room in widening circles and then collapses in a closed embrace at the hem.

'Forgive me,' he whimpers softly, over and over, the dress draped across his body in a dying tango.

Max giggles, staggers, and steadies himself against a pot plant.

'Go on,' says Gabrielle, urging him forward.

'After you,' he says.

Gabrielle selects a heart-shaped box. The chocolates were eaten long ago, but the scent remains. Max chooses a snow dome, the kind you used to find in airport souvenir shops.

'Now what?' he asks.

'Just drink more tea and look at what you found.'

Max stares at his snow dome, drinks his tea, and then stares at it again.

Inside its translucent shell is a tiny world, sprinkled white and without decay. The dome contains an open skyline in a closed city. Max brings his eyeball to the edge, allowing his whole mind to be sucked into the liquid atmosphere of the world in miniature.

His eyelashes flutter, licking the sky. Shards fall between them.

The visions begin.

••

Much later, in the small room at the hospice, Gabrielle holds Max while he bucks and spasms. Outside, the residents are having a full moon party; a bongo drum syncopates with the pulse of Tom's heart monitor. Gabrielle gently wipes Max's chin, and turns his head to the side. The fit lasts thirty seconds. The one before lasted over a minute. She tells herself that if he has another, she'll unplug him. Then he does, and she doesn't.

Tom is the only witness.

Max never records his time with her.

Most likely the Meritas mixed badly with the tea. Some watery PCPx. Or something new. Some mutant mushroom, maybe. She shouldn't have been so eager to induce the protocol. When Max starts to buck again, she injects him with more saline, removes the pulse line and probe, and flicks the patch switch into a closed circuit.

'I'm sorry, Max,' she whispers. 'If you wake up we don't have to do this ever again. Please don't make me call for help.'

Tom sleeps next to them, laid out as though on an altar. The two brothers look very alike, Tom the younger version of Max. A young man, who dreams himself as an old man, who can only dream of the young man he once was. A snake with its tail in its mouth.

The background drops from Gabrielle's vision and the room becomes a net of zeros and ones. On the journey back from the towers she had felt electrified, sure that they were on the verge of a breakthrough. She listened enthusiastically to Max's ranting. It was mostly incoherent, but occasionally he fell into such a reverie, described scenes so vivid—a trip east with his father and brother, a day of desolation before his first child was born—that she felt sure he was describing real scenes from his life.

Now she feels on the brink of shutdown.

Outside the window the music is turned up, eliciting cheers of glee.

Max stirs in her lap. 'Gabrielle,' he says, softly.

She pulls herself from hibernation. The room is suddenly bright. She sees Max's eyes meet her own, she sees she is crying.

'Why, Doctor,' he says with deep concern, but also deep satisfaction. 'You're so beautiful when you cry.'

'Are you alright?' Her voice is tiny.

'I think so,' says Max. Then, after a moment he adds, 'I think you'll be pleased.'

'I'm pleased that you're alright.'

'You are going to be more pleased to hear about my dream,' he says.

She's still fuzzy with emotion. She finds it hard to process what he says. Finally she manages to translate the white noise.

'...a cube,' he says.

Her expression freezes for a moment, then she asks, 'And anything else?'

'A place I've never seen before. An old barn somewhere. In a field. Completely abandoned.'

Max feels energy coursing through Gabrielle and into his body. It's energy she is desperately trying to control. Slowly, deliberately, she removes the pads and wires from his temple, neck and wrists. She wipes away the snail-trail of conductive jelly with a soft cloth. She drops it twice.

'Show me,' she says, finally, her voice crackling.

Max composes a scene. It's speckled, as though caught on celluloid.

They sit together, exhausted, but also transfixed by the flickering image: a ghost made of snow and static.

'You've linked,' whispers Gabrielle. 'You've linked with Tom.'

'I feel like I was sleepwalking.'

'You don't remember anything?'

'What's strange is: I do. It must have been a dream, though. With you in it, of course. And Jean. And Tom.'

'Hallucinatory dreams, disorientation, headaches and weakness. These are all minor side effects of successful reaching. Don't worry, I'm with you.'

Max glances past the image and sees his talisman. 'What's that?' he asks.

'Just some old trinket.'

He stares at the snow dome calmly.

'The city before the central district, right? Seventy-odd years old? This was in my dream. A young boy played with it. He shook it up, and I was inside. I was flakes floating across the Ecodome. Pieces of me tumbled across the whole world. It was quite psychedelic. No thoughts. No images. I had no language. It felt like someone else was thinking for me.'

'A cube, and the barn. The first bit of proof of where he comes from.'

'What do you mean the barn?'

'I meant what he has seen, what he retains.'

Max looks at her with suspicion; his body stiffens. He tries to sit, but he's too weak.

'It's okay,' she says. 'Just rest for a moment. Tell me what you saw.'

'A desolate building in a tended field.' Max stares at his composition. 'Just like this.'

Max takes her hand, squeezes it. It is cool in his.

'This is connection,' she says.

He looks at her, tired and uncertain. 'Is it?'

She stays perfectly composed.

'My son is afraid of everything, not because the future's uncertain, but because it's always certain to be uncertain. There's evidence to support every hypothesis at the time of its hypothesising. At school they had him draw up a Timeline of Misconception, and on it he marked all the things humanity once knew to be true that we now know are false. Visually, it gives doubt and certainty equal value. It even makes one look like the consequence of the other. He's so anxious about it. I would have thought total information would be total peace.'

'I suppose it depends how you use the information. What your intentions are.'

'What I mean is: what if I'm not genuinely linked with Tom at all? What if I'm just experiencing a kind of psychic feedback? The input too close to the output, the system oscillating over two intractable fields.'

'Dissociation, frustration, disbelief, panic, distress. These are all normal side effects. Don't worry.'

'What if I'm cracking up? Too many changes have occurred. Unprecedented behaviour has become an expected occurrence.'

'Doubt, fear, agitation, a distrust of one's own senses. Normal, all normal. Extrinsic signals convey information not so much in themselves, but in the way that they modulate intrinsic signals.'

'Who is extrinsic? Me, or Tom? Or you?'

'You're distressed right now. That's normal. The brain

is complex. For it to receive stimulus from an unknown source is distressing.'

'There's something frightening about you this morning,' he says, and thinks he sees her hold her breath.

'That's a completely normal reaction,' she says. 'Nothing unexpected.'

• •

They start again at dawn, as the residents don their leisure suits and begin their morning exercise routines.

'You are paralysed but conscious.' Gabrielle reads her notes back to Max. 'You have lucid moments of complete calm, but also moments of terror. You feel you have no control over your emotions. Someone washes you, clips your nails. Your blanket is heavy. You can't escape the high-pitched squeal. With your eyes closed you see things – a child, and then the adult they become. Landscapes decay in front of you. You don't want to wake up. Is this correct?'

'Yes.'

She watches on the monitor as a patch of purple swells then contracts to blue across the neocortex.

'There's a fly crawling on your lips but you are unable to swat it away,' she says, watching the green spots confetti his parietal lobe. 'You see fire. You see intruders. You can't wake. Then, suddenly, you can.'

Max nods.

'Where are you?' she asks.

'In the darkness. In the barn.' Max looks uncomfortable, tired.

Gabrielle puts the headphones over Max's ears, tuning him in to the mysterious internal rhythms of the mind. Inner ear and auditory nerves can process infinite symphonies, pre-verbal, pre-tonal, preclusive. She watches as his eyes flicker shut, then she turns her attention to the image again.

It's always much easier to measure complexity than it is to understand it. The transfer rate of information between two organic systems can be measured numerically, but describing what information does within a body is harder to quantify, and more interesting. How can we measure the rate at which stimulus moves through a disparate organic network? How can we describe it in data? The only correct method necessitates entering the network. This is the method Gabrielle defended for years.

After her study on the Sleepers was published, Gabrielle attended conferences, spoke on panels and committees. She sent proposals, papers, prospectuses. She addressed environmental benefit seminars full of bureaucrats, all wary of funding a second wave of technological pragmatists.

'I don't want to live forever,' she reassured them. 'But I do think we could be much more. Environmentally speaking, a unified consciousness is stable. It's a low drain on resources. All we'll need is calories and a space to lie down. The coma developed as a way to conserve energy. Think of hibernating mammals.'

Now, she looks at Tom. There's no visible change, but the readings she is getting from Max suggest that complex transference is going on. Tom is beyond external stimulus, perhaps. But not beyond communication. One hypothesis in the research lineage she is working on suggests that Tom could start to recruit, seeking out other systems to join the network. Perhaps she herself is a part of this process. Perhaps she has been drawn into a combined process. Tom might be a connecting, binding port. A human bridge. A kind of autopoietic environment. A biological shadow of a new human becoming.

She waits for another eighty seconds, then she brings Max back. She's learned from her mistakes, sort of. Risk minimisation. That's important. She knows this even though she finds it harder to adequately conceptualise ideas like 'risk' or 'harm' with every passing year.

'What will this do for your career?' Max asks later, after he regains consciousness.

'A successful reaching? Possibly another decade of funded operation for my research program.'

'I meant the affair with your patient.'

'You aren't my patient – Tom is.' Tom: a loose connection between events and hypotheses. His neural network is dissolved but somehow he still remains, free-floating.

'Should science reassure?' Max asks, as Gabrielle pulls triggers in synthetic nervous systems.

'No. That's not its purpose. Answers to difficult questions, uncomfortable truths – these aren't reassuring things.'

His skin looks stretched tight. His body at capacity. Even a lover's skin is still merely surface, epidermis stretched over muscles, blood, bones, nerves.

'Should science frighten?' he asks.

'Perhaps,' she says, wiping moisture onto Tom's lips,

keeping the inputs clean and lubricated.

'Is science inhuman?' Max asks, almost pleading. And Gabrielle, wanting badly to reassure him and knowing no words that can, leans in to kiss him, pressing her hot presence against his.

He needs to go home now, she thinks, he needs to leave her to her work.

• •

By night she is alone. Cords leak beneath the cupboard door and into Tom's room, into Tom's skull. Gabrielle tries to sleep, but complex processes within her are still active. She models significant shapes, significant places. A wide, broad field, a squat wooden building. She sees news clips, coroner's reports, 243 bodies.

Once she's woken by the voice of Eloise Smyth: sarcastic insights, lists of dates, and misgivings, delivered from a microscopic speaker in the ceiling.

'Perhaps he needs to get worse to get better,' Eloise is saying. 'You know, I leave clues around the house. I displace items, put them where they don't belong. I play tricks to force him to remember. Or at least ask questions. Of course he doesn't notice. He hardly seems to care.' She laughs. 'I suppose this is the question in most marriages: how do you get through to each other?'

Gabrielle reappears.

'Hello, Ms Smyth, sorry to disturb you.'

Eloise looks unsurprised. 'Dr Galleon, I'm glad you're here.'

'Where else would I be?'

'Of course,' she smiles. 'How's it all going?'

'Still inconclusive, I'm afraid.'

'That's a shame. But research is always a slow business. Jane Goodall observed chimps dancing for years before she understood it was religion.'

'Chimps dancing sounds more fun,' Gabrielle says, grimacing at Tom's shape, inert under the white sheet.

'Oh yes? I would've thought that Max was reasonably entertaining.'

Gabrielle is silent.

'And you've been following some unorthodox protocols,' says Eloise, looking bemusedly at Gabrielle, who is frozen. 'I mean the Envirotowers,' she laughs. 'Jean told me all about it. He said he followed Max there. He said he had no idea how Max came up with such a plan. It sounds so intriguing. I love that kind of thing. I read all about all the new groups. That's actually how I found out about you,' she continues. 'I read a very interesting case study. I enjoy conspiracy these days. Max has given me a taste for it. I've even tried my hand at writing some myself. Just a few short compositions.'

'You are a creative family,' Gabrielle stammers.

'We're fortunate,' says Ellie, in a monotone. 'Of course we all are. We are all survivors.' She gestures at Tom. 'And are you any more certain of his particular story of survival?'

'I still can't be sure. My feeling is that he experienced a neural catastrophe. The neurological system can only take so much before it becomes overloaded. Then the brain shuts down, protects itself.'

'Oh, I know – that's how Max has made his living.'

'How's that?'

'His films,' Ellie says. 'Neurological bombardment followed by a cathartic moment of complete rest. It helps people get on with their lives. Feeling finally and totally connected to one another is one of humanity's only historically constant desires. A lot of people are selling it. We're all potential buyers. Max too.'

'That's true.'

'There was a time when people talked about saturating the entire universe with human intelligence – do you remember?'

'Of course.'

'I remember thinking: imagine what that would be like, a universe bursting with neurosis and fear. But perhaps that's the best goal for the human mind – to detach from the individual and everyday. We're all connected now, of course, but they're not the right kinds of connections. All the obsessive self-surveillance. Just look at my husband. It leads to new diseases of the mind. But you know this. Do you think perhaps, on some level, we're all suffering from it?'

'I think you're speaking metaphorically.'

'Perhaps. I suppose scientists hate that?' Eloise says, smiling knowingly. 'Today each of us lives parallel lives. One embodied, and one as information. Of course, you're probably one of the enlightened amongst us. You understand embodied life in informational terms.' She arranges her hair, eyes far off, as though looking into a mirror. 'My husband edits his archive,' she says. 'And sometimes I edit it too. Did you know that?'

'No.'

Eloise cocks an eyebrow. 'What occurs to me is this,' she says. 'Max is so thoroughly networked that there is no reason to think he hasn't done the same research I have. Drawn the same conclusions.'

'That's true.'

'Of course, if he had, he wouldn't remember it. And there's something else to consider, too.'

'Yes?'

'Max doesn't remember this, but before Tom went missing, the two of them were becoming close. They spoke quite often. I'd only met Tom once – I didn't even know where he was living. Then, one weekend, Max tells me he's going to pick his brother up. He took a long drive. He actually dropped off the map – I was watching. I remember worrying, catastrophising actually, and trying not to. Eventually I checked Max's purchase record to locate him, and there was one recent large transfer. Then after a while he just came home. He was shaken. He refused to talk about Tom after that weekend. At least, that is, not until Tom showed up again.' Eloise gestures to the body on the bed. 'Like this.'

Gabrielle stares up at her. 'Where do you think they went?'

'I have suspicions,' she says, 'but, like I said, I'm quite into conspiracy at the moment.' She stages a rapid, contrived laugh. 'But what if he'd planned to join Tom? Wherever Tom was, wherever it was that he went, wherever it was that Tom ended up like this. I'm sure you know more than me about that.'

'I do have a theory.'

'I thought you would, Dr Stern. Your work is always meticulous.' She shakes her head and smiles apologetically. 'But it will all be over soon, one way or another.'

'What do you mean?'

'Well, Max needs to get on with his life, as unsatisfactory as it might be to him – or to us.' She laughs again. Her teeth are very white, small, and sharp looking. 'You know that he's off to the island soon.'

'Yes, I know.' Gabrielle says, trying to process the real meaning of this conversation.

'Good.'

Gabrielle senses Eloise Smyth in the room for the rest of the day. She detects her presence as she logs data into her supervision program; a stiff algorithm pervaded by a sense of failure. The program continually reassesses the promising applications of Gabrielle's research anteced-ents—brain interfaces for the sight- and hearing-impaired, parent–child neural networks, a police neural reaching da-tabase—all buried below inconclusive outcomes, dead ends, terminated subjects. She logs data with the feeling that she is also being logged and read. She fumbles observations. Twice her supervisor points to an error. 'Are you alright?' it asks in its professorial clip.

'I'm fine,' she says. 'I'm just exhausted.'

In her mind, she sees Eloise's tight, knowing smile, drawn as taut as a bowstring.

••

INT. HOSPITAL ROOM. DAY

MAX

Why did my wife send me to you?

GABRIELLE

She was curious.

MAX

About Tom?

GABRIELLE

About you and Tom.

MAX

Which part of my brain is still in love with her?

GABRIELLE

There is no part. You are in love with her when you experience a particular pattern of neural fire.

MAX

Which part of my brain is in love with you?

GABRIELLE

There is no part.

MAX

You are the fire in my neurons.

GABRIELLE

Scientists hate it when you construct lame metaphors from biochemistry.

The lens focuses on Max: he's flushed, happy. He reaches out to touch Gabrielle's thigh, but her leg flickers and becomes irresolute. He doesn't seem to notice. She says, 'Stop, or I'll sedate you.' He says, 'I love you.' Around the room, sensors bristle in response to an algorithm. The scene is recorded and logged. A statistics window shows Max's temperature and elevated heartbeat. There's no biometric data available on Gabrielle.

From another room, another place, Eloise Smyth locates her husband in the network. What she sees: Max inert, slumped in a chair, haptic lines streaming from his wrists like blood. She checks the archive.

'Love, 2:12pm.'

She smiles strangely, blinks away the feed. She picks up her bag from the porthole by the door and steps out into the day.

• •

This is how you wake up.

Paralysed. Sweating. Feelings of dissolution, fear of imminent death, the sensation of being strangled. You hear distant sirens. The blades of a helicopter.

You struggle under a damp blanket, try to slash through sleep that hangs off your bones like dead meat in cold storage.

Movement comes in unpredictable bursts. Your right hand rips the drip from your lifeless left arm, swats the mask off your face.

Cold rushes against your cheeks. Dry ice. The metal cot shakes with your convulsions. You try to wake up your body with one thought: Go.

The cot crashes to the floor. Flashlights from a corner window. You hide under a gurney.

'Stop.' A man's voice. Outside.

Lights sweep the floor. They streak across sleeping bodies, illuminate an ear, an eyelid, a thin arm, a sickly foot.

You creep silently, follow the thin crack of moonlight along the wall. Wooden slats. Small, high-set, arched windows. One open just a crack.

Swinging your body out is difficult, like throwing a sack of flour. You thud onto the ground, lie there a while, wonder if you are still alive.

'Surround.'

'I tell you, they're all asleep.'

Boots crunch through the scrub. Sticks and stones rattle like bones.

'I'm alive,' you whisper.

You run through fields, sometimes closing your eyes for seconds that feel like hours. Arms stretched out, cutting the air. Sound is your feet, your breath, your heartbeat, the wind. Are they following you? Are you going fast or slow? You stumble, rip a hole in the leg of your loose suit pants. You knot the waistband around your thin hips. Clutch it. Clench pale fists translucent.

You can't remember your name.

At moments when straight is crooked, when some obstacle rises up to block your path, you sit down, take stock. Shadows and colour flash in the periphery of your mind. Familiar shapes meld and multiply.

Water shoots out of the pipe, fierce and foamy, becoming flat like glass towards the centre. You hang your head over the side of the catchment, then jerk it up towards the sky, snapping your perspective backwards across the landscape. It's like being inside a wave. Tumbled through concrete, scorched grasslands, blue sky. Water, water, concrete, grass, sky, water, water, concrete, grass, sky.

Water, water, concrete, grass, sky, water, water, concrete, grass, sky.

Water, water, concrete, grass, sky, water, water, concrete, grass, sky.

It all becomes a zoetrope. The basic mechanics of film.

'I've lost my mind,' you say, and take off, running again.

You run a straight line on bending legs. When you turn back all you see is smoke, as though you are running from forest fire. But there's no forest. Just this road and what's ahead. Some kind of camp. Shelter. As you approach you identify things slowly: government-stamped accommodation vehicles, a giant public screen with damaged pixels. People milling. Dust kicked up by recently departed vehicles.

A restless temporality. Somewhere between sleep and life.

Slightly off to the side of the main camp you see a single tent, circular, its solar door blowing open, revealing glimpses of a void. You stagger towards it, throw yourself into the dark. You feel like you are falling for a long time before your body hits the ground. You watch a trail of ants on the roof of the tent, another trail on the floor. You watch one ant struggle, belly up, back legs flailing, front legs still holding onto some crumb.

Ants don't think. They are part of some larger pattern.

You close your eyes and data scrolls. You feel as though the ground is opening up and swallowing you. This tent is sinking. There is drowning in your bones and code behind your eyelids. There is no space to ask the necessary questions. Who are you? How did you get here? Was there a fire? A storm? Some great catastrophe?

You can conjure some relief in the dark, but not answers.

Sleep calls. Sleep like communion or surrender.

You wake periodically from dreams that aren't yours. Wake haunted. Wake in geometric tangle. Wake in high-resolution scenes, lights striking out across dried corn fields. A wave tumbling to eclipse the sky. You want to order these images into a narrative but your perspective tilts and pans. You are beset by images, sequences, a rhythmic beep. You see a light in the distance, and, far off, you hear a woman's voice asking you a question.

'What did you see?'

ACTION
SEQUENCE

'It got to the point where they had to eat each other to stay alive. Not that they killed each other – the population was way too small for that. They had to get their protein by eating the recently dead, and finally by digging up buried corpses and curing what was left of the rancid meat.'

Sitting on the landscaped slopes behind our Bay Heights home, Jonas is giving me a virtual tour of Pitcairn Island in readiness for our imminent departure. Through the lens of my gaming headset, the manicured sage and bottlebrush of our backyard has been transformed into the shoreline of a desolate island. In the distance, a smouldering wreck indicates the mutiny that occurred just days earlier. Jonas has informed his gaming companions that today he is not here to battle the Polynesian braves, or to display his survivalist know-how in a competitive arena of floods and mosquito-borne viruses. 'This is my Dad,' he says, apologetically, to an approaching topless woman.

'No worries, man,' replies the woman in the voice of a middle-aged man. She lays hibiscus on the ground beyond Jonas before vanishing.

'Is that your wife?'

'Daaaaad!' Jonas is appalled.

'I thought you had a native wife?'

Jonas shakes his head, exasperated. 'I've had eight,' he says. 'When the mutineers arrived there was no one here at all. The population was extinct. They needed women for breeding and extra men for labour. They gave Tahitian natives beads and feathers as bribes for them to move to the island. Then they stripped the ship they'd transported them in. They saved all usable timber, brass hinges and banisters, the steering wheel, iron nails, curtains, felt, wax, paper, gunpowder, rifles, springs, canvas, glass from portals, all the rope from the rig. They tore down the sails. They took everything and used it all. They started a completely new civilisation out of the wreckage of their ship, and then they burned whatever was left.'

'Well, she's very polite for a kidnapped slave.'

'Duh, it's strategic.'

'Of course. I'm forgetting this is a game and everyone is playing to win.'

'It's more complex than that, Dad. It's not like you can "win" this game.'

'No? Then what's the point?'

'The point is to progress through a series of challenges, and refine your strategies for surviving. The point is learning. About history. And about yourself.'

Jonas says the last of this under his breath, as though there is no way I could understand. He's probably right. I always thought games were a form of escapism.

'So, what was her strategy?' I ask.

'I'm currently playing in the age of disease. All the characters on this level are dying and we have to work out how to make a vaccine and develop an anti-inflammatory diet, or we are doomed. This scenario doesn't get much easier, no matter how many times you play it out. But it probably has the highest replay value, actually, because each time the resources at your disposal are different, and the solve is a different lateral equation. Also, there are other things that can weirdly help you buy time. Like, a faith healer won't cure your sick, but somehow it will keep them alive for a few more days while you prepare the vaccine, and construct the quarantine area.'

'I see.'

Jonas looks dubious, but continues. 'In the current scenario outline, myself and one other mutineer have developed a diet that protects from the illness, and we have enough supplies to save us and two other breeding women of our choosing. Naturally, all the women want to be among the chosen.'

'Can't they develop their own diets and vaccines?'

'Yes, but at this point it seems unlikely.' Jonas looks up into a rocky crag, seeing some truth unapparent to any newcomer. 'I'll save her, or she will die and have to redo the level. It's pretty hard to play a woman in this game, actually. There are a whole lot of really different strategic moves you have to learn. Anyway, this isn't that important for you. It's very unlikely that there will be a disease outbreak in the time we are on Pitcairn – and besides, you aren't an eighteenth-century Tahitian slave.'

'That's true.' I nod at my son's wisdom. 'Still, it's good to be prepared, right?'

Jonas shoots me a look.

Alone in the game now, we are free to wander around his fiefdom and take stock. Pitcairn Island is not much to look at. There's no tropical island beach to lounge on. The ocean slaps violently against the rocks. Behind us are the green peaks of the tiny civilisation; thatched huts dot the flat spaces, presumably sheltering convalescent sailors and their stolen brides.

'You can use hibiscus for rope, and ti shrub,' says Jonas. 'Ti shrub's sugary roots can also be used as an emergency food supply in hard times.'

He scrambles over the rocky crag, beckoning me to follow. From a crevice he plucks a sodden violet frond and hands it to me.

'This stuff is all important, Dad.'

'Yes, but I'm sure the island has come a long way since the century we appear to be in. I have us booked into a reputable hotel.'

'When the final storm comes, everything returns to the primitive,' Jonas says.

'Do you think it's likely to come next week?'

'What's likely, and what's not? Who decides that?'

We climb further away from the shore.

'There are all kinds of catastrophes you know,' he says.

'I know.'

'And did you know that the *Bounty* mutineers were un-witting colonialists? Even though they renounced their British citizenship when they got to the island, they were still claiming it for the empire.'

I nod. It's probable that I knew this at some point, even though the information sounds new.

I clamber after him in silence for several minutes. From what looks to be the highest point on the island we stare down into the sheltered terrain of Adamstown, the only settlement on Pitcairn, and hence its capital.

'Only a few mutineers survive,' says Jonas. 'But the island goes on to be one of the most important geographic locations of our time. Look,' he says, making commands in the game to allow us to see the island in time lapse throughout the centuries.

There is surprisingly little change in the landscape during the time lapse. Thatched roofs are replaced with tin, and then thatched again. A church is built and rebuilt in the town square, and behind it a modern-looking hotel pops up. Soon, there are meteorological measuring stations and labs in tents all over the small village. Out by the shore, a group of disaster tourists alight a small craft, excited to be, potentially, amongst the last to see this slice of land. The lettering on the side of their boat reads 'End of the World Touring'.

Jonas nods and the scenery returns to its eighteenth-century crudity. We trudge through the scrub, the wind sharp in our ears.

'You can use giant clamshells to make tools like small axes: you punch holes in the shells with bird bones and tie on the handles with hibiscus and ti shrub twine. If you don't have basalt for oven stones, you can use coral, but it's brittle and not as good,' he says.

I try to devise a respectable question to ask my son, one that shows acumen for our situation and comprehension of its implications for the future. When I turn to ask him what we are going to have for lunch, I can see he is distracted. His face is held skyward, at attention – he's reading from some urgent scrawl of information that I cannot see. He makes small snuffing noises of alarm.

'Are you seeing this?' says a loud voice of no discernable origin.

'I think so,' replies Jonas. 'Whoa.'

'Who's that?' I ask.

'That's my friend from Lutsk,' says Jonas, then: 'Yeah, I see it, but I'm in 1789 right now, so I've only got stats.'

'It looks major, man,' says the voice. 'I'd log out.'

Behind us, on the peaks, a group of spear-bearing natives are also looking with concern at the sky. They confer amongst themselves in a frenzy of inaudible chatter, and then one by one they vanish into thin air, their spears clattering into a pile. Jonas doesn't notice – he's too busy staring at projections in the sky and conferring with readings on his wristwatch. I'm not logged into the info feed from either. My own feed only gives me information about my inner-space.

'Fight or flight response, 10:45am,' notes the archive.

'What's going on?' I ask.

Jonas doesn't look at me. 'I don't know Dad, but we better get out of here. Come on.'

No sooner has he grabbed my hand than his vanishes, along with the rest of him. I'm alone on the rocks, the *Bounty* flaming impossibly on the horizon, the waves lapping at the craggy shoreline. I look around, panicked, but I'm completely alone. A triad of fishing birds dive-bomb the foam.

'Dad, come on!' yells Jonas from somewhere I can't see. 'Take off your headset.'

It takes me a moment to understand what he means. I shake my head and feel the weight of the set. I snap the buckle and flip the switch, and the island flickers and gives way to a bright, perfect day on the hills behind my Bay Heights home. I'm sprawled on the grass, breathless under the blue sky. I take a moment, trying to hold onto the difference between the real and the simulation.

'Disillusion, 10:48am,' notes the archive.

Jonas is already gone. I leave the headset on the grass and walk up to the house to join my family.

Jonas, Lilly and Ellie are in the family room, all staring agape at a news feed of Pitcairn. It's strange to see it again so soon, this time from above, alive with graphs and tables.

'It's dropped,' says Ellie without looking at me.

'That's the understatement of the century,' says Jonas.

Lilly says nothing. Her little mouth is pursed in concentration, and she appears to be holding a very important conference across several media. An infinite list of equations rolls from a block of light in her palm. Across the walls of my home, experts bob and weave.

'A spike in water temperature in the Southern Gulf has confirmed category eight probability of a category five hurricane,' says a young woman urgently.

'That's right, Mary,' says an older woman, perfectly attired in white lab coat and thick spectacles. 'But the hurricane is not what's caused the plankton extinction. The numbers I have here indicate that in the next five days we will need to add another species to the list of recently extinct if this temperature increase plateaus.'

'What are we talking?' says the male presenter, as though he might bargain the extinctions down by a few thousand or so individual organisms.

'We're worried for the krill. The krill eat the plankton. With plankton levels dropping at such a rapid rate, we will not be able to feed the domestic populations of krill. We simply do not have enough artificial plankton synthesised, and further synthesis might become more difficult as one of the key ingredients in synthetic plankton is plankton itself.'

'Can you give us a timeline for this?'

'There's a high probability that if krill bioavailability drops by more than fifteen per cent in the next week, we'll be facing a major catastrophe for the organic fish market.'

'And what will that look like? For the viewer at home?'

'Well, obviously, it's a big problem if you are a whale. But for us, it means no more ocean-based protein, Mary.'

Her jaw drops, the mouth parted in mute shock.

'Quit,' says Ellie, and Mary flickers out.

Ellie squeezes my hand.

'I never liked fish too much,' I joke.

'Who cares then, right?' says Lilly. She shakes her head in disbelief and stomps back to her room, trailing devices.

Ellie and I remain standing, hand in hand, looking around us like sad spectators who've just missed seeing the fireworks. We learn that the potential hurricane has already been sponsored – it is now named Hurricane Teardrop.

'Did Sullivan get the money from you?' she asks.

'Probably,' I say.

We learn that krill are a vital bottom-feeder, and are the subsistence of most of the large for-eating fish designed in the past twenty years. We learn that krill used to be the most abundant marine biomass, and so were a logical choice for marine designers. In fact, krill has been one of the steadiest of all marine populations for more than fifty years, with no major drops registered. Until now. We watch food stocks plummet on at least two stock exchanges. We see footage from the former republic of Russia in which short women in thick coats fight over baskets of twitching, minute crustaceans.

'I'm worried,' says Ellie.

'About the krill?'

'Yes, the krill – but also about you.'

As if to answer for me, Jean's stern expression spreads across the space between us.

'Jean – a rare networked appearance,' I say. 'Is everything okay?'

'Come back to central, Max,' he says. 'We have to get ready.'

'Get ready for what?'

'For what? To go to that island. Before it's too late.'

'Now? Are you crazy? What about the krill?'

'Forget the krill, Max. We have an opportunity.'

'Well if we're not worried about the krill, what about Hurricane Teardrop then? It's the most plausible hurricane this year.'

'All the better. We have the opportunity to make a film of the disaster that everyone is watching. But we have to move fast.'

'I'm not sure, Jean.' I can feel Jonas watching me from the floor. 'I think we should find out more first. We should wait and listen to the experts.'

'Max! You hate the experts. And anyway, this is our chance to join them. You're just being pathetic, as usual. We need to jump on this now. I'll give you two days to get organised, then we need to move.'

'Let's see how this pans out.'

'If you don't come with me to Pitcairn, it pans out with you dying in your own mediocrity,' says Jean. He turns away from me, assessing my family room as though it were a wrongly-awarded trophy. His grey gaze lingers on my grim, enraptured son, my beautiful, auburn-haired wife, and then returns to me, incredulous. 'I have to go. There are things to prepare.'

'Okay, fine.'

'Goodbye, Ellie,' says Jean.

'Bye,' says Ellie, smiling too graciously.

Jean's face flickers from view but his incredulous attitude has been transferred to my son.

'He's right,' says Jonas. 'This is a once-in-a-lifetime opportunity.'

'Jonas,' I say, 'you of all people should understand the need to have all the facts at hand, to be prepared.'

'Being prepared isn't the same as hiding,' says Jonas. 'In *Mutiny*, if you hide, you starve. You live maybe a week, tops, and you learn nothing. You may as well not even play the game.'

Ellie takes an authoritative, maternal tone. 'Jonas,' she says. 'This is not a game. This is real life, and your father is more than capable of making decisions.'

I feel buoyed by her words and reach out to squeeze her manicured hand. Somewhere, a chip measures her heartbeat and temperature.

'Intra-marital dishonesty, 11:40am,' notes the archive, producing a helpful graph.

••

By morning, three species of krill are extinct and Lilly has become a plankton farmer. She's taken over the small pond in the backyard. The holographic trout have been switched off and the pond refilled with salt water. She measures the pH hourly.

I watch her from the living room. My clothes remind me that it's too early to drink but I'm drinking anyway.

'What will she do with the plankton if she manages to raise a colony?'

'That's a pointless question,' says Jonas. 'What does

anyone do with anything? You can't know until you are doing it. The important thing is that right now she's doing something. She's raising plankton.'

I nod.

'I don't know if you've noticed,' Jonas continues. 'But Lilly gets really stressed out about this stuff.'

'She seems very in-control.'

'It's an illusion, a symptom of the stress.'

I look at my son, his hunched shoulders and grey eyes. He reminds me of someone, but I can't place it.

'We all need an outlet,' says Ellie. 'Speaking of which, Max, I've made a change in your itinerary – I've cancelled this week's sessions with Tom and Dr Stern.'

My stomach tightens and I feel a pang of anxiety like heartburn. The scent of lavender and lemongrass wafts from vents below my feet. I take exactly six deep breaths.

Ellie waits, bemused. 'I spoke with her. She said you weren't getting anywhere with Tom. Besides, I think you need to attend to the crisis at hand.'

'I don't know anything about plankton.'

'That's not what I mean.' Ellie looks significantly at Jonas, who sits, brooding on an ottoman by the window, analysing a stream of data and monitoring feeds from Pitcairn, New Zealand and the Gulf of Mexico. Isobaric indicators spread and contract around him like bacterial swarms.

'I don't know what I'm supposed to do about it.' I lower my voice, as though it makes a difference. 'I don't control the weather. Not in the real world.'

'Just involve him.'

'I need to go and see Jean.'

'Then take him to do that.'

Jonas is cocooned in stock market declines and ocean temperatures. A ruined village is picked up on a strong wind and hurled over his small head. I watch him for a while, fully aware that he knows I am watching, fully aware that all his hunching and furrowing is a message as important as any of the grim news around him.

'There was a time when parents were supposed to shelter children from the harsher realities,' I say to Ellie.

'Was there?' she says. 'How did that work out?'

I walk over to my son, closing data windows as I pass them, switching each feed from ruined homes and the scum of dead krill over to pop videos and classic films.

Jonas looks at me incredulously.

'We've had enough,' I say with my best paternal voice. 'We are all okay here. Krill or no krill, you and your mother and sister and I are safe. Let's bask in our safety and love, okay?'

He says nothing.

I flick through a folder of suitable entertainment and select Irwin Allen's 1978 classic disaster film *The Swarm*. Jonas shakes his head disbelievingly. I sit down and beckon to him to come to me. He could sit at my feet and we could bond, forge important connections. He doesn't move. A bowl of neutracarb popcorn appears on a side table. He pretends not to notice.

I ignore him ignoring me.

I can't remember how long it's been since I watched an old film – one without haptic stimulation, pre MiniCine.

The image flickers constantly, and the colours are too bright or too muted. It's a cool, old aesthetic now relegated to advertising for alcohol and authentic leather shoes. On screen, the young family relax with their picnic lunch. It's a classic setup: normality only existing to be disturbed. Actually not so different from what we use today. The bees are a noise before we see them. The camera zooms in and out on the grey-black cloud, and the buzzing dominates the audio track. All the speakers in our lounge room buzz terribly as the bees approach their prey. The family on screen notices them suddenly, their faces becoming masks of shock and alarm. They slap at themselves, they contort and spasm. Their bodies are coated with bees, obliterated with buzzing even as they thrash across the landscape. Blackened with bees, they are no longer human. They transcend, becoming something horrific: twitching black silhouettes against the bee-mottled sky. It's the shot that will be recreated for decades to come: the hysterical dance of man at the mercy of nature.

When the sequence ends, I rewind and replay it from the start.

'Why are we watching this?' says Jonas.

'It's a classic.'

'It's boring and stupid.'

'The commonly held belief is that none of Irwin Allen's films were very good.'

'I can see why.'

'Most weren't even reprinted for MiniCine. I curated a collection for the International Archive of Modern Cinema.

Before you were born. Just after *Then Rest* came out.'

'I didn't know that.'

'Does it make a difference?'

'Somewhat,' he says.

'Irwin Allen strongly believed in disaster cinema as a moral force. This was pre–climate change, pre–germ bomb, pre–economic collapse and energy crisis.' I scroll forward to a swarm of bees obliterating the horizon. 'Whether it's good or not, these films had an impact on the way we think about disaster. They certainly had an impact on my film-making.' I look at him significantly. 'I'm a filmmaker, Jonas. I'm not a storm-chaser. I'm not a politician. I'm not even a moralist like Allen. I don't know what to do in the face of an actual catastrophe. All I understand is that disaster on screen is beautiful, and to live through disaster is a great gift. I began making my films because I wanted to know if this was true in reality, but now I feel that there is too much to lose. I can't explain it.'

In my mind's eye Tom freeze-frames – not a body but a presence, a feeling.

'That's why you need me, Dad,' Jonas says, his tone soft.

'Jonas, you are twelve years old.'

'In the 1800s I would've sailed around the world by now.'

'Or you might just as easily be dead of scurvy, floating in the ocean off the coast of an as-yet-unnamed land mass.'

I surf the Irwin Allen file and bring up *The Towering Inferno*, tracking through to the first explosion.

'Look at this one,' I say. 'Allen only directed the action sequences in this film. Someone else took care of the irrelevant filler, while he got down to the serious business of showing Steve McQueen how to move his arms as he ran through the fire, conveying not only man's frailty in the face of death, but also our everyday heroism, living bravely beside the demon of nature.'

Jonas and I watch the flames lick at the curtains of a skyscraper. The sound of coughing victims and the roaring sound of the fire are constant. Even when the fire is put out it still echoes. Silence has sound.

'Allen was an expert at producing the conditions for the experience of disaster. He knew how to choreograph violent death.'

Jonas sits up on the ottoman, shuffling it a few millimetres forward.

I'm excited for him, to be watching this for the first time. I wish I could remember the first time I watched it. The climax of *The Towering Inferno* includes zero dialogue. It's a full ten minutes of nothing but destruction. Elevator shafts explode. Flaming support beams break the backs of sooty firemen. Ceilings cave in. Windows stretch and shatter. The illusion is completely real. The pleasure of disbelief that some of the early disaster films worked with—the moment where the audience picks the fault, says 'it would never happen like that'—is completely absent in the final action sequence of that film. Jonas is hooked, despite himself.

'Satisfaction, 10:10am,' notes the archive.

'When I first saw this film, I knew I had found something special,' I tell him. 'I saw no reason not to make an entire film using the last action sequence from *The Towering*

Inferno as the blueprint. Watch how the climax scene starts off with Paul Newman and Steve McQueen synchronising their watches. This is important, because at the point when Newman says there is only three minutes to go, at least nine minutes of screen time remain. Screen time is usually faster than reality, but in this sequence the camera tries to show what's going through the mind of every single character as they wait for the explosion. When the sequence is over, it cuts to a wide shot, one that's been called controversial, as it gives the viewer the privilege of academic distance from trauma. This film gives us a glimpse of the disastrous sublime.'

Irwin Allen understood the value of symbolism, I think, not for the first time. He knew the true resonance of the burning doll on the child's bedroom floor, the power of the image of the kitten licking at a trembling saucer of milk. These are shots I use over and over. Allen was also the first director to understand that narrative in a disaster film is just an accessory. On screen, another big explosion breaks the façade of the building, and a wide shot shows water pouring out into the city.

'That's pretty wasteful,' Jonas says.

'Perhaps, but it's instructive. And it's beautiful. Don't you think?'

Jonas looks unconvinced.

'This was before Panda Points,' I say, keeping one eye on my son. He is almost smiling. 'See how the Grecian statue breaks and pins the porter to the floor? I pay homage to that in *Then Rest*.'

Jonas stops smiling. He checks a peripheral feed and then glares at me, all reverie dumped from his expression.

'We've lost another 0.00012,' he says. 'The world is ending and all you want to do is watch movies.' He pulls his headset down over his eyes. 'Let me know when you've decided to deal with what's actually happening,' he says, disappearing into a more complex and earnest world.

• •

The hour of the cancelled appointment with Dr Stern approaches without further comment. As it grows closer I am distracted, pained. I can't work or focus. I can't make decisions. Fruit salads, crossword puzzles and half-empty Scotch glasses litter the house. I move around like a rat in one of those electrocuted mazes designed to test its faculties.

Finally, I settle in the bedroom and search wistfully through the archive. I bring random freeze-frames of my life up on the art deco mirror. Below the screen, on the vanity top, Ellie's potions and powders are lined up like fortune-telling apparatuses.

Without knowing why, I search Tom's doctor's full name: 'Gabrielle Stern.'

'Pleasure, 3:45pm,' notes the archive, providing no further information.

Strangely, nothing comes to the screen. I say her name again, the same feeling running across my skin. Still nothing. I log into the hospice and watch Tom for a while. If he's seen the doctor today he isn't telling.

I turn back to a random selection of archival memory, watching strange scenes from my life unfold. It all looks like a long-running soap opera. Characters dip in and out. Some are recurrent, some fade away. I try again to locate Dr Stern, scrolling through cold moments compulsively.

Now I'm not even looking for a full scene – I really just want to know what colour her eyes are. But still nothing.

I watch a long sequence of myself repeating some graceless yoga sequence, another of me driving, my fingers tapping the steering wheel in time to Schwerbut.

'Erase,' I say suddenly, not knowing why. I stand straight. Eyes fierce at scan point. 'Erase from all records.'

Even though I know I'm probably imagining it, I can hear the shock of the machine. I can hear circuits bristling. I can feel the chip beneath my scalp gnawing nervously at its edges.

In eighty-two seconds these scenes are gone.

I journey back through the record, swimming upstream, a strange breeze in my hair. I watch sequences at random, not looking at their logged dates.

I erase luncheons with actors, programmers and animators.

I erase storyboard sessions.

I erase a ten-minute grab of myself standing in front of a mirror, clutching a handful of waist fat.

Dr Stern's eyes are dark brown. Even if they are blue or green, they are dark brown to me.

I watch every dull second of a scene in which Ellie and I sit out on the balcony in pained silence. I erase it.

I erase a sequence in which a tailor fits me for golf wear.

I erase lectures on sustainability thoughtfully prepared for me by Lilly.

I head back further and further, erasing as I go, until I've located the first ever entry in my own recorded life, and settle back to watch.

INT. WIDE SHOT. HOSPITAL

The hospital room is white. Max is propped up on cushions. A tray of partially eaten food is spread across his lap. Ellie enters. She arranges recycled gerberas in an airglass vase by the bed. She kisses Max's cheek then sits next to him on the bed.

ELLIE

Recovering okay?

MAX

Fine. A little woozy from the anaesthetic. But nothing too unpleasant.

ELLIE

Good. I was worried.

MAX

I know. I'm sorry.

Max squeezes Ellie's wrist, smiling up at her.

ELLIE

I still think it was a silly risk. You could've waited until we knew something with certainty. You know, the first silicone breast implants exploded in planes. Women died from the poisonous shock of their own new breasts.

MAX

I know. I'm sorry. But we have gone through this before. I'm an early adopter. It's been a great advantage all my life.

ELLIE

I suppose.

MAX

Ellie, I'm fine. Better than ever, and now I won't miss a thing. How's Jonas coming along?

ELLIE

I wanted to wait for you before I okayed the installation. His gestation environment is ready.

MAX

You are a glowing mother.

ELLIE

Don't tease. Jean's here too.

MAX

Bring him in, then.

Max props himself up further to kiss Ellie on the lips. Jean enters, wearing a crumpled but expensive suit, clutching a hip flask.

JEAN

Well, I see Operation Skull Cam was a success.

MAX

It's not a camera.

JEAN

Whatever it is. It's another chip off the new block. A piece of synaptic plastic we apparently cannot live without. You have succeeded in widening the circuit. The predictive appliances. The communication ports, the camera, the camera, the eyes, the eyes, the ears. You have more eyes than a plague of flies. More ears than pig's ear soup.

MAX

Do you want to ask me how I am feeling?

JEAN

No. Why would I ask you that? I may wish to ask you how you should be feeling, but the question is too subtle for you.

ELLIE

Shut up, Jean.

JEAN

I am sorry, beautiful Ellie. I'm a little drunk.

ELLIE

He finished our Scotch.

MAX

He needed it to abuse me.

JEAN

I could abuse you without it, but this way it is more pleasant. For the both of us. I'm glad you're alright. Of course. You are alright? Great. Now let's move on to more important things.

'Pause,' I say.

I identify each object in the frame: Jean's tarnished hip flask, his reddening cheeks, the outmoded hospital equipment.

Around this time, somewhere far away, embryos are being injected into sacs of nutrients. Helixes are bound and labelled: 'Jonas'. And then he is foetal, ingesting the nutrient of centuries of technology. And then he is born, embodying the embryonic hope of a post-catastrophe generation.

In the screen image, just beyond the window, there's evidence of a city people recently called home.

As I continue to scroll through the timeline of my life I find myself periodically teetering on the edge of vast gaps. Parts of my life have been torn from the screen. I strain, trying to remember the missing pieces, trying to summon some trusty perception, but my mind is filled with stock images.

How can I have no memory if I have such a great imagination?

I pull up a storyboarding application.

I replace my daughter with a promising child actress.

I replace my son with a lovable and intelligent collie.

I replace Ellie with a blushing bride of high temperature and heaving bosom.

Microelectronic sensors measure the viscosity of my perspiration as I work.

In the gaps where Dr Stern should be I play out formulaic romantic entanglements with a shadowy, Nouvelle Vague looking girl:

The couple elope.

The couple drift apart.

The couple enter a suicide pact.

The couple live happily ever after.

The couple are separated by war.

The couple are torn apart brutally when one or the other party throws themselves in front of an early locomotive.

Strangely, the archive notes neither guilt nor shame.

I trawl through the highlights, cuts and outtakes of my own cinematic career – from the first images I assembled by running news footage through animation programs, through to the high-budget immersive scenarios of my seminal work. The flood. The flames. The drought.

I randomly pluck an ice-storm from the outtakes. The pellets of hail and sleet are sharp as needles. They pierce the skin, freezing the blood in your veins. *Your heart struggles, beats, struggles, throbs, struggles, stops. It will turn to ice. It will shatter.*

I splice disaster after disaster and insert them into the archive of my life, until it seems that I have moved from calamitous event to calamitous event, in an ultimate hero's journey.

Satisfied, I fall back on the bed and into the calm dark of sleep. I dream someone else's dreams.

• •

It's not that you want to hibernate like an animal. You just long to fall back into an infinite net with infinite give. To relax into a pattern of being that transcends your own small and cluttered life. You want to cast yourself out beyond the unavoidable anxiety and strain of life as an individual.

You feel the needle pierce your skin and your veins fill up with sleep. There is a moment here, on the precipice, where you can assess all the moments that came before this one. A singular collage of events. Watching your mother singing in the garden. A pile of burning machines. A long drive. The smell of smoke, the sound of sirens. All the vivid pasts, and somehow all the possible futures too. You reach out to each one but they're already gone, replaced by something more or less real. Now, as tranquillity takes hold, a feeling like returning home. The air is sweet. A vast sound fills your inner ear. Then relief takes over. You no longer feel like you, and then, you no longer feel.

• •

Pre-emptive algorithms have already packed Jonas's bag by the time I get around to checking my itinerary. He is coming with me to the central district. We will reconnoitre the scene together. It seems inevitable, now, in the desaturated light of morning, that Ellie would get her way.

'I don't want to hear any more about going to Pitcairn,' I tell Jonas, refusing to place his bag in the car until he looks me in the eye and gives me a weak smile.

'Pyrrhic victory, 9:04am,' notes the archive.

Jonas has already co-opted the trip, insisting that we visit the Pitcairn Studies Centre and make contact with a researcher he knows.

'Good luck boys,' says Ellie, smiling, as the Fleet Methane vehicle's engine silently turns over.

I glance subtly in the rear view and decide that Jonas, who's been brooding for days, dwelling in an igloo of bad data, is temporarily mollified. He appears to be looking out the window as we pull out onto the narrow road. But I know better – while the landscape of now speeds by, he's locked into events far away and important. Every now and then he gasps and dictates a note. He's constantly messaging his friend from Lutsk. His headset lies splayed on the backseat of the car like a hastily abandoned robber mask. He adds relevant information to my reading queue; an oppressive stack hangs in my periphery.

'Dad, listen to this,' Jonas turns up an audio feed.

'That's right, Wayne,' says a female voice. 'The reports say that the giant ground sloth pup was discovered in Myanmar this afternoon by a group of researchers who were updating the island's ecostats in the wake of recent heightened sea temperatures and the scourge of Hurricane Teardrop. We have the head zoologist and palaeontologist from globalUni here to explain the implications of such a finding.'

The expert clears her throat.

'Thanks, Mary,' she says. 'The discovery of a new species of megafauna on a depopulated land mass is extremely significant. It may well even be an event that signifies the end of the Holocene and the beginning of a new era for Earth.'

'I don't get it,' says Wayne. 'How can it be the end of the Holocene when we're still here?'

'Yes, Wayne, we are still here, that's true. But not on Myanmar. Hurricane Teardrop will leave vast areas of the Gulf Coast completely uninhabited but it's only the latest weather event to drastically alter population patterns. Myanmar has been depopulated for decades. The ground sloth pup we found today is three years old. It's possible she is second generation. It's probable she marks the beginning of a new geological and zoological period within her ecosystem.'

'So what are you saying? That we should look out for the return of the dinosaurs?'

'It's unlikely in the short term. But long term, potentially Wayne, yes.'

'Wow,' Mary almost squeals. 'The dinosaurs are coming back! What would that even look like? Let's put on our haptic sets and enter the world of the dinosaurs, where humans aren't in charge and survival is a daily challenge of wit and might!'

In the back seat, Jonas' headset pulses. He mutes the feed. 'It's pretty convenient, don't you think?' he says.

'How so?' I ask.

'Well, we have a species-threatening event, and suddenly some apocalyptic megafauna shows up. Out of nowhere. Like two days later.'

'So?'

'So, right at the point when we start to worry that this is the end of everything, and that it's all our fault, something miraculously shows up that suggests this is part of the grand design, that we are simply moving from one period to the next, and even that there is a possible new phase of evolution for us just around the corner.'

'You get all that from the sloth?'

'Of course. And subliminally, so does everyone else. But even if they don't, a seven-foot sloth baby is a pretty good distraction. It's hard to keep focussed on what's really going on when that thing is strutting around in the background. I mean, look at it.' Jonas casts the sloth across the windscreen.

The sloth's bright and only somewhat grass-stained teeth are visible in an uncannily human grin. Its eyes, dark and surrounded by unruly fur, are undeniably intelligent. Despite its size, there is something about the sloth that inspires a parental, protective urge. It crawls languidly through the yard of the Myanmar research facility. It sprawls in the cushioned igloo, occasionally emitting a small and pathetic squawk – a sound somewhere between a goat bleating and a human infant pointing out something of interest.

'It's adorable,' I say.

'Exactly. Because we are being encouraged to accept this giant sloth as the future dominant species.'

'The meek inheritor of the world?'

'Exactly.'

'It is comforting to know that after we are gone the world will return to the adorable megafauna – not withstanding the possibility of dinosaurs.'

'Then it's working,' says Jonas.

We pull in to the central district. In the timeshare buildings around us refrigerators order eggs, beds adjust their temperature to the body of the sleeper, and children's tears are pre-empted by calculating-candy. The car navigates the streets, each one identical: clean, empty and forgotten by the next. The streetlights beat the polished glass, metronoming space.

'Do you know what they named the sloth?' says Jonas.

'Scruffy?' I guess.

'No, Dad. They've named it Hope.'

• •

We stop the car outside the Pitcairn Studies Centre, and watch it drive away. The centre has its own biosphere, an extra shield within the blown permaglass of the Ecodome. Inside, a perfectly simulated Pitcairn Island sinks in a sea of data. Before we can get to the entrance, however, we are stopped by a rare projection of Jean, hands on hips, regarding my son and I with contempt.

'I just want to have all the information,' I tell him, trying to move past.

'Information is beside the point,' he says, blocking our path. 'Experience, that's what we need. Now is the time! We must go to where the story is. And since when did you have to consult the expert? You hate experts.'

'If ever there was a time to renounce that viewpoint, it's now,' I say.

'No, it isn't.'

'Jean, I have my kids to think of.'

'Bah! Kids are such a bourgeois excuse. Jonas knows what's going on, don't you?'

Jonas cocks his eyebrow in the manner of his mother, one eye still glued to a data-feed. 'Nobody really knows anything,' he says.

'Call this research,' I tell Jean.

'Call it whatever you want, it's still gutless procrastinating,' Jean spits. 'The world could end while you're conducting research. We should be heading to the source. The beginning of the end. God is in the place of the disaster,

Max, you know that. His very nature is defined by it. Just look at Lisbon.'

'Must we?'

'Does your son know?'

Jonas turns to Jean, interested.

'I think we have to look at Lisbon,' says Jean. 'Lisbon: the centre of a devout Catholic nation. A city known for its piety, a place of worship that never so much as lifted a virgin petticoat in the direction of God's wrath. But did that stop him?'

'Earthquakes have nothing to do with God,' Jonas says.

'Oh no?' Jean says. 'Tell that to Rousseau. Even better, tell that to Voltaire.'

'Who?' Jonas says.

'Lisbon fell. The quake shook the city to bits like a vicious dog. The ocean tore apart the docks. Sailors caught fire. It was All Souls' Day. God had chosen the holiest day of the year to wreak devastation upon a city built for worship. The churches fell to pieces. An altar crushed a priest to death.'

'Jean, do you have to—'

'Max! You know the story well enough. You're comfortable with censoring history? Shame on you. Your son should not know your hypocrisy. It will break his heart. Where was I?'

'Altar crushes priest!' Jonas enthuses.

'That's right.' Jean licks his lips. 'Crucifix impales confessor. You can imagine the rest, young son of Max. Portugal was devastated. Europe was devastated. It was the beginning of the Enlightenment. The golden age of rational thought. Alexander Pope had just written 'An Essay on Man', attempting to prove man's need to understand God and nature as irrational.' Jean stretches his arms out, filling the frame, reciting:

> All Nature is but Art unknown to thee;
> All Chance, Direction, which thou canst not see;
> All Discord, Harmony not understood;
> All partial Evil, universal Good:
> And, spite of Pride, in erring Reason's spite,
> One truth is clear, Whatever is, is right.

Then he bows low, his head flickering with distortion, before sweeping back up, hair wild and charged with static.

Jonas looks at him dubiously.

'When the initial terror of the quake began to subside,' Jean continues, 'the benevolent, reasonable God sent out an aftershock strong enough to obliterate the Carmo Convent. Crash went the Basilica of Santa Catarina, patron saint of archivists, the dying, unwed mothers and geologists. The perfection of it! The falling walls of the church flattened the huddled wretched of Lisbon. All dead.'

Jean does a church and steeple with his fingers. Then he breaks it apart and lets his hands hang, twitching, each finger a fatality.

'How can a rational God boil frightened worshippers seeking refuge in a church on All Souls' Day? The answer is simple. "God is apathy!" said Voltaire, curls bouncing above a demitasse of coffee, "God does not give a shit!" What other explanation can there be?'

'Der, there is no God,' says Jonas.

'Shhhhh! You are crazy. You want to go to the crazy house? Who else made the universe you stupid boy?'

'Uh, black hole? Big Bang even, if you want to get retro about it.'

'This is pre–Big Bang,' I remind him.

He rolls his eyes. 'Nothing is pre–Big Bang,' he says. 'That's the whole point.'

'No, no! The only other possible explanation is that God is flawed, as man is flawed in his image,' Jean says.

'So, why worship him if he's so flawed?'

'Exactly! That's what Voltaire said. If you say that God is weak then we are lost, and if you say that God is good and right you say it over the torn, bloody, palpitating bodies of the dead.'

'Must they be palpitating, Jean?'

'Absolutely, Max! You should know that. It's important to be able to imagine the experience viscerally. This is how we reach an understanding. The earthquake split the personality of God. We no longer have blind faith! We cannot! And so, what does disaster give us, benevolently, that God could not?'

'Perspective?' Jonas offers.

'Precisely. Nothing is lost on you, Jonas. With disaster comes knowledge.'

Jonas narrows his eyes. An immersion of the Lisbon quake blinks in his periphery.

'Enough,' I say, to both of them. 'Jean, my son and I are here to find out about the latest developments. We can discuss our plans for Pitcairn later, when we have all the information.'

'Information be damned,' says Jean. 'Information is the thing you collect when you've become terrified of knowledge.'

Jonas looks impressed despite himself.

'We'll talk when we are alone, then,' I hiss at Jean.

'You say you need information, and then you attempt to keep it from your son. You lack coherence.'

'It's true,' says Jonas.

'I know,' I say, waving Jean away.

He hangs between our destination and us, refusing to disconnect, and then finally, with a sigh, he fades out. We stand still for a moment, readjusting to the new perspective. Eventually, Jonas pulls on my sleeve and we walk through Jean's wake and further across the solarbitumen towards the centre.

I widen my eyes for the scanner and a glass façade whirrs and clicks. Eventually, a young woman in white, waterproof gaiters comes out to meet us. She shakes Jonas's hand first.

'This is my father,' Jonas says.

'Max Galleon? I'm Mirna.' The woman extends her hand, 'I was a big fan of your films growing up.'

'And now, Mirna?' I shake her hand, archiving a nervous, youthful heartbeat.

'Who has time for films these days?' she says.

'Resentment, 10:45am,' notes the archive.

We follow Mirna into the centre. Jonas gasps audibly. Large thermafractal renderings of the scenery and terrain of Pitcairn dominate the space. Next to a simulated sea, a group of researchers are applying cyclone variants to temperature control pads. Dead fish float in hypothetical space. A three-dimensional model of Adamstown bustles on the horizon. At intervals, speculative tsunamis hit the town and potential devastation scenarios play out. It's all very familiar.

'It's exactly like one of your production sets!' says Jonas.

'As you can see, we're studying every aspect of the island,' says Mirna.

Jonas runs over to a small plantation of palms. 'Breadfruit!' he exclaims. 'Post-*Bounty* colonists thought the breadfruit tree would solve the problem of how to feed plantation slaves back home. It didn't, of course. The slaves wouldn't eat it. Too bland. Plus too much can make you sick.'

'That's right,' says Mirna. 'You know your history.'

Jonas beams.

'Here in the botany and event science group,' Mirna continues, 'we are charting climate events based on the rings of two-hundred-year-old pines that grew in the area.' Mirna leads us to a small lab where a group of scientists examine high definition holograms of tree rings. 'Do you see how the rings closer to the edge of the trunk are deeper and wider? Those represent ecological disturbances. This one here is an oil spill almost fifty years ago – it became crucial evidence for the island's community lawsuit. Unfortunately, we can't decode what event these outer rings correspond to. This team right now is examining whether they in fact mark ecological events that we humans aren't able to identify. Sub-systemic ecological events.'

'So you have the dates for something, but you don't know what happened?' Jonas says, awed.

'That's right.'

'But if we don't know what it is already, then it's probably harmless?' I say.

'We don't believe that, Mr Galleon,' Mirna says. 'Our hypothesis is that these unknown events may form the basis of our most important and formative histories as a species, and a planet.'

'That's what I've been saying,' Jonas nods. 'You'll probably never know the most important things.'

We continue our tour. Jonas occasionally takes time out to stand reverently beside one scientist or another and observe their observations.

'You should be paying attention to all this too, Dad,' he says. 'This is what we came here for. In *Mutiny*, one of the best ways to succeed is to keep an observation journal.'

'Mirna,' I say, turning away from my son. 'The main thing we're here to find out is if the island will remain stable in the short term. I'm thinking of filming there, for my newest project.'

Mirna blinks impassively. 'At this point? I'd say so,' she says. 'But for how long is the question.'

'That's what I figured. I mean, if it was totally safe, wouldn't you be doing all this research there?'

'We have researchers on the island, too,' she says. 'But we want to be able to continue the research safely, after the possible submergence event. And besides, real environments are more difficult to monitor. The variables are uncontrolled.'

In a tank, a continuous wave swells and a model of the island sinks, again and again. It's actually quite a good effect, reminiscent of the old days of modelling for action sequences. The *Godzilla* period of cinematic disaster.

'I hope you're logged in and watching this, Jean!' I say out loud, just in case he is following us in a live feed. I can imagine him snorting in some ostentatiously darkened room but I cannot check because, though he can log in to my networks, I can never access his.

We continue into a small glass room that is filled with butterflies, hanging sacks of pupae, and the pungent stench of rotting wood.

Jonas scrunches up his nose. Impressive termite mounds and smaller, more fragile earth mounds dot the room like decaying tombstones. Another scientist, in full lab regalia, is lying flat on her stomach beside one of these mounds, her eye extended outwards via a frame-mounted fractoscope. Sensing our presence, she turns to look up at us, her eye huge and too close. Ants stream in swerving, hypnotic lines around her body.

'They're an introduced species,' she says, without needing to be prompted. 'Common to Brazil and other parts of South America. We have them here in the lab now, and we have them on the actual island. We're studying them pretty closely and getting some impressive results.'

'You're an entomologist?' Jonas asks.

'Very good!' she says. 'These ants build incredibly elaborate colonies. Some as tall as six metres.'

Jonas appraises the short lopsided mound of dirt before us. 'This one's not doing so well, then.'

'No, this one was much larger earlier in development, and that's not how it's meant to happen. The ants should build the same colony for generations, with each mound lasting and growing for decades.'

'So what happened?' I ask.

'Every colony has a kind of consciousness, a perception that is as much a structure as the mound itself. Each successive generation of ants is born knowing the blueprint of this cognitive structure. In the years where food is scarce, more soldier ants are born. When food stores are adequate, more builder and maintenance ants are born. The ants are truly remarkable. They can sense danger – they know when the anthill is under definite threat from a predator or a change in environment, and their behaviour adjusts accordingly. That's why we introduced them to Pitcairn. And we concurrently introduced them here as a controlled sample. Same temperatures, altitude, sea level, and air density. And in both cases the final results are the same, though on the real island the degeneration has been much faster.'

'I don't understand,' I say.

'We wanted to see how ecologically attuned they are. We knew that if the anthill is damaged naturally, say if some reckless human runs it over or a brutal storm damages it beyond repair, the generation of ants born during that time are lazy and forgetful – their consciousness is affected, and more often than not the colony won't survive. What we didn't know was whether the ants could predict their own extinction. But this mound and the ones on Pitcairn are exhibiting the same behaviour – the exact same apathetic malaise. It's as though the ants don't know their way around their own home. They lack the blueprint their elders were born with. They no longer possess the collective memory. Gatherers aren't stockpiling for future generations. Builders aren't making room for a growing population. The percentage of soldier ants has diminished drastically with each generation.'

'You mean—' Jonas is shocked.

'They are phasing themselves out. The ant colony has sensed its demise.'

The implication sinks in. I look at the tiny specks with a new respect, and a profound sense of empathy.

'You're saying the ants know the island will sink?'

'What I'm saying is that all these introduced colonies are diminishing. The ants are withdrawing from the everyday tasks of survival.'

'Do they know exactly when?' asks Jonas.

'If they do, they aren't telling us.'

She pushes back onto her knees and extends a hand to me. I pull her up onto her feet. The contact sends my heartbeat into a flurry. She has dark hair, dark eyes. She reminds me of someone.

'Excitement, 11:35am,' notes the archive.

'Obviously, if there was a chance of getting solid information, we'd have the ants shut up in interrogation rooms,'
she smiles. 'These critters might have the answer to the
most important question of our time but unless we can
learn to read ant, we will have to keep wondering.'

'I know what you mean. Since the hurricane, we haven't
been able to think of anything else except the island.'

'In between marathons of old movies, don't you mean?'
says Jonas, disapproving of our flirtation.

She laughs generously. 'What movies?' she asks him.

'Actually, you might be interested in at least one of them.
We watched *The Swarm* – it was about bees.'

The entomologist grimaces.

'It's about deadly immigrant African killer bees,' she says,
'who not only terrorise the communities of good people,
but also the good, old, hard-working American honey bee.
Actually, *The Swarm* is a racist allegory. I've written quite a
few papers on allegories of race that involve insects. It's a
little hobby of mine. A pet peeve, really,' she says. '*The Swarm*
was ecologically naïve too, considering that the European
honey bee is an introduced species in North America.'

'I never thought of it that way,' I say.

'You should,' she replies, no longer flirting. 'Insects are
crucial to the way we describe ourselves.'

I look down at the ants trailing through their dilapidated mound in mindless disarray. Strange growths, begun but
never completed, suggest themselves at the mid-point of
the mound. Tumescent attempts to rejuvenate civilisation,
forgotten impulses beyond history.

Mirna leads us further through the centre. In the final room—an installation space, which is open to the public— the various scenarios of post-Pitcairn earth are examined in haptic immersions. Around the room, children and their adult carers jack in to simulations just like they were in a MiniCine. Jonas runs towards a booth, dropping a headset over his eyes. After a few seconds his small body begins to jerk. His arms go floppy.

'It all ends here, no matter what,' I muse, watching my son convulse ecstatically.

'Sorry?' Mirna asks, distracted, anxious to be done with her tour.

'Well, the final result, the devastation, it can't actually be studied. We have to try to imagine it now. Because once it's happened, it'll be too late.'

'I suppose that's true,' she says.

In front of us, the end of the world strobes in the pupils of children.

• •

After lunch, Jonas and I sit next to each other on a fallen log in the temperate forest quadrant of the Ecodome. People line up to have their image captured in the four different types of endangered forests; arms splay into rainforest while short young legs are spread akimbo to cover the coniferous and montane. A holographic Pow-Pow chews a bamboo shoot and sobs quietly. A pay code scrolls beneath him, and children can allocate funds to elicit Pow-Pow's smiles and ticks of approval.

Jonas wants neither. 'If it's the end of the world, we may as well see it,' he whines. 'What difference does it make if I die on the island or through some related catastrophe a few days later?'

'No, Jonas. You are not going. The island is sinking. Right now. As we speak. I can't take you in to that kind of danger.'

'But isn't seeing the event, living through it or perishing, the whole point? Isn't that what all your films are about?'

'Films are just films, Jonas.'

He slaps his mouth in mock shock.

'The point of my films is that everyone gets to survive,' I say. 'In real life there are no such guarantees.'

'I know that,' he spits. 'But, statistically, I think I have a good chance – I have very specialised skills.'

'Oh yes?'

'Yes. I am extremely advanced in *Mutiny*. My knowledge of the history and ecology of the area is flawless.'

'Jonas, listen. This is partially my fault. I know I haven't been the best role model when it comes to setting boundaries between reality and fantasy. It's unfair of me to expect you to have a solid grip on reality. But for now, here are some things I know: you don't have a native bride. You can't really trade salted pork for materials to build a raft. You have never actually built a raft. You have never held a real hammer. You need to take protein pills at 4pm every day.'

Jonas slumps, pouting.

'Do you hear me?' I continue. 'We order your clothes for you. You are unable to fend for yourself, even in Bay

Heights. You can't colonise an island. You were not born in the eighteenth century. These are the real events of your life: eating food prepared for you by an automated chef system, Panda Points, talking over the network to shy adolescents in Lutsk, putting your pyjamas on back to front. You are not a mutineer. You are not a survivalist.'

'Whatever,' he seethes. 'I don't even see the big deal about surviving, anyway. It's not like it's an permanent thing.'

'No, surviving is not permanent. But with a little luck it lasts a long time – if you don't do stupid things.'

Jonas flushes with rage.

'Listen,' I say, softening my tone. 'You have a responsibility of your own. You need to be a beacon of hope for every adult you meet. You are a child, and children are the future.'

He picks up his backpack from the leaf-strewn soil and hoists it dramatically. 'Not anymore. Hope the sloth puppy is the future now.' He hops down from the bench and storms off, past a tearful Pow-Pow, past the happy tourists. He hacks through the damp foliage of the tropical rainforest like an intrepid explorer of old, stepping over artificial snakes until he is out of sight, descending on some artfully rendered heart of darkness.

I follow him on the GPS feed. Children of his generation live in a world where their every adventure is already clearly mapped out before them, their every discovery tracked and cross-referenced. Eventually, the small red dot that is Jonas breaches the edge of the Ecodome. On the streets outside, a Fleet Methane car will gently tail him until he gives up, gets in, and goes back to Bay Heights.

• •

When I get back to the corporate apartment I log into Bay Heights to check on Jonas.

'He's fine,' says Ellie. 'Disappointed and brooding but unharmed. There's an emotional cost-benefit analysis in the archive – its assessment concludes your excursion to the Ecodome was a success, and I agree. At least you included him right up until the point it was no longer possible.'

'Good.'

'Yes. I think so. But the question remains, Max – are you going to go?'

'I don't know. I feel strange. I'm having trouble maintaining focus. And I feel as though there's someone crucial I haven't consulted, but I can't work out who.'

Ellie blinks, smiling calmly. 'Sounds like your usual decision anxiety to me,' she says.

I nod, but I know that this feeling isn't familiar. The archive is charting it as 'unknown emotional conflict', or sometimes as 'confusion', or, bizarrely, as 'homesickness'. And the origin of the feeling can't be located, no matter how much I look. What I have found instead are strange gaps in my timeline.

'You're probably right,' I tell Ellie.

Lilly is in her room. She doesn't look up from her work when I log in, but frowns with steady concentration – a performance of unwelcome. I linger anyway. Her room has changed since the last time I visited. Gone is the Pow-Pow solar night light, the Pow-Pow holograms, the charts of Panda Points. Her bedroom has become a shrine to another animal: the walls are covered with video feeds and recordings of Hope the giant sloth puppy. Hope curled in a large ball in her enclosure. Hope squealing for food. Hope walking slow laps of her play area, dribbling a beach ball with her long-clawed paws. Covering the ceiling is a diagrammatic representation of Hope's development, compared alongside the various periods of our own ecological history, to highlight significant parallels.

After a while Lilly turns around and raises her eyebrows at me. 'Yes?' she says.

'No more Pow-Pow?'

'Pow-Pow is still important, but essentially, he is a cartoon. I need to involve myself in the real. We're living through a defining period in the history of our planet – something much more complex than conserving energy. The world is changing.'

'Hope is very cute.'

'When she's fully-grown she will be the size of a small elephant. I've subscribed to all her development feeds. I'm going to watch her grow at the same time as I watch the world change.'

'You'll grow up before she does,' I say, smiling.

Lilly does not smile back. 'You can't guarantee that,' she says.

I open my arms to her for a virtual hug but she turns back to her work.

I try to look busy too, trawling listlessly through my itinerary and the various spaces of my life. In the production office, Stephanie assures me that the film is going perfectly well without me. She stresses the competency of Sullivan, the creative energy he has brought to the whole team. I do not need to consult the archive to know how I feel about this.

'The only thing that we need to decide imminently,' she says, 'is whether we are taking this on location. I know Sullivan and Jean are very determined to go. I've prepared two reports that assess the completion of the project, based on which way we want to go with it. Without the location, we'd need another thirty days in studio. If we are going to go on location, we should pause work now until we know what kind of extra footage we are working with.'

'You hear that, Max?' Jean's voice cuts through the connection. 'We have the opportunity to take this project in a direction in which the outcome is unknown. When was the last time you allowed that to happen?'

I don't answer. A cup of coffee and a biscuit appear on the table beside me. Without thinking, I pick them both up.

'As I see it,' Jean continues, 'the island is an allegory for the whole of human history, culminating in our present predicament. I've been talking to your son about it. He has some great ideas.'

'Please don't encourage him, Jean.'

'No encouragement? This seems like an ill-conceived parenting practice. Listen, long before the *Bounty* boys arrived, Pitcairn was just part of a group of small islands that formed a mutually beneficial system of trade, enabling growth. But overdevelopment and greed interfered. Environmental resources were depleted. Starving, the native population turned to cannibalism to survive. Sound familiar?'

'Capitalism as cannibalism? Come on Jean, you're one hundred years too late to make that film.'

'Wait,' Jean continues. 'With cannibalism, the population stabilised. This is what happens when you eat each other. It's a crude but effective strategy. The island experienced a brief period of stillness. Just a flicker on the screen. Animals grazed, new growth pushed its way through the degraded soil. It looked for a moment as though there would be peace. Then the pirates arrived. Pirates, Max!'

'Pirate films had their moment at the turn of the century.'

'You are thinking too literally. Pirates are just men who refuse to wait their turn, or take orders. Once the pirates became settlers though, they automatically recreated the same hierarchical regime that they once took to the sea to escape. Worse still, they unwittingly colonised the island for the empire they hated. Of course their descendants are confused about their identity. They are morally muddled at the level of blood. How do you reconcile your descent from both coloniser and colonised, pirate and private citizen? Don't we all feel like this, somehow, Max?'

'What's your point?'

'If we work allegorically, we can frame the sinking of the island as the end of all this madness. A fresh start. Agency and hope emerging from ruination. Even Sullivan is coming around to the idea.'

'It doesn't sound like this idea does much towards promoting empathy.'

'Empathy, no. Forgiveness, yes! And, more importantly, a

clean slate. What I am talking about is a film that uses this event, this sinking island, to perfectly simulate the end of world, in terms of its history, its terrible, pathetic politics. It wipes the slate clean. If we pull this off, people should leave the cinema feeling as though their old lives are destroyed, as though they are stepping into a whole new world.'

'That sounds like what we always do.'

'Yes, of course. But this time it's real. It's actually happening out in the real world too. It's all about timing. The possibilities are immense.'

'I always thought there was something wrong with us. Now I realise we might just be at the end of our anthill.'

'What are you talking about, Max? What anthill? Anyway, at the very least I have a report that speculates we will make more money from this film than from all our other productions combined. The hysteria around this sinking island is at an all-time high. And hysteria is a great tool for us. I have even looked into getting a model of this beloved sloth pup made. I thought we could use it somehow. We could blow it up. Or have it eat people, or them it. I'm open to suggestions.'

'I need to go, Jean.'

'Max, you need to get back on board with this. Forget all your other distractions. You spend too much time fretting over your brother and practising yoga. I want to see the creative fervour you showed when you pitched this project. That's the director we need. A man transformed. You started this. You gave it momentum. Now you have to hold on for the whole ride.'

'I've got to go.'

'Fine. If I don't make it back, tell Margot that I love her.'

● ●

I search the archive for my *Mega-Tsunami* pitch and immediately a glittering image of a boardroom covers the walls of the apartment, doubling the space. The pitch is one of the only parts of my film making practice over which I have retained sole authorship. The investors like to see me in my underwhelming flesh. They like to remember that they are buying points in a Galleon production, even though I myself have long since forgotten what that means. In the corporate apartment, I attach haptic sensors to my fingertips and prime myself with three minutes of inaudible vibrations to induce a trance state.

Thirsty, I reach out for the glass of water in front of me, but I can't close my fingers around it.

'The glass is not real,' I say out loud, and a note is recorded.

The immersion begins: around me, men in suits sit in haptic executive chairs. Their bodies bend across the walls of the apartment. They are powerful men, surrendering themselves as an audience, making polite chit-chat as they wait.

And then he appears. Me. Me of electric memory. He's larger than life, hyperreal, in a suit like tailored armour. He strides across the room. His temperature registers above average, yet he does not perspire. His heartbeat is steady. His brow shows calm concentration. There's an expectant hush across the room.

'Gentlemen,' he says, his voice bellowing all around. He has the seventy-eight channel voice of a minor deity. 'Please take a moment to secure your headsets and place your hands palms down on the stimumats in front of you.'

The men shuffle with the equipment, securing straps and poking fingertips into tight sheaths. I obey him too. I sink back to watch myself, setting the perspective to play the recording not only from my implants and the external haptic pads but also the apartment's OmniCast. I slow my breath to prepare for the disorienting feeling of being both inside and outside myself.

INT. BOARDROOM. WIDE SHOT. DAY

Twelve men sit around a large table. They wear immersive cinema headsets. Their lips are pursed, expectant. Max circles the room, regarding his audience.

MAX

You're straining to hear my voice. Why does it seem so soft to you, when I am speaking at 140 decibels? The answer: a trick of the mind. Like many of the techniques employed in my films, this immersion is designed to set the conditions for a complete surrender to experience. Despite that, I encourage you to keep trying to listen to me actively, because it is my voice that engages the one part of your mind that is keeping you in control. The part that can differentiate reality from the cinematic environment. If you are successful in keeping that part alert then you will be able to experience the inner workings of the simulative model, discerning between the devices and their effects. This kind of split attention does not come easily — it requires discipline. If you feel that you are slipping and can't maintain focus, then by all means let go, surrender. There is no failure at this task. There is only experience. Those forms you can't recognise are millions of layers of stroboscopic light particles, dynamically assembling and reassembling, creating patterns, changing at a rate you can't consciously register. These patterns are engineered to draw the user into a state of altered consciousness, similar to a trance state. This technology has come a long way since the first experiments. It's more sophisticated now — but then, so are our minds. They are capable of processing the meaning of over a billion images per minute. Do you see them now, rising out of the snow? They are unambiguous. A triangle. A cube. But they are incomplete. It's a mental exercise. Your mind fills in the blanks. The images can be processed as symbols of your own experiences. You complete them. You create the association. Now you're experiencing gamma waves at a frequency of around sixty exahertz. It won't last long.

Relax. If you feel confused, just remember: there is no certainty other than that the island will sink. There is no certainty other than that the island will sink. Do you understand that? You have been woken from a dream, suddenly. Your mind is clear for the first time in your life. All your worry, stress, fear and guilt are forgotten in an instant. There is no certainty except that the island will sink. This is your fate. Listen. One hundred villagers stop to collect fish from the drained ocean bed. The villagers dance on the damp ground, gathering flapping fish in their arms. The wave is approaching, though they cannot see it yet. The island will sink. The landmass will plummet through the foaming water, pieces of coastline breaking apart and spiralling down, down, as far as the ocean floor. The impact causes a hairline fracture. This island was formed by the tip of a dormant volcano. As it sinks will it awaken the beast of fire? Red eyes blink after a thousand year sleep. Bubbles rise from the ocean. Tiny bubbles. See how beautiful they are? They are death. Those beautiful bubbles are air compression caused by earthquake. Earthquake begets earthquake. You see? The earth is a giant fault line in the universe. It was an earthquake that caused the extinction of the dinosaurs. Giant mammals explode in violet twilight. They fall into the sea, their bodies decay, the ocean bed grows over their bones. They are fossils for excavation. We are all fossils *for excavation. The tremors are barely visible from this many leagues below, but the whales see them. They call to each other through the blue. It's over, they are saying. The glaciers are melting. They crack, one after another. A family of polar bears clings to a sliver of ice. The baby bear will drown first. Where are your babies? They will drown first. The icecaps are sinking. The waves will come. In the zoo, the elephants are going wild. They raise their trunks to the sky. Huge shrapnel from collapsed buildings falls onto them, nailing the giant dromedaries to the floor of the cage. They die as prisoners. Did you live as a prisoner? It doesn't matter now. You will be nailed to the ground by shrapnel. The heavy bodies of elephants show you this. A flock of seagulls takes off. They are knocked out by missiles of water. Have you seen missiles destroy villages? This is worse. Dead birds rain from the sky. Everything you have will be gone. Flash fires spring up across the countryside. The ocean is burning. The water cannot put out the fire. Where are your loved ones? They are on fire. Can the fire diminish your love? It doesn't matter now. The mega-tsunami looks like a dust storm. It's a horizon like none you have seen before. There are no more horizons. They are gone. You only have your body. Can you hear your breath? It will be your last. Do not try to wave down the helicopters, they can't take you, there's nowhere to go. They will be blown out of the sky, become as flightless as the gulls expiring on the sand. A helicopter blade hurtles and turns the house you grew up in into splinters. Where is your childhood? It does not matter. It is now splinters. Pray. Do you have a god? It does not matter now. The water is your god. The fire is your god. There is nothing else. Pray with no words. Do not ask for anything. Look at your hands. Nostradamus was right. Finally. Are you ready for surrender? Are you ready to see the final image you will ever see? You are a second before nothing, are you ready? The only certainty is that the island will sink. Anything that has happened before this will be lost. Are you ready?*

Around the table tears splash down white shirts. Two of the twelve men have fallen to the floor and into convulsive seizures. Fingers twitch in their haptic sheaths, reaching into the interface, feeling everything. A man vomits into his lap.

MAX

The island is sinking.

More men are on the floor now. They rock back and forth. Fists are pushed into eyes. Some men struggle with their headsets before surrendering, going limp. A sixty-year-old executive reaches out from his foetal curl to pull at the cuff of

Max's perfectly pressed trousers.

I watch as the screen me bends to comfort the weeping man. 'Shhhh,' he coos, in a way I once may have comforted my children. 'Your babies are safe. We will make this film before it's too late.'

'Stop. Go back,' I tell the archive. 'Play.'

MAX

Where are your babies? They will drown first.

'Stop,' I say again.

My fingers tremble in their sheaths. My pulse quickens. Sweat beads on my skin. My vision blurs and tunnels, my ears fill with the sound of burning, with the sound of rogue winds carrying fireballs, with the sound of screaming. The whole room shakes. The immersion flickers and I can't tell if it's the boardroom or the apartment that's shaking. A glass falls off a table and shatters; a sharp sound of domestic ca-tastrophe amidst the broader tumult. Something strikes me on the face. It hurts. I put my hand up to my cheek and when I look down there's an unmistakable streak of red. I blink twice. Try to process the colour red and its real meanings.

Actual blood? Actual pain, sharp and strange. When was the last time I felt physical pain?

'Stop record.'

The boardroom flickers out, leaving me alone in the apartment. I blink several times, realising that this space, the real space of now, is in disarray. A fruit bowl has overturned and several oranges cluster under the cracked coffee table. The artworks on the walls are now just static grey squares. A damaged loop of Pow-Pow with a shattered grin buzzes by the kitchen sink, his green ticks pulsing maniacally.

There's no time to perform the standard re-entry protocol. With difficulty I pull off the haptic sensors and shake away the echo of the immersion ungracefully, pressure building in my temples. I reach for an aspirin or vitamin B amino drink, but nothing is there. Through the windows of the apartment I can see leaf debris and torn solarsheets whizzing through the air. Somewhere far below, an insistent whooping of alarm.

'Connect,' I say, and nothing happens.

I can't connect to any newsfeeds. I can't log into my home at Bay Heights, nor the office or the hospice.

'Something is actually happening,' I say out loud, but no note is recorded.

An insistent error message flashes in my periphery. A large and sentenceless exclamation point.

I tap the side of my head like it's a vending machine. Something big and unidentifiable slams into the apartment window; a threatening crack spreads immediately across the thermaglass. I try to remember the emergency protocol, any emergency protocol.

The apartment's elevator door is locked. Simulated flames

at its base indicate the risk of fire and hence entrapment. On the wall next to it, a map shows the various spaces of the apartment, dramatised, blinking exclamation points and cartoon lightning bolts illustrating unknown dangers.

At the edge of the map: monsters.

Several glowing arrows on the floor guide me through the living space and meals areas and into a small, vacant foyer that I don't recall ever setting foot into before. Here, rather than an outside-facing wall of uninterrupted thermaglass, there's a large framed window with a steel latch. I reach out for it and, registering my bioprint, it springs open. A gale blows into the apartment, carrying flecks of organic matter and unrecognisable scraps of the world below. I put my head down and, bracing my whole body across the window, I manage to shut it. Cheek pressed to the pane, I can see the fire escape below: a lonely, perilous steel staircase descending into a windy abyss.

I am not prepared for this.

I lap the apartment, gathering supplies. I take supplements and water from the refrigerator. In the en-suite bathroom, under cruel default light, I splash water on my face and press wet thumbs into my eye sockets, making blood cells wriggle.

'This is it,' I tell my reflection.

I carefully select clothing. I gather several pairs of adventurer socks, their compasses and pressure sensitivity gauges finally seeming vital. I choose a pair of trousers with excess pockets, belted by a strap of leather with full emergency functions, topped with a thermawear shirt. My shoes measure each step and would draw a map, but a red line on the toe indicates a broken connection. I pull the contents of the medicine cabinet into the deep pockets of my fully reversible all-weather emergency poncho. Its sleeves draw tight around my armpits; a whistle dangles from its neckline. I own all these things.

Nothing is telling me exactly what my heartbeat is, but I know it's fast. I don't know exactly what mixture of emotions I am experiencing, but I do know I am dizzy and exhilarated.

I'm ready.

I walk decisively to the alcove window and place my palms out to be scanned. Nothing happens. I rattle the frame. Nothing. I run my fingers around the edge of the sill in search of a manual lock. Finally, the window swings open and the cold wind sweeps through the room again. Something smashes but I don't turn to see what. I take a pair of thermaplastic goggles from the pocket of the poncho and am pleased to see they have a solar powered temperature and wind speed monitor. The numbers pulse, giving me something concrete, making me feel less alone as I cross the threshold to stand on the precarious landing of the fire escape. Has there ever been such a lonely structure? The stairs are metal grates crisscrossing the swirling street below. I clutch the steel rails. Wind whips across my skin at sixty-two metres per second.

If the elevator is designed to cushion the trauma of moving from the private space to the unknown future, the fire escape is its opposite. There's nothing gentle about it.

Even the name: fire escape, a desperate last hope. The structure itself creeps across the façade of the building, exposing the brittle, skeletal edge of all things. I shut my eyes tight, picture myself through a lens, the camera swinging in for an indulgent crane shot: a lone man clinging on tight.

I take another deep breath and push one leg out into the wind. My leg feels insubstantial, inadequate to the task. The stairs rock and bend beneath my weight. I look down and see my sock compass, pirouetting. I snap my head up and squeeze my eyes shut once more. Don't look down. That's a rule anyone should be able to remember. I move backwards into the unknown. One foot behind the other. The wind billows the hemline of my poncho suggesting I might just as easily fly to safety. Time becomes measured in breaths. My exhalations are as loud in my head as the sound of the storm. Anxious scenarios play out behind my eyelids. Scenes from films ricochet around my brain, bumping into stills of my wife and children, my brother in the hospice. A shadow-faced doctor reaches out as though she might pull me up from this precarious place and back onto solid ground. I summon the image each time I have to move my hands down the rail. A stranger's hand reaching out to mine in the space between purpose and free-fall.

'I want to go home,' I say out loud, compulsively. No one is listening.

With each terrible step I feel as though I am stepping back through the years, into the stormy depths of the unconscious. Is this my life flashing before my eyes, or someone else's? Or no one's? Where is my home? I start to fantasise about my funeral. A nervous habit.

The ground, when it finally comes, is shockingly solid. I stand, eyes still shut, unable to look for a long moment. When I do, the fire escape above me is impossibly slender, impossibly high. The top disappears into mist, the heavens, the past.

For a moment I forget my intention. I'm stopped dead by the feat I've achieved. How do heroes continue on with their heroism? How do they resist stopping to congratulate themselves after every child saved from the fire, after every leap across the abyss? Around me, small twisters strip fallen trees of their remaining leaves. Several ground floor windows are shattered, their exoshield shutters having failed to fully close. Yet somehow the street retains its cool, as though it were waiting stoically for the storm to pass. I try to conjure up images of this place during past upheavals, before it became the sanitised the central district. Images of cracked, uneven streets. The motley vendors. The crowds. The troops to hold them back. A brick flung over a line of police. A round of warning fire. But I can't locate any such images. Where are the crying children, held by angry mothers who stare straight into the camera? Where are the opportunists, stalking through the aftermath of another riot? Swept away, all swept away. This wind blows, but it carries no consequence. There is so little left to destroy.

Once, this area was sprawling and neon, then it was dilapidated and fierce, and now it is purified. There are only a few other people on the street. A man in a business suit dashes past, using his briefcase as a shield. His suit is wet, his slight body feeble beneath the fabric. A couple huddle in a Fleet Methane car, punching desperately at dials and buttons. I consider getting in with them, driving the car myself, ferrying them to safety, becoming their hero. But I'm too spent from my last heroic act.

Besides, in a crisis, a man must find his family. All others are faceless masses. Worse, as disaster movies teach, anyone outside your immediate family is not just irrelevant, but a potential threat. Such people will stomp your skull into the pavement in a panicked stampede, or murder you for your all-weather poncho. I pull the hood close around my face and run down the street. Far off I can hear the sound of steel and glass straining. A wrenching, burning screech. The soundtrack to *The Towering Inferno*.

We're entering disaster time now. Every one minute is actually three.

After a few blocks of running into the wind, I stop in the recess of a tall building to catch my breath. My lungs hurt. There's a high-pitched ringing in one ear. My eardrums might have burst, there's no way to know. I stick fingers in both ears and for a moment I hear only inner catastrophe: blood pumping, vessels rupturing, pulse beating erratically, lungs ragged and stressed. When I pull my fingers out they are speckled red, but the blood isn't fresh. It's dried – the blood of something past and forgotten.

I need a way out of here.

As if on cue, I see a Fleet Methane sedan across the road, its driver door swinging in the wind. With my forearms in front of my face, I struggle upwind towards it, blowing on my emergency whistle to reassure myself that I can breathe – and to ward off any hiding mobs. The vehicle has been abandoned. Someone else's music is playing from the speakers, vintage-sounding, with jangly, urgent guitars. The car has stalled in self-drive mode, a large warning icon flashing where the GPS and other navigation dials should be.

I can drive. Whatever else is and isn't true, I know this: I can drive.

I try not to dwell on the other skills a man in my position might need. If this were a movie, I'd need not only to drive the car but also to be able to jump it over wide chasms or jammed drawbridges. I'd need to be able to drive the vehicle tilted on two wheels, and should the need arise (and it almost certainly would), I'd need to be able to climb onto the roof of the speeding car and leap to safety.

I get in and take control. It's difficult to steer in the gale but I manage to move slowly past small groups of corporate professionals holding gadgets up to the sky. I drive past the Ecodome, its nUtitanium exoshield drawn tight around it – an all-weather emergency poncho on a much greater scale. I pass through the district's invisible gates without being logged or tracked, and drive out further, past the grim and quiet Envirotowers, noticing how much the swirling wind complements them, debris flits about like scratches on celluloid. It is as though the world has already ended and I am the last man on a jaunt through the ruins.

An insistent drum beat rolls through the cabin. A hyena-like voice cackles, declaring 'wipeout' as the world rolls past my windscreen and the storm fills my rear-view: a watching, following sea.

Do I know my way home? I couldn't draw even a basic map of this district, and yet there seems to be a pattern to my movements, to my turn signals and accelerations. I check the compass in my socks and realise that the markers—north, east, south, west—mean nothing to me.

I settle back in the seat and relax into the forward momentum of the car. It's an extension of my body. I mute the music, keep one hand on the wheel, and trust instinct because there is nothing else to trust. After a little while I begin to whistle my own tune: the 'Blue Danube Waltz'.

The wind seems to die down as I head along the road. The weather is my emotional corollary, and the background is set on a comforting loop: the same flat fields, dotted with windmills spinning so fast that they blur like vortexes opening to other worlds. This vacant terrain cradles me. I know no landmarks. The sameness suggests there are none. I let the anxiety of the storm drift away behind me.

A small and sudden glitch in the scenery causes me to slam on the brakes. In the middle of the road is a tiny something, crouching. I squint and try to make it out. It's a rabbit. A rabbit in headlights, no less. A real rabbit. Have I ever seen a real rabbit before? Where did it come from? I get out of the car and approach the creature. Its body is heaving, its pulse visible, its left leg cocked at an unnatural angle, the foot bleeding. I move closer. It makes no attempt to hop away. We lock eyes.

The small creature's lonely desperation speaks to

something deep within me. From habit I look around for a directive from Pow-Pow, but he's not there. The rabbit doesn't blink. Its ears are flattened to its skull. Tentatively, I reach down and touch it. It is quivering but it does not move.

It is dying, and it will die here. Painfully.

I think about a mercy-killing. The small neck gripped between my hands. Feeling for the fragile vertebrae, twisting hard, waiting for the crack, the body going limp in my arms. What then? Toss the body onto the roadside. A brutal but heroic act.

I pick the small creature up. It kicks twice feebly with its good leg and then, eyeing me, it surrenders, settles in my arms. I hold it close to my chest, totally unsure of what to do next. Is this how I felt when I first held my son?

I open the passenger door and place the rabbit on the seat. It makes no attempt to escape.

I get back in the car and drive on.

Bay Heights, when I come upon it, has bunkered down in readiness for the oncoming storm. An ominous sky hangs over the shadowed hills. The bay itself is switched off, little sailboats and pleasant swell are vanished, exposing a stark metal pit lined by bolted hutches where expensive equipment cowers. All the elegant houses have disappeared. Instead, the village is home to an invading race of giant armoured beetles. Inside one of these beetles is my family. They huddle together underneath this residential exoshield, hoping to survive the catastrophe and then walk with open eyes into the bright light of a new dawn – or at least another few moments in today's murky twilight.

Instinct guides me into the correct cul-de-sac. My home's exoshield is spiky with horizoscopes, satellite dishes, water-gathering funnels and small windmills. Once out of the car, the frozen stillness chills me. Thunder cracks not too far away. I silently count the seconds between flash and rumble, but forget what each second should represent. A minute? A mile? At a section of the exoshield where wide grooves suggest a door, I jump up and down and wave my arms.

'Ellie! Ellie, it's Max.'

Above me, a lens pivots to inspect the intruder. Momentarily, the voice of my daughter, tinny and hysterical, pipes from a hidden speaker. 'Daddy! You're alive!'

••

Inside, the house is dark – an energy conserving emergency services algorithm has shut down all the domestic electronic systems. There are blue standby lights flashing in the dark lobby like stars in a planetarium. It's silent here. Even my footsteps are muted. It feels like a tomb.

'Over here!' Lilly calls.

I stumble, toddler-like, arms stretched forward in the dark, groping for something solid. My hands glance another metal wall and a crack appears and broadens. Behind it, the family room is as it has always been: brightly lit, reassuring.

'Daddy!' Lilly squeals again, in disbelief, pelting towards me. 'I didn't think you would make it.'

'Thanks for the vote of confidence.'

'Why did you leave the apartment?' says Ellie, joining us, looking at me with both recrimination and relief. 'It's always safer to stay indoors.'

I kiss her forehead, feeling her slump ever-so-slightly into my lips. I wonder what the archive would notice now, were it connected.

'It didn't feel safe. Remind me to reallocate to another building when all this is over. Anyway, I'm here now and I can look after you.'

She almost laughs. 'I'm glad you made it, Max, but we are fine. For the most part, anyway.'

In the corner of the room, Jonas, in full military fatigues, is sitting on a keg of water, surfing through ironic mock–test patterns and static. His jaw is tight, his head retreating into his neck.

'When we first got news of the storm, Jonas was very helpful,' Ellie says, in a pronounced, emphatic tone, loud enough for Jonas to hear. 'He has a cupboard full of survival gear. Did you know that, Max? He took his sister and I through several emergency drills, dressed us up in the appropriate gear, showed us all the functions of the exoshield, and went through all the worst case scenarios with us. He was quite enthusiastic, quite the survivalist.'

'The basic premise of survival is that there are people who survive and people who don't,' says Jonas. 'But it's not just a matter of having the right things. You can have everything in the whole world and still not have what it takes to survive. Preparation is important.'

'Uh-huh,' Ellie coos at him, looking at me significantly.

'Physical fitness is a factor, but so is being informed,' Jonas continues, speaking rapidly, eyes fixed on the dead feed. 'Knowing your environment. Knowing how to read the signs of nature, and then also knowing that in a catastrophe situation nature is likely to send you a lot of mixed messages. You need to know how to think on your feet. You need to have special outdoor skills, and even then you don't have any guarantees. You can do all the training you like, but it won't account for chance. You could be ready for everything and then you suddenly find out you are fatally allergic to bees and you fall into a coma. It happens. There's no way to know. All you can do is be prepared and hope for the best.'

'Now, though,' Ellie says to me, lowering her voice. 'His mood has dampened somewhat.'

'We've lost our signal,' Jonas says, without looking up. 'I can't reach anyone. Anything could be happening out there. The last thing we heard was an accident at the hydro plant. I can't get through to anyone, not the Pitcairn Studies Centre, not Lutsk.'

'It's okay, Jonas. It's going to be fine,' I tell him, ruffling his hair.

He looks at me with the small, darting eyes of an injured bird. 'You don't know that!' he says.

'I drove here through the storm. I saw the damage. It's bad, but it's not world-ending.'

I'm surprised at my calm and reassuring tone.

Ellie nods appreciatively.

'That's just one person's experience!' says Jonas. 'In one,

tiny geographic radius. It doesn't prove anything. You don't know what's happening in like 99.999 per cent of the world. Let alone the universe. Let alone all the things that are happening right now that we can't see, much less understand, but that totally affect us every second of every day. That could totally kill us all, now. Finished.' His eyes dart between us and the dead feed. 'You know what they are calling this period? The Praeteranthropocene. Which means I get to live in the time where science has finally declared that human beings are no longer capable of remedying the negative impact they've made on the planet.'

Ellie squeezes my hand and leads me over to the bar. She pours me a Scotch, lowering her voice.

'He's been like this since we lost connectivity. I'm not sure what to do. I decided to let him keep searching for a live feed – at least it keeps him occupied.'

'And Lilly?'

In another corner of the room my daughter has returned to her project of frantically recording data, scrawling on the air: longitudes and latitudes, time codes and nonsensical binary notations. She grinds her small white teeth.

'I'm fine, Daddy,' she chirps. 'Unlike Jonas, I'm keeping abreast of what we know. Trying to stay busy and coordinate this data into something we can use. It's really important for us to be aware of our finite resources. I'm making calculations so we can map our consumption.'

'It's tough for them,' Ellie grimaces, speaking even more quietly. 'I'm not sure they've ever been fully disconnected. So much of their lives are in that space. We need to be understanding.' She gives me another significant look. 'How are you feeling?' she asks.

'I honestly don't know. How could I?'

The various window vistas of the family room have been replaced by soothing nature sequences. One shows an underwater kingdom, overlarge fish swimming by, unperturbed and eternal. Another shows an endless field of sunflowers. My son paces in front of a tranquil rainforest, his headset dangling forlornly from his neck, a projection of static hanging over him like a personal storm cloud.

'Jonas, there's no point getting stressed – there's nothing we can do now. Let's just relax and enjoy the time together?' Ellie pleads.

'How can we enjoy anything ever again?' He's almost shouting. 'We don't even know where we are. We don't even know who we are, cosmically.'

'No one knows anything cosmically, Jonas,' I say.

'I can't believe I've been fine with that. It's not fine. I just realised that I hardly even know any actual people. I see the people at school but I don't know them. And I see you, but you could easily be an immersion designed to keep me safe. I haven't even met any of my actual friends in real life. I just assume they exist because we communicate. A big wind comes, and puff, they're gone, like blowing out a candle. It's unreliable. What if my friend from Lutsk isn't real? What if he's not even from Lutsk?'

'What happened to these things being immaterial?' I ask. 'It doesn't matter either way, isn't that your line?'

'That just shows how theoretical my existence is. I don't

even have a position, like, in space.'

A pang shoots through my heart. Jonas keeps pacing, muttering.

On impulse, I rush for my son, stopping him mid-pace and wrapping my body around his as though absorbing a blast. 'Yes, you do, Jonas,' I tell him, feeling his small limbs twitch in mine. 'You are right here with us.'

He voices some muffled protest into my chest. I grip him tighter.

'You are right here, with me, in the family room. We are safe.'

He squawks, his body hot with panic. I make a desperate shushing sound, imitating white noise, the ocean, the sound of peace.

'We are safe,' I repeat, voicing an inner mantra both familiar and hollow. I can't make this promise to my son, but I do.

After a few moments I shuffle him over to the wall and drop us both against its comfortingly cold surface. We huddle together on the permabamboo floor, me rocking us gently back and forth. Eventually, Jonas stops protesting. His body goes slack, his breath comes in tiny gasps. I stroke his sweat-damp hair. Thunder cracks outside and he tenses up again, squeaking. I feel cleaved in two, as though I am cradling the very core of my self.

Ellie puts on Marconi Reunion and opens a bottle of twenty-year-old pinot.

The thunder strikes again. My shirt is damp with Jonas' perspiration.

'I can only find 280 litres of water stored on the property,' says Lilly, matter-of-fact. 'That's not enough for the four of us to stay well hydrated for thirty days.'

Jonas peers up from my arms, desperate. 'What do you mean?' he squeaks. 'I thought the house had a minimum of thirty days provisions! Isn't that the point of the exoshield? Do we think that catastrophe will just pass by overnight? Do we think it has somewhere else to be?'

His sister regards him with slight disdain. 'It's only a problem of consumption,' she says. 'I'm just saying, at this point we aren't dehydrated, so we can begin rationing water easily according to this chart. And because we don't know how long we are going to be here we also need to start conserving our oxygen. At this point our oxygen is fairly clean – CO_2 levels are healthy. But these are just rudimentary calculations, nothing like what I could get if I had the proper systems in place. The real problem is that even though I have the exact measurements, I can't input them into anything. It would be great to have access to a national average. Or even a neighbourhood databank.'

'That's enough, Lilly,' says Ellie. 'This house is designed so that we don't have to worry. So let's not worry. It's like a holiday. No responsibilities for anyone.' She takes a sip of her wine and sways her body to the calming music, as if demonstrating a fact.

'Responsibility is just a ruse, anyway,' says Jonas. 'And advanced design as a way to end worry? That's a joke. Ridiculous. Like kissing an amputation better.'

I grip him tighter, squeezing the fear from his small body.

'Stop it,' he says.

'No.'

'Seriously, let me go.'

'No.'

'Dad, seriously, you're smothering me.'

I hold on tight until he goes slack again. His shoulders crumpling in my grip. Eventually, quietly, he starts to snivel.

'I don't want to die, Dad,' he whimpers. 'I want to grow up. I want to see the future.'

I say nothing. My quiet fear is that this truth might suture our bodies together. My son lets out a low moan.

After a long while I gently roll him aside and stand up, dusting my pants with strong, authoritative strokes.

'Your mother's right,' I say too loudly, overcompensating. 'We have the luxury of not worrying, so that's what we are going to do. Lilly, you have no idea how the air filter works, so your calculations are skewed. Jonas, all your friends are real, they are just out of reach for now. Pretend it's the time difference. You'll be back online playing *Mutiny* tomorrow.'

I take the glass of wine that Ellie offers me and begin to rifle through a supply box marked 'entertainment'. There are strange old puzzles and several decks of real plastic playing cards. I dig up a dusty Pow-Pow buckwheat plush and toss it to Lilly, who glances at it disinterestedly. At the bottom of the box I find an old portable MiniCine console and four crude, decades-old immersion goggles.

I turn on the machine.

Lilly looks at it, and then at me incredulously. 'Dad! That is such a waste.'

'We don't need to conserve power, Lilly. All the networks are down, which means this room is running at a fraction of the house's solar capacity. The oxygen system runs its own calculations and will let us know if there are any problems.'

'For now!' she reprimands. 'What calculations have you made to lead you to believe that it will stay that way?'

'The calculations of a full adult life,' I tell her.

'I think it's a good idea,' says Ellie, distributing the goggles. 'We need something to take our minds off the situation. And how long has it been since we all sat down and watched something together?'

I can't remember when – or if we ever have. Any attempt to remember just brings forth a stock image: someone else's family, warm and happy, immersed together. An old advertisement for the MiniCine most likely. I scroll through the console's library. My own first film *Then Rest* is here, along with other early disaster immersions. But they are not right for now. Finally, I settle on an innocuous, feel-good family immersion.

With a small sigh of relief, Jonas puts his glasses on, and Lilly follows suit, reluctant but obedient. Their faces slacken, their shoulders drop and relax, and their breathing becomes regular – a tide washing away. Ellie joins them in the immersion.

I let them drift away from me, leaving my goggles off. I need to think. I push my hands forward and breathe. I repulse-the-monkey. I try to attain a state of mindfulness over my own emotions. How do I feel? I'm relieved to be here with my family. But not completely relieved. I'm not a man whose whole world is contained in his home. As I exhale and repeat the calming sequence, my mind wanders to Tom, and no sooner does it find purchase there then I begin to obsess. I need to know the status of the retirement district. Have they been hit by the storm? Are they as safe as Bay Heights? With a shudder, I picture a teepee, imagine it hurtling through the night sky. What if there was a blackout? What would that mean for Tom? Would the shock of losing fluids and breathing assistance wake him up – or kill him? Who is looking after Tom? Then, equally suddenly, I have a vision, another memory, of Tom's doctor. She's stooped over, dark-eyed and careful, tending Tom, and somehow simultaneously caring for me. I realise that I wish with all my heart to be there. To be inert in a bed, to be tended-to and dreaming. That is the home to which I truly want to return.

Now it's my turn to pace the room and search the feed. I try several times in vain to connect to Tom's hospice. On the floor, my children are oblivious, locked into the immersion. I keep pacing, the compass on my socks pointing perpetually north. I go over to the kitchen and pour myself another glass of wine, consume it rapidly, then pour one more. I need to get in the car and drive. I should head to the retirement district. Maybe I can beat the storm.

I jump, feeling a sudden cool touch on my shoulder. It's Ellie, her goggles pushed back on her head, her eyebrows raised in a question.

'Are you worrying about Tom?' she asks.

'Yes,' I say. It's half-true, at least.

'That's completely natural,' she says calmly. 'It's to be expected.'

'I think I should go to him.'

Her expression hardens; she locks her eyes on mine.

'No,' she says. 'They don't need you.'

'How do you know?' I ask in a voice that could belong to Jonas.

'Shhh,' she says, maternally. 'If you need to escape, you can do it here.'

She pulls the goggles over my eyes and the room begins to swirl. She leads me down to the floor and we sit, side-by-side, shoulder-to-shoulder, holding hands, as we lift off into a swirling, bright nothing. Soon we're a young family around a Christmas tree, everyone being everyone else: the son the father, the mother the son, the daughter the mother, the father the daughter. There's even a dog, joyously frolicking around us. We begin to unwrap presents. Each of us has trinkets particular to who we are. These objects know us and fill us with immense joy: a ribbon, a rocking chair, a smart new tie. Then it's time to open the gift addressed to us all – it's the biggest gift under the tree and we relish unwrapping it together. The dog helps tear a corner of the paper, making us all laugh. When it's unwrapped we stand, marvelling: there lies an ancient carpet with an intricate and hypnotic pattern, mandalas and deep swirls, ancient princes and princesses. We know what to do: we take it out into the yard and lay it flat across the staticky grass. The sky is bright blue, the breeze tingles the skin lightly. We all nestle on the carpet, and soon, once we are comfortable, it takes off. It flies us over the neighbourhood, over the city, and out to the edge of the world, where waves lap on a long and beautiful stretch of beach and the air smells like salt and the sun warms our skin and we are holding hands and laughing and happy.

But one thing is dragging me from the immersion. One utterance. One thing I know to be true, that I can't forget, even here: there is no beach, not like this, not anymore.

Far below me, the waves shatter into pixels. The faces of my family melt into carpet mandalas. I am disconnecting. The immersion isn't holding.

When I push the goggles from my eyes I see three individuals, bodies curled over, protecting themselves from each other and the world.

• •

The house knows that the danger has passed long before we do: we wake to the smell of fresh coffee, baking almond loaf, frying eggs. The house reassures us. We wake to real morning light coming in through its windows. The valley is dishevelled, but not devastated. Outside, the neighbour's exoshields are also lowered, thermaglass refracting the morning sun.

My children stir gradually, not wanting to open their eyes, like guests who've stayed too long at the party and fell asleep.

I get up and tiptoe through the house, checking rooms with care. The newest Schwerbut release follows me, filling each room in succession with reverb and panoramic delay. The kitchen has the wholesome and welcoming feel of being tended by a housewife from the golden age of cinema, just dashed out for a moment. Jonas' room is neat and ordered. In a cupboard by the bed, his arsenal of survival gear. On his desk there's a scrolled projection of his latest school assignment, the dreaded Timeline of Misconception.

In Lilly's room the holograms and charts of Hope the giant sloth pup map the walls, making it feel like a zoo enclosure. Hope paces. Hope plays. Hope cowers as the thunder rolls.

I find Ellie in the garden, righting plant pots, salvaging native foliage.

'Are you okay?' I ask.

She smiles, nods. 'Are the children still sleeping?' she asks. I nod.

We stare at each other for a moment, almost optimistic over the ruined garden, at ease in our mutual responsibilities.

She smiles, puts a finger over her lips and points at the uprooted vegetable patch. In it, a small rabbit squats, nibbling lettuce, its bloody foot cocked.

'It was in the car,' Ellie informs me. 'It made quite a mess.'

We watch the rabbit for a while. It is content to chew and sit. Relieved to be doing something it understands.

My daughter appears beside me, sleepy and unimpressed.

'What's that?' she asks.

Ellie repeats her shushing gesture.

'It's not native,' says Lilly, matter-of-fact.

On a whim, I crouch down and beckon my daughter to

come closer to the creature.

She scrunches up her nose, rabbit-like herself. 'It's a pest,' she says.

'It's a bunny,' I say firmly. 'It's a real bunny with a sore foot and I think it needs your help.'

Lilly humours me, crouching in the dirt like an adult who must come down to a child's level.

'Here, bunny,' she says in a monotone, but she doesn't get up when I leave.

In the master bedroom, I reconnect with the network. The newsfeed is up: two experts and a scroll of data. A graph simultaneously charts the significance of Pitcairn's most recent drop, Hurricane Teardrop, and the krill extinction event. The global micro-catastrophe chain – this is what they're calling it. GMCC for short. Medium-scale disaster events reported all over the world. Rogue winds, flash floods, bushfires.

We are all interconnected. We are all warned, again.

I try again to connect to the hospice, but I get a lost location message: the address you are attempting to log into is busy or missing. I reload and get the same message. Busy or missing.

'Anxiety and confusion, 6:45am,' notes the archive. But it's relieving to be back online.

'Thank god,' says a voice, and I look up to see Jean's face, huge, floating in the mirror. 'How long have you been down for? Sixty hours? It's very unlike you. I'd applaud your independence, but we have lost so much time to this. Why did you leave the central district?'

Anger surges up in my throat. 'My family, Jean. Some of us have families.'

Jean shakes his head, bemused. 'I'm sure your presence was vital,' he scoffs. 'Meanwhile, the production has been devastated.'

'Oh.'

'We've been set back weeks. The soundshell and the warehouse will have to be completely rebuilt. We lost equipment. We were right in one of the most heavily hit areas. We had both the flooding and the wind. At one point we had a fire. It would have been superb, but for the losses.'

'But everyone is alright?'

'More than alright! We captured the whole thing. We have footage of the destruction from the inside. And Sullivan! Sullivan had the genius idea of donning a sensation recorder and actually live-capturing the haptics of the event. It's a genius idea. I don't know why we haven't been doing it for years.'

'Not enough disasters happening close to home?' I mean it as a joke.

Jean nods enthusiastically.

'Spot on,' he says. 'But think globally! We could give recorders to underemployed citizens in disaster-prone areas and pay them to walk through the destruction, measuring the actual sensation. We could be recording the sensation of actual disasters and selling them back to the people. Disaster nostalgia! Imagine the level of realism. A new *cinéma vérité*. That's the real catharsis: reliving an event you have already survived. But more cinematic! Sharpened, and narratively resolved. A perfectly rehearsed traumatic re-en-actment. Who has time to understand the implications of their experience as it is happening? Better to go back, to go deeper. And think of the production savings.'

'Our insurance premiums might go up.'

Jean laughs gleefully. 'Not if we pay only for the footage, after it's been shot! I'm talking about fostering a new cul-ture of paparazzi – not seeking the most candid image of a celebrity, but of a disaster instead.'

I raise an eyebrow.

'Fine. Think of it another way: it's providing an outlet for community need. One thing we do know is that people need to relive disaster. Take the testimonial footage from the fiftieth anniversary of Hurricane Katrina. Or better yet, the centenary of the Hiroshima bombings. Disaster is a meme. It's viral and reproduces itself within us. We all want to hear the grandchildren of atomic survivors retelling the story of Hiroshima, Nagasaki, and Chernobyl so well we feel we are there with them. Well, imagine if we could be?'

'Is this how Sullivan incorporates the idea into his ethics of empathy?'

Jean smiles. 'That's right. It's a project of historical import,' he chuckles.

'Glitch is gone, then?'

'You'll have to ask him about that. I never understood the merits of his glitch. I'm a perfectionist, as you know. But in this case, I suppose, you don't need to remind people of the artificiality of a simulation if what they are seeing is real. Sullivan's issues were to do with production methods. But he's an ambitious young man – he wants to pioneer something. Pioneer empathic immersion or pioneer historically true immersion: real, transgenerational disasters. I suspect it's all the same to him, as long he's pioneering. And good for him! Remember when you had that kind of zeal, Max?'

'No.'

'He got a respectable haircut. He sees all this as the future of filmmaking. He'll come to the island with us. We'll stalk Pitcairn for the next month. Until it sinks. We'll mine it for all its melancholy. We'll immortalise it.'

'It's an island. It's already immortal.'

'No. Space is immortal, but place is human. Enabling place to outlast space, this is the great feat. A transcendence of nature, of the laws of physics.'

I regard Jean dubiously. His grey eyes are wide and violent, an ocean in a storm.

'There's honour in this, I think,' he says. 'More honour than there is in writing, in something as trite as composition. More honour, perhaps, than love.'

'I don't need honour.'

'No? I think you'd be surprised. Men need things today that have been extinct for years. Do you even know what you need? You probably can't remember.'

'I need to go and see Tom.'

Jean shakes his head sadly. 'No, you don't,' he says.

'I do. I can't connect to them. The signal is down.'

'Them? Did you get yourself another comatose brother? Or maybe a long-lost mother or a wandering childhood pet? I'm sure all of them would be enriching experiences for you. Maybe have Ellie look into it...'

'What? I'm talking about Dr Stern, she's been working with Tom. Remember, you met her?'

Jean shrugs indifferently, as though he has no clue what I'm talking about, or as though it is immaterial. I search his face for something repressed, some sympathy or recognition but there is nothing.

'What you need to do,' he says, slowly. 'Is to put your energy back into your real life. Into the task at hand. Into making films, not living in them.'

'What do you mean? This is my real life.'

He shrugs, looks at something below the scope of the lens. 'What I mean is that something very important is happening, and we have a chance to be a part of it. You and Sullivan and I on that island – we'll be bringing its extinction to the world.'

'But what if the sinking really does mark the beginning of the end? We're already in the middle of a global micro-catastrophe chain, and they're saying that this could result in a global mega-catastrophe. The probability is high, so is the plausibility.'

'Exactly,' says Jean, licking his lips. 'Imagine that. The last film.'

From the dressing table mirror, Hope the giant sloth puppy peers mischievously into the room.

• •

Jonas is just outside the bedroom, standing close to the door like an agent in a spy plot.

'Are you okay?' I ask.

'Are you going to the island?' His face is drawn and aged from our night in lock-down.

'Jonas, I've been through this with you. It's too dangerous and I can't let you—'

'No,' he says, alarmed. 'I changed my mind. I don't want to go.' He looks at me meaningfully, pathetically. 'And I don't want you to go.'

I have very little time to cycle through the best responses to this. I need to convey how important he is to all my decision-making processes. I need to show him that I am willing to make great sacrifices for him, but that I am, ultimately, my own man with my own inalterable agenda. Words are vital here. Our very roles are at stake.

'Okay,' I tell him, finally.

'Okay?'

'Okay.'

'I love you, Dad,' he says, wrapping his small body around me.

It is the most perfect moment, and too soon it is gone. Jonas steps away, folds his shoulders back into their hunch.

Not wanting this connection to be over, I start bargaining. 'But you need to promise me that you will try to recover from last night,' I tell him. 'I want you to take the day off. Spend time with your mother and sister. Go out and play, or something. Be a child. No Polynesian braves. No returning ice age.'

Jonas looks at his feet.

'While I'm gone I need you to look after the family,' I say, startling him.

'But you said you wouldn't go!'

'Not to Pitcairn. But I do have to go and see if Tom's okay.'

I immediately regret telling him. The panic of last night takes possession of his small frame. He begins to pace. To breathe erratically.

Beside me, a gauze mouthpiece and breath-regulating pad appear; in my periphery, a parents' guide to paediatric anxiety.

'Oh god,' says Jonas. 'I just realised something. Did I ever see Tom in real life? Have I ever actually touched him?'

When I hear this, something dormant rises up in my throat.

'Fear, 7:30am,' notes the archive.

I turn away from my son, struggling with my own equilibrium.

'We have to get on with things,' I stammer, picking a few random objects up and placing them with purpose back in the same spots.

Jonas tails me as I wash and dress and prepare to leave. He's outside the bathroom. He lingers in the kitchen. He's in my room. He squints at me as though gauging the authenticity of a painting. He says nothing. I turn on feeds of old cartoons and pop song channels, but his focus is intense.

At the front door he pauses. He will not follow me outside. He lingers on the threshold, unready to see what lies beyond.

'It's okay out here, Jonas. Everything is almost exactly as you left it.'

'I know,' he says. 'I just want to hang around the house today. You know, spend time with my sister, like you said. It'll do me good.'

He backs into the lobby slowly, as if trying not to alarm any wild animals.

Ellie grimaces from her elegant garden stool. She aerates the hydrogel, mindfully.

'He's adjusting,' I say. 'There's no re-entry protocol. He doesn't have the skills to do it alone.'

'Yes. I suppose in a novel we would call this his coming-of-age moment. But I'm not sure it works like that anymore,' she sighs. 'Where are you going?'

'To Tom.'

She sighs again. 'Do you think there's any point?' she says.

'Of course – he could be injured.'

'Isn't he already? Isn't he doing just fine without us? Don't you think it might be time to put your energy elsewhere?'

'You've changed your tune. And you sound like Jean.'

'Jean has his moments of clarity.'

'Ellie, he's my brother. I need to make sure he's safe.'

She smiles sympathetically, getting up out of the garden and coming over to me. She reaches out and touches the side of my chin, sending ripples of arousal and anxiety through my whole face. 'He's safe, Max,' she says. 'Right here with you.'

I flounder for a moment, trying to work out what she's saying. 'Ellie, do you know something I don't?'

She laughs her familiar laugh. 'Many things,' she says.

'No,' I say, hearing the anger and panic rise in my voice.

'I mean, have you heard about Tom? Has something happened to him?'

'No,' she says. 'Not as far as I'm aware.'

'Have you heard from the doctor?'

'Which doctor?'

'Tom's doctor?'

'Well, maybe – which one?'

I stare into her still, green eyes in disbelief. 'Dr. Stern,' I say, a little too pleadingly.

Ellie gives me another enigmatic, sad smile. She touches my face again and her temperature, heartbeat and minute facial tremors are caught and recorded, her pity added to the emotional chart of our marriage.

'No,' Ellie says, letting her hand drop. 'I haven't heard from anyone.'

She turns back to the hydrogarden, leaving me slumped and confused. Above us the clouds have burned off, revealing a clear and bright new day. After a full two minutes standing, waiting, unwilling to look to the archive or to my own mind, I turn from my wife and walk away.

When I open the Fleet Methane car door, I'm slapped with the stink of rabbit wee and fear. The car registers me – my personal preferences load and the deodoriser pumps. I close my eyes and let my fingers thrump on the firm steering wheel. A car should be a neutral space with no past or future: just a pitching, fast, perpetual present. But the deodoriser can't quite mask the rabbit's smells, and the seat has a distinct feeling – it's no longer just an empty vessel for a body. There's something decidedly secondhand about this vehicle now. It's no longer generic. It's specific. Filled with human and animal stink. Scratched and banged up.

It's not a car anymore. It's my car.

• •

The whole of Bay Heights looks as though it has returned from a day spa. The armoured beetle shells have retreated back into their holes and the heavy rains have left glistening and vivid mosaics on the solarbitumen.

The cabin pressure adjusts. The music goes up and the windows down. I try to focus on the horizon, a meditative, mindful point.

But as I drive along the pleasant streets, past unique, tasteful houses, I can't shake my unease. No cheerfully angled roof, no imaginatively orchestrated indoor/outdoor space, no prudently designed vegetable garden cheers me up. As I drive out of the village I realise that I have not passed a single human figure.

Beyond Bay Heights, the landscape is the same for miles, flattening out past the windscreen. Tiny saplings bow and shiver in the breeze. I search for landmarks, but the trailer packs are gone. According to the location grid they should be here, but the very earth they dwelled on has been tossed.

Waste Not Want truck crews are gathering debris. They suck up the odd shoe, a car part, a biodegradable fork. They churn the mundane necessities into mulch; flatten uneven ground into cryptic ripples. The whole area is refreshed. Rubbish. Shit. Tears. Sweat. Shame. All ploughed into the dirt. Rows of evenly planted seeds are sown across the traces.

Did the storm pass through here before or after the area was deserted?

All this is part of the emergency response plan in action, I suppose. The most important part of any disaster is its response. The great tragedies of the first half of this century taught us that. Every disaster used to be followed by a chain of secondary tragedies wrought by appalling unpreparedness or wanton neglect or old-fashioned corruption.

A freeze-frame of the last days of the city flickers behind my eyelids. People getting on buses to who-knows-where. People climbing into DigiFreeze boxes. Rats off the ship.

Any event is only as significant as its aftermath.

And so it's encouraging, passing by the vast, vacant fields and seeing the diligent recovery crews, sweeping and polishing. Just like in Bay Heights, such swift clean-up encourages us to forget the past and focus on the future. The thoroughness of our contingency plans suggest that the global micro-catastrophe chain is best understood intellectually. It's a shame, sure. But nothing we can't handle. No bang. No whimper. Definitely no Praeteranthropocene.

I drive for hours. Much farther, it strikes me, than I should need to. The scenery outside the window does not change. The sameness is hypnotic. An endless grey background loop, my satellite-positioned red spot gliding through it like an avatar in an old video game. Yawning, I put the car in self-drive and float like a man adrift on a raft.

This sweet grey monotony lulls me to sleep and I dream I'm in a vast, ancient sound stage. Studio wind whistles hollow through my ears. A high, electric squeal rings out around me. The set is an old barn, its visage dancing with scratches like ancient celluloid film stock. I walk towards it, looking for its edges, the balustrades that prop up the façade, but as I get closer I see its depth and detail. It has an acutely human architecture – great wooden doors like the long sleeves of a cassock hanging from genuflecting arms. Standing in front of these tall doors, I see that every stain and nick on them is familiar. I stretch out a hand to trace its surface. Not thin and synthetic, like a set should be, but substantial, the wood old and deeply etched. I look up and see actual stars in a real sky. I push. The heavy door creaks. Then I slump forward and lean into the warm wood. The door opens a crack, revealing darkness, a black mirror reflecting my own plump, balding head, Janus-faced against Tom's gaunt features. Our bodies melt into the darkness beneath us. Tom's lips spread and purse but his face is still, gentle lines bending into the shocked O's of my eyes and mouth. The frozen horror.

Suddenly Tom's eyes open. They are grey, flecked with noise. He smiles without recognition, puts a finger to my mouth, and nods towards a window on the far wall. Flinchingly, I follow his gaze and through the pane I see Gabrielle: her hair strangler vines, her eyes black holes, mouth moving like a ventriloquist's doll.

She's beckoning me.

I step forward and a crack of light from the window illuminates parts of the room. Dismembered body parts floating in the dark.

Gabrielle speaks. 'This is how you wake up,' she says.

Searchlights sweep the floor.

'Something has knocked you out,' she says. 'You use the language of direct violence. Of assault.'

I stagger towards her, arms outstretched, feeling my way through the dark.

'Watch out!' she says, laughing. 'You're slipping into another, more beautiful reality.'

I grope around in the dark. I slap at the darkness between feet and elbows, the curve of a nape, a spill of hair.

'Imagine the cube,' she says, from everywhere, and then, petulantly: 'I'm waiting.'

I'm suddenly exhausted. Unable to keep staggering in the dark.

'Good,' she says. 'Relax. Count to ten. Imagine the cube.'

• •

I open my eyes to the empty world rushing past the windows. For a moment I can't discern whether I've woken or not. I check the archive: a storyboard of brief and excited sleep, and a definite wake-up point. Clammy hands. My heart rate is eight above.

The grid still doesn't show a location for the retirement zone. The car must have sustained some connectivity damage in the storm. I reassume control of the wheel and pull onto a side road, hoping to find a place to turn and head back the other way. But there's no place, and I don't turn. I continue on without knowing why. The grass on either side of the road is long, unkempt. It brushes the side of the vehicle. I check the feed but the map is a featureless grey. I try to stop, to put the car into reverse, but a series of exclamation points appear on the dash, and then suddenly the car stops in a vast clearing. The engine switches off and the door opens.

I pause for a moment, unwilling to leave the known space of the car.

Outside, the clearing narrows into a long path. It's not a road suitable for a car, but deep grooves suggest the traffic of smaller vehicles. I step out into the quiet scrub and the car doors close gently behind me.

The path is lined on either side with flattened and parted native grass crops; my shoes inform me of their genus. This continues for five hundred metres, before the scenery changes again and I notice the piles of rubble. The piles are small at first, just detritus in mounds by the track, but as I continue the piles grow larger, like funeral pyres, and then like demolition sites. Small buildings imploded and stacked.

This place, then, was just decimated by the storm. The branches of trees hang jagged and broken. I try to take in the traces, work out what once stood here. Parts of the area are littered with what look like the interiors of homes from golden-era films. There are torn velvet paintings and hand-carved coffee tables, weaving looms and charred fondue sets. In another part of the field there are piles of elaborate and ruined electrical equipment. Balls of knotted wire and tubes of all sizes. Shattered fractaLight panes like grounded galaxies.

Waste Not Want skipsorters move around silently, heaping like with like, recyclers following closely, sucking each pile into one of their many metallic guts, belching an innocuous and non-polluting steam.

Instinctively, I look around for Pow-Pow, but there are no children here to draw him out.

Beside me: a tower of mattresses, a midden of prostheses, a pile of soft furnishings with a burnt-out piano on top. The crews work efficiently and without human appendages. I'm the only man standing.

Over to my far right I notice the remains of what must have been a train stop, the shell building flattened and sorted into its components, colour-coded, as in a children's educational tool. A long, oblong box moves slowly along a rail, picking up the tracks behind it, folding them like a picnic blanket and churning them into small briquettes of carbon as it rolls forth.

Only one building is still partially standing, having seemingly evaded the storm and the wrecking crew. It's a medium-sized pyramid-shaped building; an accidental monument to our changed attitude to the ruin.

On one wall, a flickering holograph reads 'Harmonic Convergence Hut'.

Something stirs in me. Some ghostly image pushing to the forefront of my mind. My shoes analyse the surface terrain of the ground, and register the pressure of ants smashed under my feet as I traipse across the dirt.

I've been here before.

The archive spits out a colourful chart of conflicting

emotions.

'Where am I?' I say out loud, and a note is recorded.

In answer, a broad yellow banner unfurls in the fore-ground. 'This district has been rejuvenated!' declares its cheerful, county-fair cursive.

In my periphery, a feed scuttles, skims, and fixes on a pleasant, presentation-style montage.

'I'm glad you asked!' says a chirpy blonde woman. 'Towards the end of the twentieth century this area was part of the urban sprawl that surrounded the city. The centralis-ing push of affluent families, followed shortly by another recession, left these once well-maintained neighbourhoods to the creep of urban blight and decay. Within a decade, after several small-scale social and environmental events, this whole area became uninhabitable wasteland.'

In the background, a helpful montage shows a residen-tial neighbourhood taken over by crime and poverty. Every now and then the presenter turns to see, looking back at me with mock alarm, conspiratorial distaste curling the edges of her lips.

'Less than a decade after these grim scenes, this area was rezoned as a health and community sector and the plans were laid for a unique residential zone for older people.'

The background is now a faded sepia slideshow. Behind the presenter a slight old man with long braids pays a country tune on the ukulele while a gang of geriatrics dance with unbridled passion, dragging bracketed limbs and life-style assistance boxes with each shimmy and sway.

I feel sick.

A group of silver-haired sprites dance topless around a large bonfire. Shadows flit through the trees. An effect has been laid on the image, pixelation that gives it the look of a historical document. Celluloid from another time.

'Cognitive dissonance, 11:50am,' notes the archive.

'Most recently, another event activated the area's rejuvenation protocol,' continues the woman in the montage. 'Soon, a final rezoning will see a new temperate forest, the third cultivated in five years, making this district one of the most densely rejuvenated in the nation.' The presenter smiles broadly, proudly.

Behind her, senior citizens melt into a forest like characters of ancient folklore. Lovely trees grow in time-lapse, moss spreading across their thickening trunks. A mist descends on the canopy.

I drop to my knees.

'Are you okay, sir?' asks the presenter on screen, alarmed, detecting my sudden movement. She cycles into her first aid algorithm: 'Are you experiencing sudden shortness of breath? Is there any pain or numbness?'

I wave her away and the world flattens into three dimensions. I'm low to the ground, the base of some other kind of pile, loaded with the weight of so much detritus.

'This must be memory,' I say out loud, and a note is recorded.

With great effort, I pull myself upright and try to see the scene in wide shot.

'I am the lens,' I say out loud, for the record.

I try to dolly back on the world, to see myself as only one small part of a greater scene, but an unprecedented emotional surge explodes into narrative within me. I wander between mounds of detritus. Unreliable fragments stick to this scenery. At seemingly random spots I find myself frozen in romantic flashback. I become their voiceover, translating them as they seize hold of me.

'This is the place where you and Gabrielle first spoke,' I recite beside a pile of thermobricks, laid out in piles according to size and colour.

'And this is where you kissed,' I tell a stack of gurney frames, and a note is recorded.

'A classical tune. Repeated perfectly,' my voice cracks as I pass the broken piano.

I recite each hazy association like they were positions in Jonas's endless game.

I am stumbling by the slipping shoreline.

I am harvesting the flyblown crop.

I pause beside the ruined temple.

'And this is the room in which she asked you to erase her. This is Tom's room.'

••

It's only much later, as Ellie and I pull into the parking lot outside the grief centre, that I realise I've become grateful for the rabbit-stench in the car. Against Lilly's better judgement, I made a submission to keep the car. I regard it as evidence. A primitive archival technology. A machine that bears traces of human history. Ownership notwithstanding, I haven't been permitted to drive it for some weeks. Now, from the driver's seat, Ellie touches me, pats me, giving me small, hardly reassuring contact.

'Are you ready?' she asks.

I'm not ready. But I am sedated.

The archive documents my decline: the day I came home raving, carrying a bag of refuse, parts of the past saved and bundled.

INT. WIDE SHOT. NIGHT

In the dimly lit family room, Max sorts through his broken objects, unbundling and rebundling parts of the past by type. He is intent on his work as members of his family walk cautiously past him carrying sports equipment or bowls of cereal. Ellie stands over him for a long while, observing his strange project.

ELLIE

We can't go on like this. You need closure.

Jonas, loaded with supplies for the school day ahead, pauses by his sorry parents, shaking his small head sadly.

JONAS

It's improbable that any of us knows what he needs. And besides, what he needs today might be the opposite of what he needs tomorrow.

On the floor, Max continues sorting.

I review the feed, but I don't need to. I remember all this. The clarity is painful.

When I lose interest in the bags of rubble I begin hiding out in Jonas's room during the daytime. I like to do his homework. My work is methodical but not up to his usual standard. He refuses to hand it in but I keep doing it anyway. I need to keep my mind out of the newsfeed, to keep the flood of memory at bay. I work on my own Timeline of Misconception, wallowing in the existential resignation of the task. First, I plot love in its incarnations throughout history. I note the platonic, idealised boy/man love of ancient Greece (renounced as paedophilia), and the pagan bisexuality of the Romans (declared heresy). I make a mark on the timeline to represent Saint Augustine and his confessional, guilt-ridden love (dangerously repressing the Id), the courtly, bittersweet love of the Renaissance (idealising and objectifying women), the chaste, hard-working love of the puritans (blind to the dictates of progress), the nuclear love of the atomic decades (bang!), the free love of flower power (drug-fuelled promiscuity), the driven, ambitious love of the end of last century (perfume and watches), and the doomed love of the next ('until the end, my love' – finally a shortfall in commitment.)

On the corresponding line, at a point parallel to my own,

I write: You think you're in love but you're just experiencing a chemical and hormonal synthesis. Then I lie down on my son's tiny bed and cry.

When Ellie finds me there in the damp sheets she decides it's time.

'Closure,' she repeats now, evenly, soothingly, as the car powers down.

Every night I dream Tom is a pile of parts and I am a Waste Not Want machine, sorting him into something recognisable.

Ellie steers me from the car with soft touches. We walk together into the foyer of the grief centre, where small groups of mourners linger, waiting stoically on puffy, hungry couches or milling by trays of tea and biscuits. I will go anywhere, do anything. It might be the sedative, or I might have no desire left. I pause by a stack of lightly salted protobites, a row of calming chamomile.

Ellie does not like to wait. Her green eyes sweep the room like searchlights, picking out a director where he chameleons against the drapes. Ellie zeroes in, dragging me behind her. 'We are the Galleons.'

The director blinks, his face a veil of unwavering sympathy.

'Of course,' he says. 'For Mr Tom Galleon.'

'Yes.'

'And Dr Gabrielle Stern,' he adds, making me flinch. 'Right this way.'

He explains the process in a gentle murmur, gesturing for us to follow him down a long corridor. We trail past thickly draped doors. The odd mourner stepping out into the hall, blotting tears, sniffling.

'Each room is equipped with six variable-predictive functions. If you have an archival chip it will be registered upon entry in order to help us tailor your experience to suit your unique mourning requirements. Please let me know if you do not wish this to happen and we will simply provide our extremely high-quality standard service.'

'I think recognition is important,' says Ellie. 'My husband is fully compatible.'

'We have Mr Galleon in a smaller room, as requested,' the attendant waves towards one door, 'Dr Stern is right opposite. Please remember that I'm your personal attendant so if you need anything at all, don't hesitate to ask.'

'Thank you,' says Ellie.

'Shall we?' the attendant gestures.

At a nod from Ellie he holds back the heavy drapes and we step into a dark room. It's small, yet opulently fitted. An access request flashes in my periphery and I accept. After a few moments the air becomes close and heavy with electricity. Particles of light pour in from somewhere behind us and arrange themselves on the podium at the front of the room. A virtual curtain draws across the projection.

'Are you ready?' Ellie asks again, through a veneer of patience.

I shrug. I feel numb, ready for nothing.

Ellie waves the curtain away. Behind it, Tom sleeps, a linen-wrapped sarcophagus, his breath the only motion in his body, a wall of monitors bleeping rhythmically behind him. We sit down on the pew-like bench. Ellie takes my hand and we watch him, just as we did remotely from our house in Bay Heights or from the central district.

After a while Ellie says, 'I thought they were going to take data from your archive.'

'This is the only memory I have of him.'

'Well, would you like to play a simulation?' Her voice is like a sigh. 'They have a number of generic family loss immersions.'

'No,' I tell her. 'I want to stay true to the memory. At least I know it's real.'

Tom's body is placed in a perfect representation of the hospital room the last time I recorded it in the archive. On the walls, liquid photo frames scroll through pictures of my family: Ellie as a young woman in a fashionable bathing costume; Jonas in a Humidibasket on a kitchen table. A picture of me as a young man on the red carpet at the opening of *Then Rest*. In glass casings by the bed, the few remaining relics of my parents are displayed – a photograph, a locket. A plush talking Pow-Pow, donated by Lilly, props its buckwheat-stuffed body against a bonsai orchid. Tom is one more object in the pile.

I get up and circle the bed. Everything is perfect. A haptic glove on a tray beside him allows me to reach in and hold his hand in mine. His hand is warm and limp. I imagine us in wide shot: a portrait of common grief.

The wires and tubes extend from Tom's fingers like strings on a puppet. I get another inconvenient flash of memory: an efficient machine sucking up ruined wiring like spaghetti.

Ellie's face, her eyes fixed on Tom, is another unblemished terrain. I try to remember what she looked like when we met. The idea then that time will one day register on her face seems crass and old-fashioned.

I want to cry, but that too seems crass and old-fashioned.

The room is filled with respectful silence.

'I'm going to go next door,' I say eventually. 'Do you want to come?'

'Do you need me there?' Ellie says.

'No.'

'Then I'll stay here. I always liked watching Tom. I might talk to him a little. I always found it so calming.'

I squeeze Tom's hand three times as though transmitting a message. Then I drop it, watching it flicker, becoming irresolute as it falls. I put the haptic glove back and push through the drapes into the corridor, into the room opposite.

This room is larger and lighter, with a real funereal feel. It's better suited to an immersion with a subject in possession of a large data set. It could even accommodate a small audience.

The room detects my presence and what I assume is a generically coded relative appears to give a eulogy.

'Gabrielle was a quiet person,' says the woman, sombrely dressed, with high cheekbones and a steady gaze. 'She valued her privacy, but had a reputation for kindness amongst those fortunate enough to know her. She had a formidable intellect, and her work in the field of Temporal Lobe Hibernation Epilepsy was highly regarded.'

The relative sniffs, as if she is holding back some deeper,

more eloquent truth. It's a well-delivered speech, almost as though it were taken from something real. It also serves as an opening act, an entry protocol to prep the immersion. I can see the swirling shapes behind the eulogist. The curtain is heavy with hypnotic suggestions. I pause it, shake my head and look away from the patterns.

I don't want to be immersed. I want critical distance. It might be the first thing I am conscious of wanting since I returned from the retirement zone.

'I want to see Gabrielle,' I say, and then almost immediately regret it.

All around me, projected Gabrielles spring to the walls, dance towards the lectern, unaware of each other, passing through themselves. There's a teenage Gabrielle by the beverage station. There's a serious thirty-something Gabrielle accepting awards for excellence near the curtained entry. On the ceiling, a formidable Gabrielle delivers a paper to an assembly of scholars.

I feel light-headed, dizzy and euphoric.

The most captivating image is a long, yet almost still, close-up of Gabrielle. In it, she is serious. A consulted expert reporting to a room of colleagues. The audio is off. Gabrielle just stares, flickers of recognition and response ticking across her face, her lips mouthing a silent conversation.

Her dark eyes look through me.

At the beverage station a cup of relaxblend tea is waiting for me. I sip it slowly, breathe deeply, and count. I restart the eulogy, try to let it drift over me like a voiceover: *You are at the funeral of someone you loved, you are close to the bittersweet brush of mortality.*

'In recognition of her work,' the eulogist continues, 'Gabrielle was awarded research program integration and will continue to be an invaluable part of databases in global research institutions.'

'Pause. Replay.'

'Gabrielle was awarded research program integration,' says the eulogist with the same sad pride. It takes me a moment to begin to understand the implications of this statement. I search through to a register, a datafeed of names. In my periphery, the feed scrolls through images of scholars and artists now integrated into various program subsets. All brilliant. All dead, or rather, undead. An army of immortal intellectuals. Dr Gabrielle Stern just one among them.

My pulse slows. The immersion patterns are causing the edges of my vision to blur. I feel a cold wetness on my cheeks.

I scrutinise the eulogist. Her sincerity is real, and in her face, there's something uncanny. I look up her name. Clara Stern. A real relative. A real eulogy. A recording from an archived event. A replay.

A pang shoots through my body, dropping me into a chair, where I automatically slump into the emergency brace position. Hanging down, facing the thick haptofeel carpet, I realise that I'm not at all surprised.

I should leave, but I don't.

I get as far as the viewing platform before my legs buckle. Clara Stern doesn't notice – she is not programmed to be interactive. She is only a recording, can only repeat the past. I stumble forward and steady myself on the side of the coffin. Inside, Gabrielle's façade wavers almost imperceptibly.

Nothing I know is real. All of it is designed, stolen. Gabrielle's dialogue was probably sampled from some primitive picture book that gave me my first intimation of the language of the erotic. I couldn't find her in the archive of my life. But perhaps my problem was that I was looking for a whole when I needed to search for parts. Perhaps I would have been more successful scrolling through flat-screen films and commercials advertising carcinogenic breakfast pastries. We are all made of this stuff. Nothing exists beyond the archive.

Gabrielle's dark hair falls loose around her head. There's no mind in there. Not for years. It lies dissected somewhere, illuminated by inappropriate metaphors, progressing the species to its stainless destiny. In circuitry, somewhere, the river is contained. Algorithms analyse wave and ripple, produce a helpful graph.

I take my breath in panicked gasps. I can't get enough air. I gag, trying to suck it from the climate controlled atmosphere, but it's thick with frequencies. I'm choking. My eyes fill up with tears. I blink them out and they splash down off my nose, falling into the arrangement of light beneath me. The sad eyes, the long hair and dark, shadowy features.

Such pretty light.

A bracing arm encircles me, steadies me on my feet.

'I'm sorry, Mr Galleon, perhaps you would be better off to spend some grieving time with the reconciliation module,' says the attendant.

He half-carries me away from the coffin and into another, darker booth, where he seats me on a broad, comfortable haptic armchair.

'I'll be just outside when you need me.'

I sit obediently, quietly shaken by sobs, trying to steady my breath. As I regain calm, the light in the room pulses and reorders and soon I'm no longer alone. Gabrielle is standing in front of me, so perfect and real I could reach out and touch her.

'Hello, Max. Are you okay?' she smiles.

'I'm struggling.' My voice wavers.

'That's natural,' she says. 'You shouldn't feel any guilt about struggling. Grieving is a natural part of death and death is part of life.'

The script for dealing with grief makes no sense coming from Gabrielle's mouth. I reach out to her.

She backs off slightly to maintain aspect ratio.

'You're not dead,' I tell her. 'You are probably working simultaneously on four or five patients as we speak.'

'Today, death is a word that marks a transmission from one state to another. It's important to grieve the absence of loved ones.'

We stare at each other. Invisibly, systems meet and catalogue, searching for traces of Gabrielle coded in my archive. Were she accessible there, this image in front of me could comfort me, would be able to deliver some speech of recognition. I remember when we walked in the park, she would say, that was one of the nicest days of my life.

But she has been erased from my memory. Or, perhaps

worse, she may never have been there at all. Not tangibly. Not in any way you could record.

Gabrielle stares at me with designer compassion.

'What did I mean to you?' she asks, so sweetly, so nostalgically, her tone digitally interpretive to at least six operators of entendre.

I almost laugh.

'What is it?' she asks.

'It's unlike you to be so sentimental.'

'Death is a complex emotional process.'

'That's a little better.'

'Who am I to you? It's important to say it out loud to get a sense of closure.' She's imploring now, using that word, closure, Ellie's word-of-the-month. 'What did I mean to you?'

I sigh. My testimony is required. It's a necessary input for proper program implementation. In the pseudo-code, lodged in a network of tiny cameras, scanners, monitors and microscopic sensors that record individual brain pattern, there is still a place for the word.

From my inadequate mind I pull a flimsy, malleable, compromised notion. I yell into a network so comprehensive that it already includes my speech, thought, action and intention. One programmed so ingeniously that it predicts my desires, rendering me as mere formality.

I am a tribute to the way things were.

'You were my brother's neurologist,' I say out loud, and a note is recorded. 'You were also my lover.'

Gabrielle's dark eyes melt into me as she fixes me with a look of pure and perfectly composed devotion.

'I understand now,' she says. 'I love you.'

'You aren't real.'

'My love is real,' she says.

I stand up. We would've made the perfect couple.

I pull open the curtains behind me, stepping into the bright room beyond. The child version of Gabrielle flits across the walls, loops, crumples and flits again.

Ellie is still sitting on the bench, watching Tom. I join her, take her hand in mine, rest my head on her shoulder. Tom is not moving. I listen to Ellie's pulse through her slender neck, in primitive concert with Tom's monitors.

'Let's finish it,' she says.

She inputs a command and lets me sink against her. She reaches her hand up to stroke my hair.

In front of us, Tom rises and falls, silent and complicit. Gradually, the rhythm of his vitality changes. The steady bleep of the heart monitor becomes syncopated, and then erratic. His body twitches, a small leg jerk, a finger flicking against its tremorplastic sheath.

Just as they did in my dream, his eyes flicker, and open. They are irresolute for a moment before they snap to an icy blue stare, locked onto mine. He reaches out for me. I rush to his bedside and reach in, but without the haptic glove his body is just cold light to fall through.

He smiles anyway, grateful. I lean in.

With difficulty, he opens his mouth. 'I wouldn't worry about the past now,' he says. 'The weather is fine where you are going.'

He looks at me with perfect love.

'I miss you,' I tell him.

He nods. He has the face of a saint, full of gratitude and certainty. He slumps back, exhausted and satisfied. I stay by him. I manage to get the glove onto one hand and feel his warm skin.

My brother takes a big, raspy breath. The bleeping evens out into a steady tone, the breath releases. The image flickers and dims, the curtain closes. And I am alone in a velvet cocoon.

A calming re-entry sequence plays around me. Tom is gone.

• •

Ellie and I are quiet until we reach the bright and inspiring fringes of Bay Heights. Only then does she speak.

'How do you feel?' she asks.

I shrug. I've got no more tears, nor words. We both look stare out to the road ahead.

'I think it will all feel real soon enough. This is closure. At least we know what happened now.'

'Know?' the word triggers contempt, and then anger. I wave away the pie chart. 'What do we know? We have no idea. I've been walking around in a dream.'

'Not a dream, Max,' Ellie insists. 'Her research was impressive. And her program had so many additional applications. I thought you needed a change.'

We pull into our neighbourhood. Each house in Bay Heights is unique, but the uniqueness is of a kind.

'Have you even looked at her work?' Ellie persists.

I say nothing.

My wife adds a number of peer-reviewed papers to my reading queue. I wave them away. Focus on the road being swallowed up by the windscreen. It's no accident that car seats are still placed parallel. People want to be able to move forward without looking at each other.

'How do I know that's not just extra text?' I ask. 'A re-entry protocol to close the immersion.'

'I suppose you don't,' she says. 'But if there were a protocol for re-entry, wouldn't you like to do it, for the sake of integration?'

'Resignation, 2:50pm,' notes the archive.

A video tutorial on the five stages of grief pops up in my periphery, but I lay another file over the top – my Timeline of Misconception.

I scroll to the last note on the timeline and change it: You think you are in love, but that's just the parameters of the immersion.

• •

At home, Lilly is sitting quietly in the hydrogarden, patting the rabbit.

'Hi, Dad.' Her voice is small and sad.

'Hello, little Lilly,' I reply in my best parent patois.

'Hope's dead,' she says.

Ellie drops her handbag on the bonnet of the car and rushes over to kneel beside her daughter.

'I'm sorry, darling,' she says, massaging Lilly's back in long strokes. 'That's terrible news.'

Oddly, the rabbit does not hop away. It remains stoic in Lilly's lap.

'She died in the night,' Lilly says. 'They still aren't sure what happened. There are theories that Hope failed to adapt to her captive environment. Even though they thought they got everything right.'

'That's what they always think,' says Jonas, standing in the front doorway with a bowl of spirulinacrunch.

Ellie puts her arms around Lilly and holds her. After a second, Lilly's little body starts to quiver and she begins a hearty, childish cry.

It's cathartic to watch.

I move towards them quietly so as not to disturb the scene. When I am there, I stroke Lilly's hair, feel the vibrations of her tears. She looks up at me with big, earnest, reddened eyes.

'It's not fair, Daddy,' she says. 'Hope was innocent. Hope never hurt anybody.'

'I know, sweetheart.' After a while I follow Jonas back into the house. 'Your sister is devastated.'

'She shouldn't be,' he shrugs, seemingly back to his old self. 'She's not usually so impractical.'

'She was very attached to that sloth puppy.'

'Yes I know. Impractical. It would've been the same if Pow-Pow died.'

'But Pow-Pow can't really die. You can always reboot him.'

'Exactly,' he smiles. 'Now they are saying that the Praeteranthropocene might have been prematurely declared.'

'Who is saying that?'

'An expert faction. They think we have nothing to worry about, that this whole thing has been blown out of proportion.'

'But the island will sink.'

'Oh, it'll sink. But now they are saying it might not be that important. Somehow, the death of Hope supports this.'

'How?'

'Well, human beings don't need successors anymore. Better to save that drill for the main event.'

'What are you saying?'

Jonas sighs. 'I'm saying I don't think there ever was a Hope. I think the whole thing was a distraction, a consolation. I've told you this before.' He waves away a connection request from some third party, perhaps a fellow mutineer, perhaps Lutsk. 'What's interesting is that they have changed their minds about that island. I mean, what purpose does that serve? If it sinks and it's the end of everything, no one will hold them accountable for being wrong.'

'And if it blows over?'

'Well, I suppose they will get to be right. Which gives them more authority for the next thing. The next sinking island or crumbling coastline or whatever.'

I take a moment to consider this. Jonas goes back to watching the feed. His entrenched scepticism has returned, but there is more certainty to his nihilism, less fear.

'Do you want a snack?' I ask him.

'Sure.'

The death of Hope has raised his spirits.

I bring him protein balls and kelp milk and then open his Timeline of Misconception.

'Show me how you are going,' I urge him.

He looks at me, a little suspicious at first, but then something crosses his face, some memory perhaps of our recent family kindnesses. He smiles a little, grateful smile. 'I suppose I should really add all this to it, keep it up to date. Teachers like that.'

'Everyone likes to keep abreast of the latest information.'

He scrolls to the last entry on the spreadsheet. Under 'Event' he has already written, "The discovery of Hope the giant sloth pup", and below 'Conception' "Signifies the end of the Holocene and beginning of the Praeteranthropocene."

He highlights the 'Conception' and changes it to 'Misconception'.

In the new cell he writes "Hope dies and the Praeteranthropocene is critiqued as prematurely declared. Conspiracy afloat?"

The spreadsheet creates an auxiliary chart of events that my son has also marked as potential conspiracies.

Jonas changes the viewing mode and the Timeline of Misconception stretches around us, ringing the walls of the family room like rope around a bale of straw.

'Not everything is a conspiracy,' I tell him. 'Lots of things in life simply don't add up.'

'That's the number one fallacy about a conspiracy,' he replies. 'That it has to add up.'

I stare at his assignment. The great sweeping arc of it. All true and untrue insofar as we can make these claims.

'Just because something is humanly designed doesn't mean it will be complete, or accurate, or even successful,'

Jonas continues. 'That goes doubly for knowledge.'

He looks at me with thoughtful compassion, taking in my darkened, slackened features, my dishevelled clothing.

'Actually, I think that's the major lesson for this assignment,' he says out loud, and a note is recorded.

••

Even though it no longer marks the beginning of the end, we all still watch the feed from Pitcairn. At home, in Bay Heights, we lock the feed to the wall in the family room. Jonas, Lilly, Ellie and I make a point of walking past it without making too much fuss. We are performing our stability as a family.

Jean is performing something quite different. He sends me breathless transmissions from Pitcairn. The emphasis of the mega-tsunami epic has changed again, as well as the name. Jean and Sullivan are making great shakes with footage collection. Jean feels young again, invigorated.

'The natives were hostile,' he says, grey eyes staring through a mosaic of solar panel and thermaglass. 'But I explained the stakes of this film, and things have changed. They see the value in it now. They want to enter a broader network, assimilate into mass consciousness. I have several squads gathering data. We have haptics from all over the island. We'll be able to incorporate multiple empathic positions on this. The free-floating perspective in which the viewer can be, a fisherman, or a tourist, or even an animal for a few seconds at a time, will actually be real this time!'

'Sullivan has gotten to you then,' I still feel disconnected from the project, but I'm comfortable to let it go, too.

'It's the logical next step for this technology. Why restrict ourselves to one perspective? "You": it's old-fashioned. Anyway, what is really interesting here is not that the island is sinking. If you have ever been on a sinking island you would know that it feels solid underfoot. What is intriguing is how the knowledge that it is sinking affects the emotional atmosphere of the place. That's the challenge for the immersion. How can we use this data set, and the haptics we have gathered, in combination with a narrative that will produce the same effect? This emotional miasma. The sense of being at the centre of everything. It's impossible to describe. You have to feel it.'

'I look forward to it,' I tell him. 'But if anyone can describe it, you can. I want my own private retelling when you return. Preferably combined with a good Scotch.'

Jean looks away. Behind him, an ominous cloud hangs over the craggy green of Pitcairn.

'I sent a composition to Margot,' he says, still staring off into the distance. 'I wanted her to feel this place.'

'Oh yes?'

'Yes,' he says. 'It was an immersive love letter.'

'And was it a success?'

'You can see it for yourself,' he spits, looking back at me with a hardened expression. 'She shared it with everyone.'

In my periphery a muted scene appears. Jean is dressed in rags, knee deep in foaming brine, hands clutched to his heart. I can see that there have already been 5,783 derivative versions made, replete with humorous captions and overdubs.

'It's so hard to make grand gestures these days,' Jean shrugs. 'We no longer speak of intention in any meaningful way.'

'That's true,' I say.

Jean shakes his head. 'You can't know what I'm talking about,' he says.

When he logs off the house is quiet. The children have accompanied Ellie on a walk to the bay. Even the rabbit is with them, wrapped in Lilly's protective arms, chewing through Panda Points like chaff.

I am alone.

I bring up several feeds at once, obscuring the vista, swaddling the inner pangs. I lean back further in the chair, trying to get into character: a family man at home alone. I change half the feeds to sportscasts, but they don't hold me, and I start flicking absently though my reading queue, past the *Art of War* and self-help books on grief and memory.

In the 'short reads' category my eye catches on something: Gabrielle's articles on Temporal Lobe Hibernation Epilepsy, helpfully marked and highlighted by Ellie. I begin to read one, but the academic jargon and the figures and tables are beyond me. I am a man of images and clear symbols. I key a search for Temporal Lobe Hibernation Epilepsy and find a short current affairs report.

A bowl of kale nuggets appears beside me. I throw them into my mouth, hardly chewing. My nutrient score goes up.

On screen, a wide shot of a large research hospital is cut against images of official-looking people walking through clean corridors.

'Less than fifteen years ago, the very first case of what

would be diagnosed as Temporal Lobe Hibernation Epilepsy was reported to *Neurology Today*,' says a female voice. 'The article documented one doctor's work with an adolescent female. The patient reported fits in which she would fall suddenly into sleeping binges from which she could not be woken. There had been no traumatic event preceding the onset of the condition and no indication of prior PTSD. The child had no injuries. There was no detectable reason why this bright, well-adjusted school student of seventeen would sink into an impenetrable coma state, lasting anywhere from a few hours to a week.'

The image underneath shows an intelligent looking teenager, prostrate beneath a floral quilt, as her anxious mother looks on, attempting to give her water, occasionally trying to shake her awake.

'This was the medical community's first encounter with TLHE, now a well-documented syndrome most often diagnosed in patients with a T/T variation of the CHRNA4 gene, who have also been subject to a prolonged state of neural overload. Sufferers are typically unresponsive to electro-stimulation therapy or hormonal charge. Once the brain has established a pattern of TLHE attacks at the point of overload, seizure becomes a common neural response to high levels of stimulation. However, with preventative protocol and treatment measures in place, the reported cases of TLHE have diminished drastically.'

The screen shows the same intelligent child in a montage: walking and talking with friends, putting her hand up in a classroom, playing indoor soccer with a pleasingly multicultural team.

'The syndrome would perhaps have remained an issue for only relatively small sections of the population if not for a dangerous new recreational trend.'

A handheld camera shot, taking us down suspicious and depraved-looking back-alleys, replaces the soccer team. Where are these places? I cannot imagine such an alley running parallel to the pleasant streets of the central district.

'Recreation club and bar licensees were reporting cases of customers blacking out for long periods. Emergency wards reported similar cases. Soon, these attacks were classified as drug overdoses and patients were excluded from emergency room care under Article 84. The drug overdose protocol known as "day dreaming" is brought on by a combinatory dosage of PCPx (a street drug with similar properties to the anaesthetic agent phenylcyclohexylpiperidine) and Meritas, a commercially available hypnotic. The chemical reaction and neural patterning within the brain at the point of administration of the narcotic combination is almost identical to a TLHE seizure.'

The screen now shows a laser-lit nightclub. Young people in garish costumes twitch and convulse, locked in private or small group entertainment immersions.

'It's like slipping into another, more beautiful reality,' says one doe-eyed boy, waving his impossibly thin arms above his head, tracing fingers across the strobing light.

'More like,' says another brightly clothed youth, 'being knocked out cold and then having the best dream you ever had. It can take you anywhere.'

The image cuts to the alley again, a shadowy and frail figure slumped in a disgusting doorway.

'Once the drugs PCPx and Meritas were added to the monitored illicit substance database,' says the narrator, 'electronic detection mechanisms saw them eradicated within twelve months.'

Shots of legal buildings. An animation of policy documents scrolling through a database.

'Once again, the condition appeared to be under control.'

The soundtrack grows ominous, the colour grade darker – the climax is coming. I watch a long, skull-mounted shot showing movement through an overgrown landscape at night. The landscape opens to a clearing. There is some chaotic and abrupt background noise.

The image is dark, deliberately obscure, then it steadies somewhat, closing in on a building, drawing back into a wide shot from another source.

I bite my lip and taste a trickle of blood.

A glass of saline gargle appears beside me. I stare at it for a long while, not wanting to return my eyes to the image and confirm what I already know. I pick up the gargle. I rinse and spit. Then I look up again.

The camera circles the area before zeroing in on its target. It moves towards it at a walking pace. The doors to the large old farm building part and the light changes to night-vision green.

INT. WIDE SHOT. NIGHT

A spider web links fragmented bodies in the
green gloam. A chopper hovers overhead.

REPORTER
This is the headquarters of the drug cult that
came to be known as The Sleepers—

I can only look for a moment before my whole body
begins to tingle, as though I am about to pass out cold.

'Close,' I almost-yell.

The image snaps to black.

My heart pounds a primal rhythm. My face is cold, my
hands clammy. Several prescription pills appear on the arm-
rest of the chair. I take them, one by one, sounding out the
name of each pill, each optimistic commercial contraction.

I count backwards from ten and try to focus on a
familiar object – the perfect cube of a pill container. It only
makes me feel worse.

I close my eyes and see the screen image in reverse. Is
this a memory, or is the archive playing these scenes for
me? My head swims. In the dark room a web extends from
one body to the next, extending towards me, ensnaring me.
I can feel it, sticky on my skin. I can see Gabrielle, concen-
trating on a tiny wire. I can hear her voice, rising above
the steady electric squeal, the rasping exhale: The human
brain is capable of processing the meaning of over a billion

images per minute.

Imagination is part of what makes memory, I have heard somewhere, who knows where. This, then, could be a memory, or a fantasy, or both: Gabrielle pushing me back into the folds of the hospital bed. Kissing me, brushing her lips across my skin, her breath fluttering over my eyelids. Her body rocking back and forth, building momentum so gradually that it takes every part of me to feel the nuances of her movement. My whole body tries to isolate each tremor, appreciate every surface minutely. When I know the movement completely I will come, I decide – then, almost immediately, Gabrielle bucks sharply against me and crumples, falling as if from a great height into my chest and then further, into my blood and tissue, into my nerves and neurons until she is gone, nothing but frequency, messages circulating.

She knows more than I do.

I remember Gabrielle, her voice laced with mirth. I hear it as clear as if it were recorded in the archive: 'Then you can just erase him. You can erase all this right now and save us a lot of trouble.'

'She's right,' I say out loud, and a note is recorded.

I hold my gaze steady for the retina scan. I look towards the vast and expectant horizon.

Somewhere, light moves through sound before becoming something else. Something lost. We are all lost in data. Lost: a snowdrift space between people.

'Process complete erasure,' I say, emptying it with a final, decisive sweep.

'Nostalgia, 6:45pm,' notes the archive.

I sit back in the armchair and stare out at the blissful, lossless blue.

A little later, as dusk draws around Bay Heights, Ellie gently wakes me to say that Pitcairn Island has sunk.

'Jonas and Lilly are asleep,' Ellie tells me. 'I don't want to wake them. There's no use causing panic. So far the consequences are minimal. The extreme weather is continuing in some places. There's flooding somewhere too. But we're safe. In any case, there's no need to repeat the other night. We've dealt with a lot lately.'

'We have,' I nod, placing my hand on her shoulder.

'Well,' she says.

'Well.'

'I think I'll go to bed then.' She smiles a resigned smile.

'I'll be with you soon.'

She kisses me lightly on the top of my head. Warmth spreads out across my chest.

When she leaves, I steal down the hallway to my son's room. I watch him sleeping unusually calmly in a cosmos of indicator lights and panels. Quietly, I pull up his Timeline of Misconception. I search and find the item on Pitcairn. Sinking marks the culmination of the global micro-disaster chain and any possible final global catastrophe. I change the entry data cell type from 'Conception' to 'Misconception' and add a new entry.

'The island sinks,' I whisper to the network, 'and yet, we go on.'

In my periphery a query blinks. It's a video package from Jean. A giant file. The subject title: The Last Film.

DIRECTOR'S
CUT ENDING

t is the last opening night. A three-level ferry, the inside decorated to recreate the ballroom of the *Poseidon* cruise ship from Irwin Allen's 1972 film *The Poseidon Adventure*, carries the guests across to the small harbour island. On our return the ship will be rearranged. A team of production designers have mapped a fastidious blueprint of how it would look after the fictional tsunami ruptured the deck and soaked the cabins. We will journey home as survivors of a cinematically sunk cruise.

Cocktails are served. Trays of drinks form toxic liquid rainbows.

People circulate, shaking my hand and Sullivan's, gazing at us in rapt anticipation.

Cindi Mac floats by with her novelty microphone. She asks me how I am as an invisible camera zooms in on my pupils, registering my emotional state. Somewhere, a psychiatric expert makes a running commentary.

'Wow!' Cindi squeals, her voice preceding a rain of synthetic applause 'We are here with master filmmakers Max Galleon and Sullivan at the premiere for their new film, *The Island Will Sink*. Max, do you want to tell our viewers a little bit about what to expect?'

'Expect drama,' I say. 'Expect action. Expect suspense. Expect to experience The End as you have never experienced it before.'

'Awesome!' squeals Cindi. 'Now a little birdy told me that this is the most realistic, most profound experience of disaster we will ever have. Can you tell everyone at home why?'

'Well, Cindi, as you know, my partner, the late, great Jean Di Vita, was on that island.'

Cindi claps her hands over her lips in a gesture of shocked sympathy.

'And he captured the entire event.'

The canned audience coos and murmurs.

Cindi looks pantomime-sad.

'Jean Di Vita was a true artist,' she says. 'We are so lucky to have known him.'

'That's right, Cindi. He died for what he believed in.'

'That is such an honour.'

'Well, Cindi, thanks to Jean, this film is as close to death as you can come and still get a drink afterwards.'

Risqué laughter cuts across the ebbing tide.

'This is a cutting-edge immersion content gathering system that Jean and I pioneered,' Sullivan chimes in. 'We are now using it all over the world to gather content from every site in the global micro-catastrophe chain.'

Cindi looks deeply moved.

'That chain links us all,' she says.

'That's right, Cindi.' Sullivan's smile is shark-like. 'And through this technology we have managed to create the conditions for total empathy. There's no longer any distance between us. You can feel the pain of someone on the other side of the world, without leaving your lounge room.'

'That is sooo important,' Cindi gushes, turning to me. 'I am so excited about this film, Max. The sinking island is enough to make this a must-see, but do you want to share any more of the premise with us? No spoilers though, okay?' She waggles her finger coyly.

'Sure, Cindi. In *The Island Will Sink*, you are born fully grown, with the consciousness of an adult.'

Cindy's mouth forms a thrilled O. A hollow cheer echoes through the night.

'But you can't speak. You can see all the truths of humanity, but you can't say a word.'

'Amazing!'

'Yes – and there's another catch too. You are born on an island—a sinking island—on the final day for planet earth. You are forced to interpret the meaning of a whole lifetime during the final moments for the only biosphere where it makes sense.'

'Wow,' says Cindy. 'Deep.'

'But you can still expect explosions!'

The applause intensifies.

'And full body immersion. You can expect to feel the truth in ways you never felt possible.'

Screams erupt from the appreciation machine. Cans of thrill pop and whiz.

My heart rate is steady.

My blood is peppered with a designer hypnotic.

The island is only a ten-minute ride from the old city harbour. Forty years ago it was a garbage-processing facility. Boats would have arrived daily, stacked with steaming mounds of refuse. Crushed bicycle wheels, offal, dead animals, the butts of a billion cigarettes, used lipsticks, and prophylactics all came to the island to be compacted into innocuous cubes.

Tonight, it's clean.

Tonight, the red carpet spills from the ferry like blood, spreading quickly over a custom-built pier where people of note alight. Razor-sharp stiletto heels make bullet-hole impressions. Dresses swoosh in the evening breeze.

I walk along the pier flanked by Ellie, Sullivan, and his date, some fashion model-cum-philanthropist. They wave to the people, left and right. Invisible crowds of eager fans wave back, enraptured. Their applause optimised and mastered far above the gentle lapping of the waves on the shore.

There's no one here, but in residential districts, even in trailer camps, we are streamed.

They've done the garbage island up to look like Pitcairn, or to look how Pitcairn looked to Jean. It's a balmy evening, and the moonlight is elegantly designed, flattering. Notable people make their way across the beach towards the round-house, glittering like zirconia. Out across the black harbour a light flashes, bobbing on the tide. Ellie squeezes my arm.

'Tsunami!' she says.

A group of event staff dressed alternatively as fishermen and noble savages stand at the doors to the roundhouse. They hold trays teetering with flutes of twenty-year-old Champagne. Tiny bubbles rush to the surface and break into the atmosphere.

The interior walls of the roundhouse are a continuous screen on which ambiguous patterns tangle and order. As soon as they find their places, each member of the esteemed audience begins the task of strapping themselves into haptic suits, adjusting headsets, attaching sensor pads to their temples and jugular. They morph into wire creatures, antennae bristling, smooth shells reflecting each other's buzz and switch. They fall bug-like into the web that binds them.

Ellie assists my metamorphosis. She helps me slide, one arm at a time, into the most technologically advanced immersion suit to date.

'It's perfect,' says Sullivan, satisfied.

'No glitch, though,' I say, a little meanly.

'The glitch will be more disrupting if it's disguised in a perfect continuum.'

'I see.'

If Jean were here, he would laugh.

Ellie adjusts the pressure of my goggles and headset, narrowing my vision into a long tunnel that focuses finally on the pulsing walls of the room. Shapes bounce and weave in the distance. Patterns flicker briefly, becoming visions of scenes from my day. Familiar objects to prompt short bouts of recollection; the drill is built into the immersion. Through pixel-dust I watch Ellie parade me out into the living room in my charcoal suit. She shows me to the children. Jonas and Lilly stand close together, regarding me suspiciously.

The shapes melt into each other. The ground begins to tremble underfoot. Or perhaps I'm jumping. My heart hammers beneath my skin.

A chopper shoots footage from above Pitcairn straight into my eyes. The blades disturb the aerial view, dissecting it into minute detail, making a study of shadow and glare.

The island is trembling. Far off, I can hear Cindi Mac's shrill squee.

I watch a grove of palm trees bow to each other as though dancing. Strong winds lift a thatched roof into the sky.

A deep rumbling from under the sea sounds like tanks heading out to war. Schools of fish panic and scatter.

The tsunami is building.

'Nothing is certain except the island will sink,' a familiar voice whispers.

I yank on the chopper pilot's sleeve.

'My friend is down there,' I implore. 'My best friend is trapped on that island.'

Beneath me I see Jean, kneeling in the foam, arms reaching the sky as if in exultant prayer.

'Love, Max!' he yells out, his voice drowning in the storm.

In a nameless desert, a mine collapses, killing two hundred machines.

Sweat beads on my skin. I'm dead cold underneath

the immersion suit. The initial panic is building. I feel the sudden need to locate my family. I want them with me.

'Where are you?' I shout.

From somewhere outside the screen I hear Jonas reply.

'You'll be okay, you are the third most famous Dad I know.'

Children file in through the gates of a school, unaware.

Where are my babies? I search faces for a trace of myself, my legacy.

A woman gossips to an old friend while every bottle in her cellar implodes.

A couple climaxes simultaneously.

A flock of crows take off in a blizzard of feathers, squawking.

Light flashes behind my lids. I am left on the edges of partially assembled visions. My arms grasp at the violet darkness, searching for missing pieces.

I look down into the palm of my hand and see that I am holding a cube. I consider it. Six even surfaces. Always the same.

The background drops away.

I'm only vaguely aware of the assault of images beyond my body, only vaguely aware of the chaos of sound and light and what it means. Reaching up to wipe my face I touch the headset instead, then pull at it, struggling with straps and buckles and wires.

I yank it off and throw it on the floor.

I blink, adjusting my eyes to the widened perspective.

All about me, strange electric moths shiver and shake in

chrysalises. I stare at them like a scientist examining spec-imens. The moths loom; they are trying to get closer to the light but they hiss and singe at its periphery. Notable people hunch inside these chrysalises. I mentally strip away the apparatus and see the contorted limbs and desperate faces. The eyes wretched with tears. The teeth gnashing.

The walls of the roundhouse spit light across the bodies. In the splinters of illumination I decode motion. Women tear at their designer gowns, ripping fabric away from their hearts so as to beat their chests with more vigour. On the ground, people convulse in epileptic fits. Still figures are suddenly overcome with nausea and spit bile onto the carpet. A great moaning begins. A howling chorus of grief. There is shivering and rocking. All about me are heaving bodies, mewling and puking, doubled over in pain. Inside moth silhouettes, men masturbate furiously, grunting and hawing, chests puffed up at the oncoming destruction.

Crawling across the image, a moving stripe creates a glitch in the light. Tiny ants are marching towards a dark patch. Their trail creates trickling dead-space in the picture. I follow them with my eyes, and then my body, compelled to move towards them, to track their journey. I weave through the dust-covered sacks. The carpet is patchy and wet with tears and sick. Piles of powdery dirt from collapsed anthills stick in the tread of my shoes, interfering with their measurements.

I have no depth perception. My shoes are mute.

A woman stands, fixated, tearing out her slick blonde hair one strand at a time. As each strand falls it turns to hay scattered across the floor of a slaughterhouse or a barn.

When the film is over, no one will view the remains of this destruction as anything out of the ordinary. No one will see the torn frocks and the destroyed hairstyles. No one will care to notice the skin scratched to a bloody mess. No one will judge any other person. We will all be washed clean. Turned like the earth.

Shirtless men toil in a field, blissfully unaware of a growing rip in the planet's crust, an opening like a zipper.

All anyone can ever know at any one time is that, against all odds, they are still alive, and, in this they are chosen.

I follow the ants towards a dark patch in the room; a small break in the resolve of the scene. It's flat, a hole in my vision. A forgotten, grey place. As I get closer I realise it's a small door, hidden at the bottom of the screen. It must be a fire escape or a service exit. Ants trail underneath it, past their ruined and abandoned colonies.

I step over arms and legs to get to the door. I snake around a group of men and women stamping their feet on the floor in a protest rhythm.

The door gives easily on well-lubricated hinges, swinging open and allowing me to step inside. Behind the screen, the room is dark and filled with plain sleeping cots. A broad electric net ensnares each sleeping body.

Sick-rest overcomes me, as if my limbs are dead. Barely audible whispers hiss in my head: arguments, promises, orders, strange notions.

'Shhhh.' I spit white paste onto my chin.

Here, behind the screen, the shapes are clear in reverse:

hypnotic patterns. And emerging from them, the figure of a man, prostrate in his cot. His limbs twitch. His eyes flicker.

Somewhere, lava is bubbling up from an underwater volcano. It will explode into the blue, causing tornadoes of water to tear across the ocean floor.

There's a shriek in my ears like aftershock getting higher and dangerously higher.

One billion windows shatter at once, glass shards falling through the air like rain.

A mysterious girl with haunted eyes waits in the sparkling subway for an explosion that will turn everything to rubble.

The man sits up, yelling, 'We need the disaster! We need the final catastrophe!'

The tsunami builds, gathers momentum. It surges across the harbour from the decimated city. It lifts up the shore, changes the shape of the coastline forever. It shatters the pier, each plank collapsing on the other like dominoes falling in fast-forward. The tsunami rips across the small island and shatters the walls of the roundhouse, sucking up Champagne flutes, pearl earrings, full-body haptic suits, designer silks, screaming men and women. Electric currents loop through nerves, causing frothy spasms in the freezing blueness. Splinters of wall lodge themselves in flesh. Broken figures tumble through the water, and blood ribbons unfurl. DNA scatters, spelling out centuries of literature.

The man leaps out from the darkness and I move without hesitation to take his place. I pull the thin blanket up to my chin.

The wave surges up, splits the image apart. A wall of water eclipses the horizon, forms a screen.

I'm sinking.

The lens widens and pulls back and now *it's you who jumps out of the darkness. Your feet roll on the hard floor and you take off running, far, far, farther, out of frame, into the desert, becoming smaller and smaller, then tiny, a fast speck in the endless grey. The credits roll like thunder.*

You close your eyes.

FADE

Acknowledgements

I am so grateful to all the readers of this work in its earliest forms, particularly Aden Rolfe and Geoff Lemon, whose editorial instincts are sharp and fine. Thanks also to Steven Amsterdam, Luke Davies, Levin Diatschenko, Jennifer Mills, Peta Price, Anna Vost and Olof. I started this book one afternoon at the green fibro shack in Wombarra and rewrote it many years later at the Wooden Dog in Austi, so to Pat Grant: our excellent conversations must be good fuel – thanks for all the pies.

I'm so lucky to have had some excellent teachers and mentors over the past decade, especially Mick Broderick whose perspective on the end of the world has shaped my own, and the late Martin Harrison, who ignited something fierce and bright when he said, emphatically, 'I think more sci-fi, yes, I think so, yes.'

Finally, a million thanks and bunches of golden roses to Julia Carlomagno and David Golding at Scribe and to Sam Cooney, Rosetta Mills, Chad Parkhill and the whole crew at The Lifted Brow – it is a great honour to work with people who are so passionate about what they do, and who do it so damn well.

Briohny Doyle

Briohny Doyle is a Melbourne-based writer.
Her debut novel *The Island Will Sink* is the first
book published by The Lifted Brow. Briohny's
writing has appeared in publications such as
The Lifted Brow, *Overland*, *Going Down Swinging*
and *Meanjin*, among others, and she has
performed her work at the Sydney Festival and
at the Museum of Contemporary Art, Sydney.
Her first book of non-fiction, *Adult Fantasy*
(Scribe Publications, 2017) will explore the
cultural underpinnings of adulthood.

—THE LIFTED— **BROW**

We are a not-for-profit literary organisation from Australia, and we acknowledge that we gather, work, learn and play largely on the lands of the Wurundjeri people of the Kulin nation, and we pay our respects to First Nations elders past and present.

We publish magazines and books, produce events, run writing prizes, and post new content on our website every day. Our quarterly magazine *The Lifted Brow* features the best writing and artwork from literary, demographic, and cultural margins, and is distributed nationally and internationally.

Alongside new and unusual writing and writers, we have published work by Christos Tsiolkas, Helen Garner, David Foster Wallace, Neil Gaiman, Rick Moody, Karen Russell, Wayne Koestenbaum, Joy Williams, Tom Cho, Douglas Coupland, Heidi Julavits, Tom Bissell, Tao Lin, Rebecca Giggs, Margo Lanagan, Jim Shepard, Frank Moorhouse, Anna Krien, Romy Ash, Natalie Eilbert, Diane Williams, Margaret Atwood, Sam Lipsyte, Eileen Myles, Sheila Heti, Andrés Neuman, Blake Butler, and Benjamin Kunkel.

We are based in Melbourne, with eyes all over the world. This novel in your hands is our first book.

www.theliftedbrow.com